W9-ANT-984

A
NOVEL
DISGUISE

A NOVEL DISGUISE

A LADY LIBRARIAN MYSTERY

Samantha Larsen

CROOKED
LANE

NEW YORK

Copyright © 2023 by Samantha Hastings

Published in the United States by Crooked Lane Books, an imprint of The Quick Brown Fox & Company LLC.

Crooked Lane Books and its logo are trademarks of The Quick Brown Fox & Company LLC.

Library of Congress Catalog-in-Publication data available upon request.

ISBN (paperback): 978-1-63910-346-1
ISBN (ebook): 978-1-63910-349-2

Cover design by Sarah Horgan

Printed in the United States.

www.crookedlanebooks.com

Crooked Lane Books
34 West 27th St., 10th Floor
New York, NY 10001

First Edition: May 2023

10 9 8 7 6 5 4 3 2 1

To Isaac

Chapter 1

Miss Tiffany Woodall's fortieth birthday commenced rather sourly. She awoke with the sun to make bread, only to find that her starter had gone off. With a huff, she began a new one, delicately picking out the weevils from the yeast. She warmed the kettle over the fire—her kitchen was already hotter than the devil's dancehall. Wiping sweat away from her brow, Tiffany poured the warm water into a wooden bowl and carefully added the yeast. While waiting for it to bloom, she fetched eggs and boiled them. The yeast was bubbling, so she added the flour and salt from the dry cupboard next to the hearth.

She began to knead.

Punching.

Grabbing.

Squeezing.

Tiffany often imagined it was *his* face and it gave her a great deal of solace.

Most days she felt more like Uriah's servant rather than his half sister. For more than twenty years, she'd kept house for him. Ever since her father died and she'd had nowhere else to go. Uriah had done his Christian duty by her, and together they had shared a life of genteel poverty, shifting from one poor-paying curate situation to another. Until finally, not six months ago, Uriah had the luck to be offered the position of librarian to the Duke of Beaufort at his principal residence, Astwell Palace.

The situation even included a lovely cottage of their own. It was the first time since her father's vicarage that she'd lived in her own house. Usually, they had only been able to afford a room or two in another's lodgings. It was a luxury that almost made serving Uriah worth it.

Almost.

She gave the ball of dough one last punch of frustration before covering it with a cheesecloth to prove.

The kettle whistled. Tiffany grabbed a rag and took it off the chain hook by the fire. But she couldn't add the tea leaves until her half brother unlocked the tea box. Since they did not keep servants, there was no need to lock up the tea. Uriah, however, was miserly and wanted to make sure that Tiffany did not drink any without him.

Swiping at the sweat on her brow once more, she began extinguishing the fire in the stove.

"Uriah!" she called up the stairs. "I need to add the tea leaves while the kettle's hot."

He didn't answer.

Tiffany placed the boiled eggs into their bowls and waited. Uriah did not allow her to eat before him. He was the *man* of the house after all. She rolled her eyes. Her half brother unfortunately felt their remote connection to his employer rather too strongly (third cousins, twice removed). Uriah behaved as if *he* were a duke, and everyone else in the village, including herself, was beneath him. He would no sooner respond to her call than he would fetch a bone like a dog. He was truly the most dreadful of brothers. Even half ones.

"Uriah," she called up the stairs again, "your breakfast is getting cold and you're going to be late."

No response.

She waited and waited until the eggs were beyond cold, her temper rising with the heat of the day. She was hungry and irritable and it was *her* birthday.

Forty years.

A depressing thought. Tiffany had so very little to show for it.

Picking up the spoon, she cracked the egg in front of her. This small act of rebellion brought a smile to her lips. She poured herself some hot water from the kettle to drink.

If Uriah didn't come down now, he would be late for work. She shook her head and had to bite her lower lip to keep from giving her half brother a piece of her mind. No one cared for the opinion of dependent relatives and confirmed spinsters. Which was silly. They saw more than anyone else because they were always on the fringes. And she would be hanged before she allowed him to ruin this wonderful position and lose her cottage.

With trepidation, she stole up the stairs and knocked on his door.

There was no answer.

She knocked again, even louder. Still no response. A fear that something was amiss began to grow in her mind, tightening her chest until it ached. Uriah had been a bear the night before, yelling that someone had stolen his diamond pin and complaining about the pain in his belly. He possessed a weak stomach and often vomited. And rarely did he clean up his own sick. That *pleasant* task was left to her.

Slowly, she opened the door and saw him in his bed. She sighed in relief.

"Uriah, you lazy sloth! Get out of bed before you lose the best position you've ever had."

It was at that exact moment that a rather unpleasant smell met her nostrils. He had been sick in the night, and a great deal of it was now on the floor that she had scrubbed the day before. How Uriah could sleep in a room with this noxious smell, she couldn't believe. Pinching her nose, she walked closer to him and put a hand on his shoulder, giving him a shove.

"Wake up!"

His body moved a little but fell back in place. Inanimate. The fingers that had been pinching her nose, fell to her side. Uriah wasn't moving at all. There was no rise and fall to his chest to indicate that he was breathing. She put two fingers on his neck and felt for a pulse. There was nothing.

Her half brother was dead in his forty-fifth year.

The smell and the shock overcame her, and she ran from the room, down the stairs, and through the kitchen to the back garden. She breathed in and out slowly. Deeply. Trying to convince her stomach not to lose its precarious contents.

Uriah was dead.

Tears fell down her cheeks, but they weren't tears of sadness for her half brother's death. She sobbed and gasped for air because she felt so guilty that she didn't feel any sorrow. As a good Christian woman, she should be mourning the loss of a family member. Weeping and wailing for the dead. Praying that his soul would be safe in the arms of his maker. But Uriah had not once thought of her comfort or preferences in all of her forty years. She might have been a chair or shoe—useful, but of no particular importance. Certainly not worth soliciting or listening to her opinions.

No. Tiffany could not pretend she felt any sorrow at his passing. As much as she wanted to.

More tears of shame fell from her eyes. She would mourn the loss of Bristle Cottage more than that of her half brother. It was the first place that had felt like home since her father's vicarage. It was perfect. Far enough from the town of Mapledown for privacy but close enough to walk to. Its situation was well appointed and pretty, overlooking the artificial lake that adorned the grounds of Astwell Palace. The same water that Uriah had forbade her to even place a toe in.

Bristle Cottage, with its three bedchambers, lovely parlor, and newly outfitted kitchen, was everything she'd ever wanted. She would never be able to afford such a lovely open-range stove. She would never have her own kitchen again. She had no money. Her father had left his diamond cluster pin, their furniture, and a small legacy to Uriah, but he had spent the money within five years of their father's death on little luxuries that a poor curate could ill afford.

Tiffany had inherited nothing.

There were a few coins left in the cottage from her food money. They were supposed to keep her and Uriah fed until the end of the month, when he received his quarterly salary next. But now there would be no money on the first of October. The remaining money the last month of every quarter was always meager, for Uriah had no turn for economy. She might be able to feed herself for the remainder of the month, but she didn't have enough money to rent a room in town.

She would have to find a paying position. Maybe as a housekeeper or a companion? But how did a woman even set about advertising her availability? And would her future employer expect her to have some experience to qualify her for such a role? She'd managed two servants at her father's vicarage, those many years ago, but they had been more like family than help. And she had no idea how one set about running a large house. A cottage was the perfect size.

More tears fell from her cheeks until Tiffany felt as if she had run out of water. The Duke of Beaufort would give her lovely cottage to his next librarian.

Her gaze fell on the crack willow tree on the edge of the stone fence. It looked all weepy and the sort of tree you'd see in a graveyard. She sighed. She didn't even have enough money to pay for Uriah's burial, let alone his funeral. Their local rector, Mr. Shirley, was not the sort of person who would perform any church duty without pay. He would want the coins in his hand before he opened his Bible.

Perhaps she could dig the hole in the cemetery herself and save the fee of the grave diggers?

She looked down at her hands. They were rough from housework, cooking, and the garden she'd planted behind the cottage. Her hands were used to hard work. She could dig that grave. She was a tall woman. As tall as her brother. Taller than most men. Tiffany had often thought if it weren't for her dress and panniers, she could be taken for a man. Her resemblance to her half brother was unfortunately quite marked. They both had oval faces, light blue eyes, and overgenerous lips. At the suggestion of her school friend, she had once put on her half brother's clothes and tricked her parents for a whole hour before they realized that it was her. Father had not been amused by her prank. Like Uriah, he lacked a sense of humor. Mother had laughed until she cried. She died later that year.

If only Tiffany could put on Uriah's clothes now and take his place!

She laughed out loud at the thought. How ridiculous. How perfectly wonderful and ridiculous. If she could wear his clothes, she could keep his position as librarian and her cottage. She would not have to lose her home and be dependent on another's charity. Laughing harder, she was bordering on hysteria. Tiffany thought of all the books she could read if people thought she were a man. She could read anything she liked! No one would tell her that she was not intelligent enough to read a treatise or that she was too delicate to read the contents of a salacious novel.

Tiffany laughed so hard that she cried and gasped for breath. No one would miss her half brother. She didn't. The duke, if he'd ever actually met Uriah, probably wouldn't care about the death of one of his many servants. Uriah had made no friends in the village. He'd tried to befriend the Baronet of Shaftesbury, Sir Walter Abney, but he'd been snubbed. And Uriah thought he was above everyone else who would have included them in their society, forcing Tiffany to be excluded as well. The only sort of a friend he'd made was the rector, Mr. Washington Shirley. But they didn't have much in common besides both being in their late forties and thinking rather too highly of themselves. The rector had buried two wives and acquired fourteen dour-faced children in the process.

Wiping at her eyes, she sobered. Her half brother's body was upstairs in the cottage, and he already smelled wretched. He was covered in his own sick and defecation. Death had not been kind to him. She needed to clean and take care of the body to prepare it for burial. And with his body, she would bury her hope for a better life.

Unless . . . she took his place. The idea was too fantastic to even be considered, but once it climbed into her brain like a mouse, it refused to leave. If she took Uriah's place, she would keep her cottage. She would have money of her own and freedoms as a man that she had never experienced as a spinster.

Choices.

Power over her own destiny.

CHAPTER 2

Tiffany ran her fingers through her messy hair as she paced around the back garden for several minutes, contemplating the risks involved and the chances of success in such an outrageous charade. She could not masquerade as Uriah all of the time. What excuse could she give the villagers if they asked after the real her? Somehow, she would have to play both herself and Uriah so well that no one would realize that it was only one person. Not that anyone knew her. She was only the librarian's sister, the quiet spinster who never spoke without her half brother's permission.

What if she were caught?

Would they accuse her of murdering her brother? Would she hang for being so wanton as to disguise herself as a man?

The sound of church bells awoke her from her dreary thoughts. Uriah should have been at Astwell Palace for an hour now. She reentered the house and saw that her bread dough had risen above the side of the bowl. She shaped the dough into two loaves and put them in tins for a second prove. Removing her apron, Tiffany straightened her hair and put on her shawl. She would go to the palace and tell them that Uriah was ill. Buy herself a little time.

Tiffany put on her Bergère straw hat and placed an unwanted shawl on her already hot shoulders. With a deep breath, she opened the front door to the cottage and followed the path around the lake. Her heart beat in her throat. By the time she reached the servants' door of the palace, she was shaking from her hair to her toes. She'd never set foot in the grand building before, only looked at it from across the lake. It was so much bigger and more forbidding in person. The stone was light, looking almost white in the midmorning sun. Endless columns and windows were lined up in perfect unity and symmetry. She could not have imagined a more beautiful place. Even in heaven.

Standing at the door, she tried to work up enough courage to go in, when a woman a little older than her came up to her. The woman was dressed very finely but wore a frilly white apron and a Bonnot á la Jeannot cap made from a sheer organdy. She was short, but her figure was trim, and her eyes a sharp green—the sort of sharp that did not miss the little details. The flour underneath Tiffany's fingernails. The mud on her worn pair of boots from the rain the night before—the wooden pattens strapped to the bottom of her shoes hadn't been high enough to keep it off.

"May I help you, miss?" she said politely.

"I—I am here to tell you that my brother, Mr. Woodall, is ill today and unable to work."

The woman nodded. "I could tell that you were Mr. Woodall's sister even before you spoke. You have not only similar features but also mannerisms."

She *was* sharp.

Tiffany curtsied. "I am Miss Tiffany Woodall."

The woman returned her curtsy. "I am Mrs. Wheatley, the housekeeper."

"Will you pass my brother's message on to the family?"

She nodded. "His Grace is not at home right now. He is taking his young son to London for school, but I will inform the butler that Mr. Woodall is not to be expected for dinner today."

Tiffany blinked, temporarily stunned. "You eat dinner during the day?"

"Usually at two in the afternoon," Mrs. Wheatley said. "That way we have plenty of time to be ready for His Grace's dinner at four."

She could only manage a wry smile in response. Uriah had insisted that they economize by not having any midday meal. Clearly, that economy had only been meant for her. Any guilt she'd felt about contemplating burying her brother in the garden seemed to evaporate like boiling water in the air. Her half brother had always thought of his own needs first. Maybe it was time she did the same.

"I am sure that after today's rest, he will be fit as a fiddle for work tomorrow," Tiffany said.

"Very good."

She remembered her half brother's pin. "Oh, and Uriah has misplaced his diamond pin. If any of the servants see it, will you let him know? He's worried sick over it."

Mrs. Wheatley stiffened, as if she thought Tiffany was accusing her of the theft. "And what does it look like?"

Tiffany swallowed. "It's very small. The head is a circle with a cluster of small diamonds, and the pin is made of gold. Uriah often wears it on the lapel of his coats. It must have fallen off. Perhaps in the library or in a hall."

"I will keep an eye out for it, Miss Woodall."

Tiffany smiled and gave another graceless curtsy before leaving the doorstep, her heart feeling lighter than before. When she reached the cottage, she did not go back inside. The smell of Uriah's body and sick had already reached the front door. Rather, she went around back to her garden shed to collect her shovel.

She scooped the first shovel of dirt from underneath the crack willow. Then the next. Over and over until her hands blistered and began to bleed. Still, the hole was not deep enough for her brother's body. Taking a break, she washed her hands in the bucket by the house and prepared to bake her bread. Not even the delicious aroma could overcome the noxious smell that permeated the cottage. She ate her brother's boiled egg from breakfast and drank the leftover cold water from the kettle. She would need the energy to continue to dig.

Waiting until the bread was done baking, she tried to remember what Uriah had told her about the Duke of Beaufort, his family, and staff. The duke, he had assured her, was the perfect nobleman. The duchess was always extremely affable to him—which could have been an exaggeration. Her half brother had been terribly pretentious. Uriah had not mentioned any other members of the duke's family nor the staff. They were servants, and *he* was a gentleman. How useful it would have been if she even knew their names or positions!

Tiffany returned to the garden and dug until the hole was at her own eye level.

She climbed out, covered in mud and dirt from her hair to her feet. The sun had begun to set. It would be dusk soon. The perfect time to bury a body. She entered the cottage and picked up her scarf and wrapped it around her nose before climbing the stairs to her half brother's room. Eight hours had not improved the sight or smell of him. Steeling herself, she pulled his blankets and sheets around him, then began to drag his body across the floor.

It was so heavy!

By the time she reached the top of the stairs, she was breathing hard, already exhausted from digging his grave. The sound of his body thumping against the wooden treads made her heart jump, but she could not stop. She dared not stop. Freedom was within her grasp. She would be able to make her own choices. Have her own money. Such a heady, marvelous feeling to have the same privileges as the male sex!

She dragged his body through the parlor, through the kitchen, and out the back door. She pulled her half brother's corpse to the hole and rolled him in. Filling the hole with dirt went much faster than digging it. Still, the sun had completely set before she finished, and the moon was rising in the east.

Kneeling, she said a prayer over the grave. She pleaded with the Lord to accept her half brother's soul and to forgive her for not burying him in sacred ground.

Tiffany returned the shovel to the shed and reentered the house. The smell had not abated. She rushed through the cottage and opened every single window. The last one was in Uriah's room—the source of the unpleasant scent. She saw that the mattress was irredeemably soiled. Her father, rest his soul, always said that death did not treat even the greatest of men with dignity. Her half brother had not been the greatest of men, but she couldn't help feeling he might have deserved better than this.

She scrubbed the floor with old rags and then rolled them up in the mattress and carried it down the stairs. After a corpse, it was not too difficult a burden. She set it on the freshly turned soil of the grave and then lit it on fire. The feathers and tick burnt fast and fiercely. Hopefully covering the smell of the body from any animals.

The embers were still smoldering when she realized that her own clothing was quite impossible to save. Stripping down to nothing but her second-hand boots, she threw her ruined dress, scarf, and shift onto the fire. The flames reared up again but, after a few minutes, faded until there was nothing but ash. She stomped out the rest of the sparks.

Smoky, dirty, and smelly, Tiffany looked longingly at the forbidden water of the lake. Her half brother was dead and he could no longer tell her what to do. Purposefully, she strode toward the lake and walked in. The cool water stung the sores on her hands but also numbed some of the pain. She walked deeper until the water reached above her waist. Sitting down, she tried to shake off the grime of the day like a duck shook rain off its feathers. The cold water felt marvelous. She allowed her head to go underneath it and for the lake to swallow her up entirely.

It was peaceful underneath the water—until two rough hands grabbed her around the waist and hauled her back to the pebbled shore.

"Let me go!" she shrieked.

"A fine thank-you," the man said. His face had been obscured by his hat, but he did exactly as she had asked. He released Tiffany in a heap on the beach.

"Why should I thank you for ruining my swim?"

She scrambled to her feet; realizing that, for the first time in her forty years, she was completely bare in front of a man. Mortified, she placed her hands and arms strategically, attempting to cover herself. The full moon did not give much light, but enough for her to make out the face of the man who thought he had rescued her. She recognized the warm brown skin and handsome features of Mr. Lathrop, the bookseller. He must have thought she was drowning and had entered the water to rescue her.

They stared at each other for a moment before he turned away and demanded, "Where are your clothes?"

"I didn't bring any."

He glanced back at her uncovered form, and Tiffany felt the heat rise to her face, before he averted them again. "You walked all the way from town in nothing but your boots?"

"I don't live in Mapledown!" she spat out, before she could stop herself.

"What is your name?"

Mr. Lathrop hadn't recognized her. Not that they had ever been formally introduced, but she thought that he would at least know her name. The town of Mapledown was fair sized, but it was not that large. But she was invisible. Clothed or unclothed, she was just another spinster.

"None of your business."

"Then I shall make it my business to learn it."

She gasped in surprise. Personal inquiries about her at this time would prove disastrous. "Miss Tiffany Woodall."

He bowed to her as if they were being formally introduced. Since he was facing the other direction, it gave her a rather nice view of *his* backside. "Well, Miss Woodall, I suggest you run, so you don't catch a chill."

"I will as soon as you leave," she gritted out.

The wretched man laughed but returned to the path. She waited until he was well and truly out of sight before doing exactly as he suggested: running for it.

CHAPTER 3

Tiffany spent the early hours of the morning delousing her brother's wig. Wearing a wig was itchy enough without the addition of vermin. Once she was confident that no small critters were going to be on her head, she opened her brother's wardrobe. Like everything else in the cottage, it was finer than hers. Disrobing from her nightdress, she pulled up the linen breeches and buttoned them by her knees. They were a little snug, but not too bad. Tugging on his silk stockings with embroidered clocks, she secured them to the garters, before adding the false shin paddings that her brother had worn to make the back of his legs appear more muscular. He'd also used similar padding to make the front of his breeches look larger, but she wasn't about to stick that thing in her pants. She would pitch it into the morning breakfast fire.

Next, she put on his shirt, only to realize that, although the good Lord had not endowed her with much in the upper area, there was enough to make her not look like a man.

With an exasperated huff, she went to the linen closet and took the only spare sheet and started ripping it into long strands. Then Tiffany bound her chest until it hurt. After, the shirt fit mostly well. Luckily, Uriah had also worn stays to slim his waist.

She put on the matching waistcoat and the double-breasted coat with a full skirt, quilted collar, and cuffs. Glancing in the mirror, she saw that the coat went nearly to her knees and covered her hips pretty well. She looked remarkably like her brother; except he wore face powder.

Opening the jar of white lead somehow felt more intrusive than wearing Uriah's clothing, but it had to be done. She covered her face in white powder and then used liquid rouge made from alum, benzoin gum powder, and brandy to redden her cheeks and lips. The last things she added were three circular black patches on her left cheek. Her brother had had a small pox scar there that he always covered. She placed his wig on her head. This time when she looked in the mirror, she had to glance twice. Looking at her own reflection was like seeing her half brother's ghost.

Satisfied that she could deceive even the most discerning, she went down the stairs. She slid on his high-heeled boots; they were a little loose, but not too much. She took a deep breath and then put on his brown hat with a small crown and wide upturned brim, and grabbed his cane.

The walk to Astwell Palace took longer than it had yesterday. Tiffany had to try to keep Uriah's boots on, which proved much harder on the pebbled path. At last, she reached the servants' entrance. She took one more sustaining deep breath before entering. The door opened onto a small landing before descending into a sunken, square dining room with two large banquet tables. She walked down the stairs. From one side of the dining room, she could see an archway into the kitchen, which was bustling with servants and delicious smells.

She walked up the stairs on the other side of the room, where she reached a hall. One way led to a large room and a staircase that went both up and down. The room had many mismatched chairs and must have been a common room for the servants. The other direction led to a hall with several doors on either side and one on the end. Tiffany assumed that the last door led to the main house.

As she passed the first door, Mrs. Wheatley opened it up. The room looked like a little private office for the housekeeper. "Mr. Woodall, are you feeling in better health today?"

Tiffany almost curtsied, but remembered in the nick of time to bow. "Much better, Mrs. Wheatley," she said in her lowest voice, almost a whisper. "Thank you for inquiring."

The housekeeper smiled and walked the opposite direction.

Tiffany reached the door that led out of the servants' quarters, but then realized, to her horror, that she did not know where the library was. Astwell Palace was enormous, and the hall she found herself in seemed to be lined with an endless row of doors on both sides. Trying not to call attention to herself, she started to surreptitiously open doors. She found three drawing rooms, two dining rooms, and a ballroom, all sumptuously furnished, but no library.

She was about to open another door, when she heard a voice behind her with a curious cadence.

"Did you need something from the duchess's private parlor, Mr. Woodall?"

Turning, Tiffany saw that the voice belonged to a very tall young man of African descent. He was dressed finely in the livery of the house and wore a white wig that accentuated his dark skin. His soft brown eyes watched her with interest. Her own blue eyes were scarcely less curious. He was the handsomest young man she'd ever seen, even though he had to be at least fifteen years her junior.

Trying not to smile at him, she cleared her throat. "I was ill yesterday. And today, I am all turned around and can't seem to find the library. Would you be so good as to show me the way?"

He raised his eyebrows at her but nodded. "Of course, Mr. Woodall—this way."

She followed behind him. The young man had to be at least six feet tall, with broad shoulders, and very fine calves. But she was supposed to be a man, who didn't notice those sort of things, not a spinster who had very little contact with anyone besides her half brother and had, in the space of two days, goggled at two very different men. She needed to pull herself together! She'd spent too much time alone.

The young man opened the door to the library, which was only three doors down. "Let me know if you need anything else, Mr. Woodall."

Tiffany could not repress a smile this time. "Thank you very much."

She entered the room, and he closed the door behind her, which was good, for she could have shrieked with delight. Never in her life had she seen so many books! They lined the walls of the large room and went up two stories high. She walked to the closest shelf—the books were in Latin.

"Oh dear," she whispered aloud. She hadn't thought about that. Uriah had been taught Ancient Greek, Latin, French, and German by her father; and then he had attended Cambridge University. She had only learned conversable French at the young ladies' school she'd attended. And she was lucky to have learned even that, as her father would not have spent a farthing on her education. Her mother had prevailed on their vicarage's benefactor, the Earl of Topham, to send Tiffany with his own daughter, Tess—Lady Theresa—to school.

She continued to walk and found that the next section of books were written in French. Luckily, she could make out most of the titles. The section after that she assumed was in German. She walked around the rest of the library. To her relief, the majority of the library was in English. Uriah, with his usual attention to detail, had organized it by the author's last name. Every shelf was tidy. Every book was put away.

There was no sign of Uriah's diamond pin anywhere. Perhaps it was still in his room at the cottage. She would have to check for it when she got home that evening.

But what was she supposed to do all day?

She'd once asked Uriah about his librarian responsibilities, but he'd summarily snubbed her. "The complexities of my position are too much for your female brain."

Sighing, she examined the room a second time and found a desk with some papers on it. She recognized Uriah's scrawl on the paper. It was a list of books for Mr. Lathrop to order from London. She picked up the list. It was not a very promising one. All of the books were either lectures on morality or philosophy.

Uriah had let it slide one night, after too much ale, that there were certain people at the palace who needed to repent. Who they were or what they had done he would not say, deeming it too lewd for his sister's ears. Everything interesting he'd deemed inappropriate for her ears or eyes. She glanced again at the list; there was not a novel to be found on it. She bit her lower lip. How she longed to read a novel!

The door to the library opened, and it was the same young man who had helped her find the library. He held the door for a lady who looked to be around her age, possibly a little older. It was hard to tell because the woman's face was heavily painted, and she had an enormous white wig on her head. It was an elaborate coiffure of ribbons, feathers, and so many curls. But it was her gown that made Tiffany truly envious. It was striped with thick green and gold lines and thin maroon ones. It gathered in bunches around her waist so that the golden petticoat underneath showed. The sleeves reached to her elbows and were adorned with lace.

A young woman followed her into the room. She was not as finely dressed, but she was undeniably beautiful, with unpowdered, craped golden curls in a coiffure friseur and a heart-shaped face.

The older lady made an impatient noise.

Tiffany had been gawking at the finery when she should have been bowing. She gave a slow, low bow before glancing at the woman's face. A smirk lingered on her lips. Unbidden, Tiffany felt herself blush. This had to be the Duchess of Beaufort— the lady of the house.

"How may I assist you, Your Grace?" Tiffany asked in a low whisper.

The duchess sniffed. "I have a house party arriving in a fortnight, and I should like a book or two to be in each of their rooms."

"Very good, Your Grace."

She wrinkled her nose once again. "Not any of these dusty, dull ones. My guests only want the latest novels. Perhaps you can go to the local bookseller and purchase some."

The blood rushed to her face when she thought of Mr. Lathrop and how embarrassing it would be to see him again. But *Tiffany* wouldn't see him again. *Uriah* would. She would be dressed as a man and therefore had no need to feel embarrassed. Nor to wonder what he thought of her unclothed form. Or her person at all.

"Of—of course, Your Grace," she stammered.

The duchess gave her one last look of disdain before leaving the room. The pretty young woman followed her; she was probably a servant. The footman closed the door behind them all. Tiffany let out another sigh, which turned into a laugh. Of all the ridiculous predicaments to find herself in.

★ ★ ★

She passed several hours going through her brother's notes. It didn't take her long to realize that none of them would be at all helpful in finding popular novels for the duchess's guests. Uriah was a snob when it came to literature, and only the very finest playwrights and poets could be found on the shelves.

Her stomach grumbled. She'd been too nervous that morning to eat, but now that it was the afternoon, she was positively famished. Tidying up the papers, she left the library (careful to remember exactly which door it was) and wandered back to the sunken dining room. Mrs. Wheatley and the female servants sat at the left table. An older man (presumably the butler) with a second chin sat at the top of the right table. He stood up when she entered the room, slightly favoring his right leg.

"Mr. Woodall, I wondered if you were going to join us."

"I am sorry to be late, sir," she said, and walked to the only open seat in the room. It was on the right side of the older man. Even though Mrs. Wheatley sat at the adjacent table, her sharp eyes were watching Tiffany's every move. Tiffany's stomach roiled with hunger and nervousness, but she managed to serve herself some stew and meat pie. She took a bite of pie. It was fresh and soft and so delicious. The miller hadn't added any dry bones or filler to the white flour of that pastry.

"Well, Mr. Ford," the cook said in a strong French accent. "We'll have our work cut out for us the next two weeks preparing for the house party."

The butler's name was Mr. Ford. Tiffany could remember that.

"How many guests should I prepare for?" the cook asked.

"Only five," Mr. Ford said, "but they'll each have several servants that we must arrange meals and accommodations for."

Five guests.

Tiffany would only need to purchase ten books from Mr. Lathrop. That wouldn't be too difficult. She continued to eat the stew, and each bite was like a symphony in her mouth. Whether it was the quality or the variety of the ingredients, Tiffany had not experienced anything so delicious before. Once her appetite was satiated, she slowly took a drink of water and looked around the room.

Sitting left of Mrs. Wheatley at the other table was the pretty young woman who had followed the duchess. She must be Her Grace's lady's maid. Beside her was a row of women of differing ages and body types, all wearing a white mob cap and crossed apron over a simple dress. They talked to each other and threw glances at the male servants' table. Not that she could blame them. The man seated across from her was a meek little fellow with protruding eyes, but the strapping young man on his other side was well worth a glance. He had blue eyes, a strong jaw, and thick lips. He smirked back at the maids. Beside Tiffany sat the handsome young man who had helped her find the library. He also glanced at the other table, but his eyes seemed to be only for the pretty lady's maid.

The two tall men were about the same size and judging from their placement at the servants' table, they were footmen. Perhaps Uriah had been offended by their flirtatious manners, but there was nothing immoral about a handsome smile.

The small man seated across from her must be the duke's valet.

Mr. Ford sat down his cup with unnecessary force. Every eye at the table snapped up to look at him. "Bernard, you will wind the clocks."

The footman with the strong jaw stood up, still smirking.

"Thomas, you will polish the silver."

The other footman nodded as he stood up, casting one last glance over his shoulder at the lady's maid. The pretty young lady smiled back him, her cheeks turning a flattering shade of pink. It appeared that the handsome young man was already taken.

A pity.

Chapter 4

Tiffany had never before been so grateful for a Sunday. She was able to scrub down Uriah's room and wash all of his clothes. She carefully checked every item for the diamond pin before placing it in the soapy water, but the pin was nowhere to be found. Where could he have lost it?

She would also not need to spend another nerve-racking day trying to figure out what she was supposed to do and guessing the names of servants that she should already know. For once, she didn't mind the tightness of her stays; they were less restricting than the binding around her breasts. She pulled up her panniers—without them, she barely had noticeable hips, something that definitely helped when she masqueraded as a man. She pulled on her plain gray dress and could not help but think of the duchess's exquisite day gown. Her brother had not allowed her to spend her money on fine materials. He'd insisted on simple, sturdy, and basic cloth for her. Well, she was her own woman now, and she would buy herself the prettiest material in the shop as soon as she received her quarterly wage.

Walking to church, she was grateful for shoes that fit her feet. She contemplated skipping the Sunday meeting, but if both she and Uriah were missing, the rector would call to see what was wrong. And he was probably the only person who had known her half brother well enough to see through her disguise.

Still her heart caught in her chest when she entered the chapel, as if all the statues of the saints were looking down and condemning her for her charade and for not burying Uriah in consecrated ground. And then a man stood up in his seat and tipped his tall black hat to her.

It was Mr. Lathrop!

The heat rushed to her face, and she knew it must be as red as fire. Trust a man to only recognize a woman after he'd seen her unclothed. He smiled widely, as if he were delighted to see her again. He was even handsomer when he smiled. She managed to give a sharp nod in return and slunk into her brother's pew, her mortification complete.

Tiffany barely heard one word in three of the rector's sermon because of her guilt, embarrassment, and fear of discovery. Not that she missed much. Mr. Shirley called them all to repentance every Sunday and insinuated that most of the town's occupants would be burning in hellfire in the next life. She'd always assumed that she would be one of the few that wasn't in flames, but after her deeds this week, she would be blazing with the rest of them. At least she wouldn't be lonely.

The service ended, and she tried to make good her escape, only to have the rector catch her by the elbow.

"Is your brother unwell this morning?"

She clenched her teeth but then forced herself to lie. "I'm afraid that he is. His old stomach complaint is afflicting him again."

"Perhaps I should come and visit him?"

"Oh no!" she said quickly. "It would embarrass Uriah for you to see him . . . like this. But be assured that I will pass on your concern for him. Thank you, Rector."

Tiffany tried to step away, but his hold on her elbow was like a vise, and he was not letting her go easily.

"Miss Woodall, if you would wait until I have bid farewell to my parishioners," Mr. Shirley said, "I would be pleased to walk you home, since you do not have the company of your brother."

She wouldn't be pleased at all but couldn't think up a plausible excuse fast enough. So, she gave him a pathetic smile and a small nod. At last, he released his grip on her elbow and moved to the door, where he could talk to people as they left the church. Tiffany let out a sigh and shook her head.

"You don't fancy being the rector's third wife?"

Tiffany knew that voice. It was beautifully cultivated, clearly educated, but with the slightest foreign lilt to it. The bookseller, Mr. Lathrop, was standing beside her, grinning like a child with a piece of cake. He was dressed very elegantly in a blue coat with golden embroidery on the cuffs and the tails. His shoulders were broad and filled out his coat quite beautifully—not that she noticed. She felt herself blush again. Curse the man!

"You talk nonsense," she said, giving him a much-needed set down.

He only grinned more widely at her. She sighed again and rolled her eyes. For six months, no man had even bothered speaking to her in Mapledown, and the one Sunday she came without Uriah, she was accosted by two of them.

"Of course, you did not know the rector's first two wives, as I did," he said, still watching her with a look of unholy joy at her discomfort. "But you would fit right in. Light hair, blue eyes, pretty, and with a great deal of spirit. The spirit he will drain out of you quickly enough, if your fourteen stepchildren don't, first."

She blinked and it took her mind a few moments to process his words. Mostly, because he'd called her pretty, a word that she hadn't heard since she was a young woman and her mother had been alive. Did he really think she was attractive? Even at her age, with the wrinkles that had started to form around the corners of her eyes and mouth?

Fourteen stepchildren. The thought of being responsible for the rector's never-ending line of dour-faced children brought her to her senses. "Good heavens."

Mr. Lathrop had the audacity to laugh.

Tiffany was forced to bite her lower lip because, for some unknown reason, she longed to laugh with him at the ridiculousness of it all. *She* marry the rector? That would be worse than living with Uriah. At least, with her half brother she was only supposed to clean his house and cook his meals. The rector would expect her to take care of his children and share his bed. She shivered at that repugnant thought.

"You'd best watch your step with him, Miss Woodall," Mr. Lathrop said, his voice sober but his eyes still dancing with merriment.

"I don't need to."

He blinked at her, as if surprised by her answer. "You fancy a husband?"

"No," Tiffany said, and this time she was the one smiling. "But I have *you* to watch my steps, as you did at the lake."

She had the satisfaction of seeing his brown skin flush with red. He looked rather sheepish.

"Miss Woodall," Mr. Shirley called out, and then walked up to them. "What have you and Mr. Lathrop been discussing?"

"Books," she said, the first thought that popped into her head. "The Duchess of Beaufort is eager for my brother to purchase some modern novels for her upcoming house party."

"And I have a great variety of novels at my shop," Mr. Lathrop said.

"I don't approve of novels," the rector said, shaking his skull-like head. "Their content is often quite lewd. Especially for ladies, whose minds are already too weak and susceptible to the devil's influence. I hope that you do not read novels, Miss Woodall."

She shook her head. "I have not read one."

"A pity. I think you would enjoy them," Mr. Lathrop said, then touched his tall black hat, with a hatband and narrow curled brim. "Miss Woodall. Rector."

Tiffany watched him leave the church. With his departure, the room seemed to darken. Mr. Shirley smiled at her—it would have frightened a rabbit. His teeth were yellow and rather sharp. It made his already thin white face look even more skeletal.

"Shall we go, Miss Woodall?"

"Yes, please," she said, and started to walk for the door without waiting for him. She did not want him to offer his arm. Touching him for the entire walk to her cottage would have been worse than digging another grave with her bare hands.

"Did you enjoy the sermon?"

Oh dear. She hadn't really listened to it. "Very much."

"It was quite a balm for me to look down from the pulpit and see your lovely face watching me speak the Lord's words."

When Mr. Lathrop had called her pretty, she'd been pleased. But when Mr. Shirley called her lovely, she felt sick. All Tiffany could do was turn her head away from the rector.

"You are too modest," he said. "Another one of your many virtues."

If "modest" meant that she never got to say what she thought or truly felt, then she was the embodiment of that word.

"Most women of your age are not very attractive," he continued. "But I suppose that it is because you are unmarried that you have not lost your bloom. Nor have you experienced the difficulties of child breeding and rearing, which age a woman greatly. You are no doubt past such a time in life."

Tiffany choked at his forwardness. At his offensiveness. She knew not how to answer.

"I assume a woman of your age no longer has monthly bleeds?"

She was only forty. She still bled every twenty-eighth day. It was a dreaded monthly reminder that she would never be married and have children of her own. "Mr. Shirley, it is hardly appropriate for me to answer such a question."

The bony-faced man had the grace to color. He cleared his throat. "I apologize if I have been too rough in my language for a lady. I have been meaning to speak to your brother about a most important question."

Mr. Lathrop had been right. The rector did want to marry her, and after fathering fourteen children, he did not want to father any more with her. At least *that* feeling was entirely mutual.

"I-I would ask you not to speak to my brother quite yet," she stammered. "I-I should like to get to know you better before any . . . decision is made."

Mr. Shirley gave her another frightening smile. "That is very prudent, Miss Woodall. Yet another one of your stellar qualities for me to admire."

She gave a false, little laugh. The rector seemed pleased enough with it, for he continued to speak at her for the rest of the walk to her cottage. He even seemed inclined to linger on her doorstep.

"Thank you for walking me home, Mr. Shirley," she said, unlocking the door and turning the handle. "I bid you good day."

She closed the door before he had a chance to continue the conversation. Breathing heavily, she leaned back against the wood. What a tangle she was in! How was she to end the rector's suit without offending him or, worse, without him discovering that her half brother was dead? And why had Mr. Lathrop suddenly shown an interest in her?

His behavior, unlike the rector's, was harder to understand. He had attempted to rescue her from the lake. Had he also attempted to save her from a disastrous marriage to the rector? Why else would he have warned her about Mr. Shirley's intentions and previous wives? Mr. Lathrop was a conundrum, but a handsome one.

CHAPTER 5

At least in breeches, Tiffany didn't have to worry about the rector's unwanted attentions. She had stuffed linen in the toes of her brother's boots, and now they did not slip and slide as much. In fact, she had started to enjoy the walk to and from Astwell Palace, always keeping her eyes peeled on the path for Uriah's lost pin. It had been their father's, and his father's before him. The only heirloom of their family—irreplaceable. The most valuable thing Uriah had owned. For her, it had always been a lovely reminder of her father. He'd worn it every day of his life on the lapel of his coat.

Dressed as a man, she could go wherever she pleased, with no one to tell her what, when, or how to do anything. It was a freedom unlike anything she had ever experienced, and she reveled in it.

She no longer needed Thomas's assistance to locate the library, which was probably a good thing, for she spied him and Miss Doddridge kissing in the shrubbery on her way to the servants' entrance. Her heart lifted at the sight of young love. She had also once been young and in love. *Nathaniel.* Like, Thomas, he'd been tall and handsome. A wave of emotion swept over her, and she felt like crying. But this was not the time or place. He had been dead for twenty-two years.

Sniffling, so as not to touch her face (she didn't want to smudge the white powder), she picked up her list. The door to the library swung open.

"Where is Miss Doddridge?" the duchess demanded. She was still in her night clothing, with an embroidered silk robe barely covering it. She was not wearing a wig, and Tiffany saw that the true color of her hair was brown with a few streaks of gray.

Tiffany stood and bowed. "I have not seen her this morning, Your Grace," she lied. She was not about to tattle on the footman or the lady's maid.

The duchess huffed. "And where are the books that I asked you to purchase for my guests?"

She swallowed heavily. "I was making a list."

The duchess picked up a rather heavy volume from a table and threw it on the floor. "I don't want a list! I want books in those rooms. I want everything the way it should be—the way it was always meant to be!"

"Now, what's amiss, my duchess?" a polished voice from the door asked. It had to be the Duke of Beaufort. He must have returned from taking his son to school. He strolled into the room with a winning smile. His curly hair was powdered white and his face heavily made up, but she could see the lines of age around his eyes and mouth. Every piece of his clothing was beautifully embroidered and perfectly tailored, but his finery couldn't hide his paunch.

"Miss Doddridge is nowhere to be found this morning, and your silly librarian hasn't purchased books yet for our guests," she said. "We are already going to have an uneven number, so every other detail must be correct."

The duke took his wife's hand and gently kissed it. "Would you like some snuff? It always calms you down."

She shook her head vehemently.

"I can assure you that everyone will have a perfectly marvelous time at your house party, and I saw Miss Doddridge in the hall," he said, "so I believe she will be in your rooms before you are."

The duchess sighed and then glared at Tiffany. "I want those books today."

"Yes, Your Grace," Tiffany said with another awkward bow.

The angry woman left the room, but the duke stayed. Tiffany remained standing. She didn't know what she was supposed to do or say.

He took a small snuffbox out of his pocket. It was as beautiful as his clothes, delicately painted with red robins. He flipped it open with only his thumb and took a small pinch of snuff, placing it on the back of his hand. Raising his hand to his nose, he inhaled the snuff in one nostril and then the other. The duke held out his snuffbox to Tiffany.

"Would you care for a pinch, Mr. Woodall?"

She knew that her brother had on occasion taken snuff when his social betters offered him a pinch of their sort. But the one time that she'd tried it, she'd spent the next hour sneezing. Snorting dried tobacco leaves soaked in scented oil was not her idea of a treat. She shook her head.

"Don't take the duchess's words to heart," he said. "Tomorrow is early enough. There is no reason to make you journey out here twice in one day. Please excuse my wife. She is simply upset that our dear friend, the Duchess of Surrey, is unable to attend her house party."

"Tess," the word escaped Tiffany's lips before she could shut them. Tess had been her first friend and only confidante. They had been as close as sisters when they were girls, but Tiffany hadn't realized that it would all change when they grew up. The daughters of earls did not associate with poor spinsters. They became duchesses.

The duke's eyebrows popped up, and he eyed her closely. His eyebrows were so perfectly shaped that they must have been made from mouse fur.

"You know the dowager Duchess of Surrey?"

Tiffany shook her head. "No, Your Grace. Um, my sister attended finishing school with her when they were girls. The duchess's father, the Earl of Topham, paid for my sister's education."

"And have they remained in contact?"

"No, no. Not since they were seventeen," Tiffany managed to say. "Many years ago."

"And what is your sister's name?"

"Miss Tiffany Woodall," she whispered. It felt strange talking about herself in the third person.

"Never married?"

"No. She was engaged to Third Lieutenant Nathaniel Occom, but he died before they could marry," Tiffany explained, although why, she couldn't say. She hadn't spoken Nathaniel's name out loud in years. Perhaps, it was the duke's gentle tone or sympathetic face. "My sister has kept house for me for the last twenty years or so."

The duke stroked his smooth chin. "Your sister is currently residing in Bristle Cottage with you?"

"Yes, Your Grace."

"With your permission, I shall write to the Duchess of Surrey and let her know of your sister's location and see if that doesn't change her mind about coming to the house party after all. She is still mourning the loss of her husband; but perhaps seeing an old friend would be enough to stir her out of the dismals."

Tiffany hadn't spoken to Tess in twenty-three years. Not since the dreadful day when her best friend had returned from the London season and told her that they could no longer be friends, that Tiffany's station in life was too far beneath that of the daughter of an earl. Tess had been engaged to a duke and hadn't so much as nodded to Tiffany at church. It was as if she hadn't been able to see her. The memory still brought Tiffany pain. The last person she wanted to see was Tess, especially since her visiting would make it impossible for Tiffany to be dressed as Uriah. The very idea was a disaster, but the duke was her employer, and she didn't dare refuse him anything.

"Of course, you have my permission," she managed to say. "Whatever you wish, Your Grace."

The duke gave her another winning smile and left the library. It wasn't until the door closed that Tiffany felt like she could breathe again. She wouldn't think about Tess right now. The house party visit was over a week away, and it wasn't certain that she would come. And even if she did, she would probably only bow to Tiffany as an old acquaintance of a lower rank.

No, Tiffany needed to focus on her immediate problem—purchasing novels. A smile curled on her lips. She would read every single one of them, and no one could stop her!

★   ★   ★

She waited until after eating her two o'clock dinner with the servants before setting off for Mapledown. She was hot and thirsty by the time she passed her cottage and stopped inside to get a drink. Slipping off her shoes and then her clock stockings, she could see blisters forming all over her feet. Uriah's shoes did not fit her at all. And the thought of wearing them all the way into town, where they would chafe and fester her blisters, seemed to be a poor idea. The fact that she was changing her raiment from Uriah's to her own best blue dress, had everything to do with her feet and absolutely nothing to do with the fact that Mr. Lathrop had called her pretty. He was a seller after all; he probably told every lady customer that she was pretty.

Still, she had to be presentable after all. She washed off the full white-face powder that characterized her half brother's appearance. But then she added a little bit of rouge to her cheeks. She pulled on her best pair of boots that were worn in all of the right places. They felt blissfully comfortable, even with her blisters.

There were two roads that Tiffany could take into town. She opted for the longer one that did not pass by the rectory. The last person she wanted to see today was Mr. Shirley, nor did she wish to have him attempt to renew his addresses.

Mr. Lathrop's bookshop was a cobblestone building on the corner of main street. The only outward sign that it was a bookshop was a small black plaque with white letters over the door that read "Books." She'd passed the building so many times after going to the market and had always longed to go inside. Her heartbeat quickened, and she suddenly felt rather breathless. She'd allowed one minor compliment to go entirely to her head.

Her hand shook as she turned the handle to open the door. On three sides of the room, floor-to-ceiling bookshelves filled the walls. The leather binding of the books' spines shone in the sunlight. It was like paradise.

Mr. Lathrop came into the room, from an interior door, and stood behind a counter. It was the first time that Tiffany had seen him without a hat. His dark hair was quite wild and curled in every direction, with a short ponytail in the back. He smiled at her, and Tiffany could have died happily on the spot.

"Miss Woodall, an unexpected surprise."

"Mr. Lathrop," Tiffany said with a curtsy, after recalling that she had stared much too long.

"What can I help you with?" he asked with another smile that did all sorts of things to her inner organs.

Help.

Yes, he was the proprietor of this bookshop.

Pull it together, Tiffany!

"I'm—I mean, my brother has been tasked by the Duchess of Beaufort to procure some novels for the guests of her upcoming house party," she stammered. "I was hoping that you would direct me to your latest and most scintillating novels."

"I see now why your brother sent you," he said with a laugh. "I cannot picture him even touching a novel. The indignity!"

Tiffany laughed too, and she looked him in the eye. Despite the shortness of their relationship, she felt like she'd found a kindred soul in him, someone who appreciated her sense of humor—which her half brother had not. Uriah had even gone so far as to try to squeeze it out of her. She hadn't realized how confined and suppressed she'd been, until his death, when she was finally able to make her own decisions, to think her own thoughts, and to laugh at jokes that *she* found humorous.

"Do you have many novels on hand?" she asked, her eyes greedily looking over the shelves.

"Of course," he said with a smirk. "They sell much better than the philosophical treatises or the foreign language titles that your brother is so fond of ordering from London. Still, the duke's patronage is what allows me to have a bookshop in such a small town, and I'm grateful for it."

"He seems like a kind man."

"And a fair one," Mr. Lathrop said. "I've seen him pardon many a young man for mistakes that others would not have."

"That is generous."

"I am sure he would forgive a lady for swimming in forbidden waters."

She huffed. "Will you stop bringing that up?"

He shook his head, the smile still on his soft, pink lips. "It was *you* who brought it up last time, and I'm afraid that memory is entirely unforgettable."

Tiffany felt heat rush to her face. And the more flustered she felt, the wider Mr. Lathrop's smile became. *Hateful man.* She cleared her throat. "I am . . . my brother is looking for ten to twelve novels."

"Very well," he said, and walked over to the east shelf. He pulled out one book after another and stacked them on his arm until they reached his chin. There was a little bit of dark hair there, and Tiffany wondered whether it would feel scratchy or soft.

Shaking her head to clear that thought, she held out her arms. "I'll take those, and you can send your bill to the palace."

"They're much too heavy for you," he said. "I will deliver them first thing in the morning."

"Very well." Tiffany picked up the top book on the pile. "I'm taking this one with me."

"*The Castle of Otranto* by Horace Walpole is an excellent choice," Mr. Lathrop said. "You will have to tell me what you think of it."

"I should like that very much," Tiffany said, clutching the book to her chest. "Good day to you, Mr. Lathrop."

She turned to leave and heard him call from behind her. "And to you, Miss Woodall."

CHAPTER 6

Mr. Lathrop had been right; Tiffany did enjoy reading novels. In her mind, there was no greater pleasure than escaping between the pages of a book. She quickly finished *The Castle of Otranto*, by Horace Walpole. She passed on *The Vicar of Wakefield*, by Oliver Goldsmith, because she already had quite enough clergy in her life. But she wasted an entire candle to finish reading *The Old English Baron*. Her whole body had shivered with suspense as she turned each page. It had been thrilling.

The duchess's house party was still a few days away, but the new books from Mr. Lathrop's shop had already been placed in the guest's rooms. Tiffany ought to have waited until after the house party, but one of the books was called *The Two Mentors: A Modern Story*, and it was by the same author as *The Old English Baron*. She couldn't wait two days, let alone a fortnight, to read it.

She entered the palace through the servants' quarters and the sunken dining room, lingering until she found the housekeeper, Mrs. Wheatley, in the common room.

"Ah, Mrs. Wheatley—just who I was hoping to see."

"Mr. Woodall." The housekeeper's green eyes watched her with suspicion as she gave an obligatory curtsy.

"I was hoping that you could show me where the guest rooms are," Tiffany said with a smile, hoping to soften the housekeeper's demeanor. "I decided to switch out one book for another. I want the duchess's guests to be entirely pleased with my selections."

Her eyebrows raised a fraction. "Very well, Mr. Woodall. If you would follow me."

Tiffany trailed behind the housekeeper through several halls and up a flight of stairs. The first floor was just as grand as the main floor. Tiffany couldn't help but marvel at the width of the halls and the intricate woodwork and paneling. It was as if Astwell Palace itself was a work of art. Every inch was painted and planned to perfection. Mrs. Wheatley stopped in front of a door that was at least ten feet tall and beautifully carved with cherubs. She turned the golden handle and pushed open the door.

The housekeeper gasped.

Tiffany couldn't help but peek into the room to see what had surprised the woman. Blinking, it took her a few moments to realize precisely what she was seeing. Miss Doddridge and the second footman, broke apart. Their clothes were rumpled, and it appeared as if they had been interrupted at a most inopportune time.

"Bernard," Mrs. Wheatley said, her voice tight, "you will report to Mr. Ford immediately."

The tall, blond footman hastily buttoned up the front of his breeches as he left the room.

"Miss Doddridge," the housekeeper said, "I should like a word with you."

The pretty young maid's face was flushed, but her expression was defiant. She opened her snuffbox with roses painted on the top and took out a pinch. "Fine. I have several words for you as well."

Tiffany cleared her throat. "Let me switch out this book, and I'll leave you two alone to discuss whatever it is you would like to discuss with each other."

Walking into the room. Tiffany found the brown leather book she wanted and traded it for the red one in her hand. Returning to the door, she gave both of the ladies a brief nod and then left the room, closing it behind her. She took three strides forward and then stepped out of one of her too large shoes.

"I will not tolerate your wanton behavior." Tiffany heard Mrs. Wheatley say through the door. "First, I caught you dallying in the shrubs with Thomas Montague, and now here you are with your skirts up with Bernard Coram. Are you determined to debase yourself with every male member of the staff? This is your last warning. I risked everything to bring you on, and I won't have you ruin it."

Embarrassed to be overhearing a private conversation, she slipped out of her other shoe and quietly tiptoed back for the lost one. She had it in her hands when she heard the next line.

"If you try to get me sacked, I will tell the duchess about your little secret, and then you'll be tossed out on your ear after thirty years of service."

With both shoes in hand, Tiffany was about to make good her escape.

"You have more to fear from exposure than I," the housekeeper said, her voice quieter than before but still threatening. "I'm not the only one who has noticed things gone missing around the palace."

Missing things?

Could Uriah's diamond pin have been stolen by someone at the palace? And maybe both Mrs. Wheatley and Miss Doddridge knew something about it? Tiffany couldn't help but listen to find out more.

"There are more grievous sins than a few lost trinkets, *Mrs.* Wheatley," Miss Doddridge said. "But you're not really a missus, are you? It's only a courtesy title for the housekeeper."

"I will not bandy about words with you," Mrs. Wheatley said. "I have work to do."

Tiffany did not wait to hear the young maid's retort. She dashed to the end of the hall and went down the stairs before she put her too-large shoes back on. Luckily, her presence in the hall wasn't discovered by either lady. What she wanted to know was what else had gone missing and what both ladies had to do with the thefts.

Making her way back to the library with her new book, she passed Thomas. She gave him a smile, and he stood taller before returning it. He had such a beautiful smile. Miss Doddridge was a fool if she let him go for the likes of Bernard Coram. The second footman smirked and flirted with all the female servants, while Thomas only had eyes for Miss Doddridge. The two footmen were both tall and handsome, but Thomas Montague's worth was so much the greater and his affection, pure and honest. But perhaps Miss Doddridge would have to learn, like so many young ladies before her, the differences between a Montague and a Coram. Her Nathaniel had been a Montague. Several young ladies from their village had vied for his attention, but he had never wavered in his loyalty or his love for her.

Tiffany opened the door to the library, feeling like a sage old lady. She found a nice comfy chair and sat down to read her new book. It seemed almost prophetic that when she turned open the cover and read the title page, it said, *"A man cannot possess anything better than a good woman, nor anything worse than a bad one."*— *Simonides.* The same thing could be said about a woman; and despite his teasing, she thought that Mr. Lathrop was a good man.

CHAPTER 7

Attending Mr. Shirley's sermon on Sunday was the last thing that Tiffany wanted to do, but if she and Uriah were both absent, the rector would surely pay a call on them. So, she put extra white powder on her face and carefully placed the three patches that Uriah used to always wear. Pulling on his full-skirted coat, she glanced in the mirror and thought that no villager would be able to tell the difference between the two of them. She would have never thought a month ago that she would someday be glad that her brother had snubbed the inhabitants of Mapledown, but now she was.

She strode into the church with her chin up and a look of disdain on her face, passing several shopkeepers she purchased from on a regular basis. They appeared not to recognize her, ignoring her as she was snubbing them. She sat down on the pew and held in a sigh of relief. She'd made it so far.

Then Mr. Lathrop came into the church. How or why she knew to turn at his entrance, she could not say. But he was looking particularly handsome this morning, his dark curly hair wild and untamed in the front, a smile lingering on his full lips. The smile faded when his eyes met hers. As if he recognized her. Tiffany swallowed heavily and turned back around. She was simply being fanciful. Of course, seeing Uriah was what had wiped the smile from his face. Seeing Uriah had always taken away her own smile.

Determined not to glance back again at Mr. Lathrop, she focused on the dour countenance of the rector. His balding head looked even more skeletal as he pounded the pulpit with his waxy yellow hand, which caused his front hairpiece to slide back a few inches before he righted it. Mr. Shirley told them all to prepare for the hottest of hell fires. He was truly eloquent on the eventuality of their eternal damnation and spoke with nary a pause for nearly two hours.

Tiffany felt like the church in September was itself as hot as hellfire. She longed to pull at her collar or fan herself with a hymnal. She did neither. They would draw unwanted attention. So, she simply sat up straighter and felt the sweat pour down the side of her face. When at last, Mr. Shirley said, "Amen," on instinct she repeated the word loudly.

Every eye in the chapel turned to focus on her.

What a foolish mistake. She wanted to hide her face in confusion, but Uriah would never have done that. He was a man. He could say and do whatever he wished. He could call attention to himself without being seen as brazen or outspoken.

Tiffany lifted her chin even higher, and eventually the stares left one by one. The villagers began filing out of the church as if they too felt like it was on fire. The rector's family walked past her pew, from tallest to smallest, all wearing black and with pinched looks on their faces. She wondered if any of the children knew how to smile.

Exhaling, she stood up and began to walk slowly to the door, so as to not step out of her too-large shoes. Mr. Lathrop was still sitting in his pew, watching her like a spider watches a fly stuck in its web. She felt her color rise but continued walking to the door. Uriah would not have given Mr. Lathrop a second glance because of both his profession and the color of his skin. His father was English, but his mother had been Indian. Tiffany, however, thought his skin was a beautiful color and only increased his already handsome looks.

Mr. Shirley was decidedly unhandsome as he scowled by the door. His black cassock hung on his narrow frame, and he looked like a sinister judge waiting to pass sentence on every person who came near him. Only three more steps and she would be past him. Tiffany touched the corner of her tricorn hat and continued walking.

"I should like a word, Woodall," Mr. Shirley called out.

"Of course, Rector," she said, turning to see the blazing brown eyes of Mr. Lathrop right behind her. It was as if they could see through her makeup, through her very skin, into her soul.

He blinked and gave a sharp nod. "Mr. Woodall."

Tiffany was too dazed to even respond or return the gesture. Her growing feelings for the bookseller were affecting her judgment and risking her masquerade, her position as a librarian, and her cottage. She could not allow herself to give into them. Besides, she did not know if Mr. Lathrop even returned her preference.

"I'm glad that you have recovered from your stomach imposition," Mr. Shirley said, adjusting his slipping toupee again. It did not fit quite right, and Tiffany wondered if he had purchased it secondhand.

"I appreciate your concern," Tiffany said gruffly.

"I hope that nothing is amiss with your sister this morning?"

Nothing beyond an aversion of you.

She cleared her throat and tried to speak in a lower register. "Alas, my sister is suffering from cramps caused by her monthly bleeds and was unable to get out of her bed."

The rector nodded and appeared not to be shocked by the mention of her monthlies. Even the smallest complaint about her feminine struggles had caused her half brother to go into strictures on propriety and appropriate behavior for females. Mr. Shirley was clearly made of sterner stuff; but he had been married twice before. They strolled together down the road.

"Er, . . . yes, her monthlies," Mr. Shirley began slowly, as if trying to find the right words. "I hope that I didn't offend the delicate sensibilities of your sister when I asked her last week if she was still fertile at her age."

Tiffany cleared her throat again. "She was initially surprised, but I believe she appreciated your frankness. It is better to be in full possession of the facts before one pursues a courtship. Now that you know that she could still bear several children, I— she—that is to say, *we* would not at all be offended if you were to turn your eyes to another woman on whom to bestow your affections and your name."

"I shan't deny that the thought of more children does present a financial strain to me," Mr. Shirley said. "But at her age, I doubt that she would be able to bear more than one or two children. Three at the most. Especially if they should be girls, it would not present too great a cost."

Girls were not as great a cost. For they did not inherit, nor did they receive much of an education. Tiffany couldn't help but be grateful to Tess's parents, who had paid for her education. Her own father would not have spent a groat.

"My sister is barely forty years of age," she said. "It is impossible to say how many children she could have, but I believe the number to be as many as five. Such a number of children, in addition to your other fourteen, I cannot think a prudent thing."

Tiffany did not know if she would be able to have any children, but anything that would scare away Mr. Shirley, she would happily use. They reached the fork in the road that led to Bristle Cottage. The rector stopped walking. Reluctantly, she turned to face him.

"I assure you that I am well able to support a wife."

"And all the children?" Tiffany pressed.

"I shall be frank with you, Woodall," he said. "When I initially planned to marry again, I thought to find a woman past her childbearing years, for all of the pecuniary reasons that we have already discussed. However, since seeing your sister's beauty and observing the excellent manner that she keeps house for you, I believe that I have quite fallen in love with her, and at this point, no other women could do for me."

"She has no dowry."

Mr. Shirley didn't so much as blink. "That was expected. I assumed, since she was a spinster, that she was penniless. A pretty woman like her would be otherwise married."

"My sister was once engaged to a naval lieutenant, and the young man died at sea," she said, trying to dissuade the rector. "I believe that she will always love him."

"I, too, know what it is to love those who are dead," he said, touching the location where his heart should have been. "I will always love my first two wives, God rest their souls. And while it is good for a woman to mourn, it is better for her to wed. Like Eve, she has no other purpose on this earth."

Tiffany stiffened. "I am not sure that my sister returns your regard."

Mr. Shirley smiled, a frightening sight. "A woman of her age does not have many options. She is very fortunate to catch the attentions of a man of the cloth and to have the opportunity to be a wife, the highest and holiest calling available to a female. I am certain that I can depend on you as my friend to help with my suit?"

She nodded and touched her hat once more. "Good day, Shirley."

Slowly and painfully, Tiffany walked away. Once he was out of sight, she kicked a rock and sent her boot flying across the road. She hobbled over to it and dusted it off before putting it back on.

How on earth was she going to get rid of the rector?

CHAPTER 8

It was with relief that Tiffany went to Astwell Palace on Monday morning. There was no chance of seeing Mr. Shirley there, for the duke had his own personal clergyman who gave sermons in his private chapel. She wished that Uriah had chosen to attend the duke's services with his servants, instead of joining the church in Mapledown. But her half brother had not thought of himself as a servant, even though he was paid for his services. He had always considered himself a gentleman, with a gentleman's tastes.

The library was blissfully quiet as Tiffany opened a new novel that she'd found on the shelves. It was the first volume of *Clarissa; or, The History of a Young Lady*, by Samuel Richardson. Ironically enough, this book about a young lady was typically forbidden for women to read. The contents must have been shocking or salacious and only appropriate for a man's eyes. Tiffany couldn't wait to find out why!

She was about to warn Clarissa verbally about the libertine Robert Lovelace's dubious attentions, when the door to the library opened. Tiffany sat up in her seat, but it was only Miss Doddridge, who was looking pale and piqued in a striped and embroidered dress of peach and cream that had probably once belonged to the duchess. She walked toward Tiffany liltingly, as if she was trying to get Tiffany to notice her body. The lady's maid was much more like Lovelace than Clarissa.

Tiffany set the book down on the table beside her, noticing for the first time that the golden candlestick usually placed there was gone. "May I assist you with something, Miss Doddridge?"

She came even closer, until her dress brushed up against Tiffany's breeches. Tiffany stiffened awkwardly. Miss Doddridge either didn't notice or didn't care, because she placed a hand on the arm of Tiffany's chair and leaned forward until her chest was directly in front of Tiffany's face.

"Mr. Woodall," she practically purred, "I'm afraid that you might have gotten the wrong idea about me."

Tiffany held up her hands to make some space between herself and the amorous lady's maid, but Miss Doddridge instead pressed her stomach against them. If Tiffany wasn't careful, the young lady was going to be sitting on her lap, the last thing in the world that she wanted. Scooting back her chair while still holding Miss Doddridge away from her, Tiffany stood up.

"I do not judge, and I do not gossip," she said in a whisper.

Miss Doddridge stepped toward her. "I should hate for you or anyone else in the house to assume that I receive preferential treatment because Mrs. Wheatley is my aunt."

For the first time, Tiffany noticed that Miss Doddridge's eyes were the same green as the housekeeper's.

"I did not know that she was your aunt," Tiffany said, stepping back again. "You have nothing whatsoever to fear from me."

Miss Doddridge giggled, and it sounded practiced. "Mr. Woodall, I once feared you, but now I can see that you are a kind and understanding man."

Tiffany might have been both kind and understanding, but she certainly wasn't a man. Nor was she at all interested in Miss Doddridge's attentions. She couldn't help but wonder if Uriah had encouraged this young woman somehow. She was exceptionally pretty, and he might not have been immune to her young charms.

Miss Doddridge licked her lips, and Tiffany gulped uncomfortably. Had Miss Doddridge taken the diamond pin from Uriah? She was standing close enough to Tiffany now to touch the lapel of her coat. If she'd been this close to Tiffany's half brother before, it wouldn't have taken much to steal the pin. The housekeeper's threatening words to the young lady now made perfect sense. Mrs. Wheatley knew about the thefts, but she hadn't reported them because Miss Doddridge held something over her. But what?

"Thank you, but I do need to get back to work."

Flipping open her snuffbox, Miss Doddridge took a pinch out and placed it on her wrist. She slid her hand underneath Tiffany's nose. "Care for some of my sort?"

Tiffany stepped back again and bumped into the bookcase behind her. "I don't take snuff."

"We both know that's not true," Miss Doddridge said with a wink, raising her wrist to her nose, and snorted the snuff in on both sides. Then she began to cough.

Tiffany had no idea what that meant, but she used this opportunity to escape from Miss Doddridge to the other side of the room. Whatever Uriah's relationship had been with the young woman, it needed to end now. She was relieved when the door opened again and stopped her tête-à-tête with the lady's maid. The Duke of Beaufort strode in with his usual winning smile. Miss Doddridge pocketed her snuffbox and picked up a book from Tiffany's desk, *The Two Mentors: A Modern Story*.

At least it wasn't *Clarissa.*

"Thank you for the book," Miss Doddridge said, curtsying. "The duchess is looking forward to reading it."

The lady's maid curtsied low to the duke before simpering past him and through the door.

"A persistent flirt, isn't she?" he said. "Doesn't seem to know how to take no for an answer."

Tiffany could only nod as she came closer to where the duke stood. Bowing to him, she thought that Miss Doddridge was a persistent thief.

"Oh, none of that, Woodall," the duke said with another charming smile that set her nerves perfectly at ease. "I have come to thank you personally."

"Whatever for?"

"Lady Surrey is going to attend our little house party after all, and it is all thanks to your sister," he said, his smile widening. "She is particularly interested in renewing her acquaintance with Miss Woodall."

Tiffany's heart raced, and she tried to keep her face as neutral as possible. If anyone could see through her disguise as Uriah, it would be Tess, or rather Lady Surrey now. It had been Tess's idea all those years ago for Tiffany to dress in her half brother's clothes and fool her parents. Tess had thought it the best kind of lark and had even applied all of Tiffany's face powder and patches. They had both laughed until their sides hurt.

"My sister would be honored to see her," she said formally.

The duke held out his hand. "For your sister."

Tiffany stepped closer to take it and her jaw dropped when she felt six guineas land into her palm. She'd never held so much money in her entire life. Blinking, she looked at the duke for an explanation.

"I thought perhaps your sister might need a new dress or two," he said. "It's not every day that you're visited by a duchess."

"Of—thank you, I am—she will be thrilled to have something new," Tiffany sputtered. "It's very thoughtful of you."

"Lady Surrey has had a difficult year with the death of her husband and her son's conversion to strict Methodism," he explained. "I am happy to do anything in my power that will bring her the smallest of comforts."

She bowed again. "You are a true friend, Your Grace."

"Why don't you take the rest of the afternoon off," the duke said. "Lady Surrey writes that she will be arriving before the rest of the party, in only four days; and no doubt, your sister will need all of that time if she is to have a new dress ready."

He was right.

How was she supposed to sew a new dress and be a librarian all week? Tiffany would have to sew until the late hours of the night, but to do that, she would need new cloth.

"I shall go at once, Your Grace."

"Very good," he said with another of his warm smiles. "Give your sister my best regards, Mr. Woodall."

"I will."

Tiffany definitely held the duke in her very best regards. If she had to see Tess again, at least she need not be embarrassed by her dress.

CHAPTER 9

The shop clerk wrapped the cream-colored silk, a matching spool of thread, and seven different embroidery yarns. This dress would be the finest that she'd ever worn. Ever owned. Tiffany gave the clerk the three guineas, and he eyed her with suspicion.

"Does your brother know that you are here?"

"The Duke of Beaufort wishes for me to have a new dress," Tiffany said, glancing at her plain wool gown. There could be no greater difference between the two materials. "His guest, Lady Surrey, was my schoolmate long ago."

The shop clerk brought one of the coins to his lips and bit it, presumably to test its authenticity. He must have decided that it was good, for he put it and the other coins into his drawer. She placed the remaining guineas back in her reticule before picking up the package and leaving the stuffy shop.

Next door was Mr. Lathrop's bookshop. She glanced through the window and saw him stacking books onto a shelf. Her heartbeat quickened. She longed to talk to him again. To see his smile.

He turned around and saw her watching him through the window. Mr. Lathrop waved to her, and she guiltily waved back.

Tiffany had no choice but to open the door and walk into the bookshop.

He bowed to her. "Miss Woodall."

"Mr. Lathrop," she said with a small curtsy. "I should like to purchase my very first novel. My very first book even. I have never owned one before."

"Your very first book," Mr. Lathrop said. "This is truly a privilege. Do you know what you are looking for?"

She thought about *Clarissa*, which she was enjoying, but the heroine was a rather stupid character for all of her virtuous ambitions. "A novel about an intelligent woman would be nice. Do you have any like that?"

He smiled and something inside her melted. "How about three of them?"

Mr. Lathrop walked to the opposite shelf and scanned through the spines of the book until he found three in a row in brown leather. Pulling them out, he flipped open the one on top. "Here it is: *Evelina: Or, The History of a Young Lady's Entrance into the World*. It was published in three volumes."

She set down her package and stepped closer to him, to see the pages. He smelled of leather, books, cardamon spice, and everything nice. "And the author?"

"Miss Fanny Burney."

"A single woman?" Tiffany could not keep the excitement from her voice. She'd never dreamed that such a thing was possible. That a woman, without a husband, could become a published author of renown.

"Yes," he said, grinning. "Some might even call her a spinster, for I believe she is over thirty, like yourself."

Tiffany was a great deal over thirty, but she had no intention of owning her exact age to him. "Has she written anything else?"

"A few plays and another novel only last year, called *Cecilia: Or, Memoirs of an Heiress.*"

"Do you have that book as well?"

"All five volumes."

"There's five of them?" she said, touching his arm.

Mr. Lathrop turned his head. His face, including his lips, were so close to hers. It had been so long since she'd been kissed, that she had no idea how to start. She stood so close to him that she could barely breathe, but she didn't move a muscle, waiting for him to make the first advance (as a lady is trained to do). His acorn-brown eyes glanced down at her lips.

The bell on the door rang as it opened, Tiffany released her hold on his arm and stepped back from him to an appropriate distance. The person who had opened the door was Mr. Shirley. Tiffany felt her face grow hot, and the fluttering in her heart now had nothing to do with pleasure.

"Miss Woodall," he said in a low voice. "I thought that I glimpsed you in here."

"Yes," she said, attempting a forced smile. "I am buying my very first book."

"Books are a treasury of knowledge that can be passed on to future generations," Mr. Shirley said. "Which work have you chosen?

Trust the rector to take the joy out of the purchase. "*Evelina.*"

"A novel?"

"Yes," Tiffany said, lifting her chin a little. "I am—"

"Does your brother know?" He cut her off with a question. "Does he approve of you using your money on such a frivolous and immoral purpose?"

"It is not my brother's money," she said, frustrated that, for the second time that day, she had been treated like a child who needed her brother's permission to act. "If you must know, it is the Duke of Beaufort's."

Mr. Lathrop's eyebrows raised a fraction, and Mr. Shirley scowled, which did nothing to improve his sharp features.

"Then why do you have it?" the rector demanded.

She longed to tell him that it was none of his business, but in the world in which she lived, a woman did not speak freely to a man who was her senior and above her in station. "He gave it to me—to my half brother—to Uriah. The Duchess of Surrey is visiting, and she is an old schoolmate of mine, and she wishes to see me. The Duke of Beaufort kindly gave me some money to purchase materials for a suitable dress."

Mr. Lathrop gave a low whistle.

"You are intimately connected with the Duchess of Surrey?" Mr. Shirley said, now standing in front of the bookseller.

Tiffany shook her head. "No, no. Tess and I—the Duchess of Surrey has not spoken or written to me in over twenty years. I would never presume to call her a connection."

"Miss Woodall," the rector said, as if she had not spoken, "I had no idea that you once moved in such elevated circles. Meeting with a duchess? What an advantage you will be to me in the future. And your humility is exactly how a wife of the clergy should behave."

"Mr. Shirley," she said, "I have much sewing to do, so if you do not mind, I should like to purchase my book and be on my way."

"Of course," he said, smiling ghoulishly. "You must spend all the time that you need to prepare a gown that is appropriate for the occasion; and perhaps you might even wear it again on another special day?"

The rector didn't say "wedding," but Tiffany knew exactly what he was insinuating. She didn't dare refuse him outright and yet, she didn't want to encourage him, so she smiled weakly and walked around him. Mr. Shirley then bid them both adieu and left the shop. The bell on the door ringing was the only noise in the room.

Mr. Lathrop still had the three volumes in his hand, but his eyes were watching her face closely, as if trying to interpret her emotions. She hoped he could see that she did not care for the rector's attentions and that she did not want his good opinion. It wasn't hard to transform her pathetic smile into a real one when she looked back into Lathrop's beautiful brown eyes. *He* hadn't demanded to know if she had her brother's permission to do what she wanted with her own money.

"How much for the books?"

"One guinea."

Tiffany reached into her reticule and pulled out the coin, placing it in his outstretched hand. It was a thrill to touch his skin, even for a moment.

"Thank you, Miss Woodall," he said. "Let me wrap these for you."

"Please, and how much for *Cecelia*?"

Mr. Lathrop set the books on the counter and wrapped them with brown paper and twine. "*Cecelia* is two guineas."

She had enough to purchase it as well, but she needed to be practical and save the money for food, even though she was spending a great deal less at the market now that she was eating at the palace and her brother was gone. However, Tiffany no longer wished to live hand to mouth. She wanted to save money for the future and feel safe in case something went amiss with her masquerade.

"I shall have to convince Uriah to purchase it for Astwell Palace."

"Excellent idea," he said, handing her the bundle, and their hands brushed again.

It was like touching the flame of a candle: a spark of pleasure mixed with pain. She needed him to know that Mr. Shirley's wishes were not her own.

"I am quite happy being a spinster like Miss Burney," she said. "I have no plans to wear my new dress to any occasion but to visit the duchess."

Mr. Lathrop smiled for the first time since the rector had entered the shop. "I'm glad to hear that, Miss Woodall."

His smile made all rational thought leave her mind. She deftly picked up her other package and went to the door. Mr. Lathrop got there first and opened it for her.

"Thank you, Mr. Lathrop."

"You're welcome, *Miss* Woodall."

The walk back to Bristle Cottage was shorter than ever before.

CHAPTER 10

For three nights, Tiffany sewed until the candle guttered in its socket, and the tips of her fingers began to bleed. It was well past midnight when she finished her dress, but it needed to be embroidered, which took the most time of all. Still, she was pleased with the result.

The next morning, Tiffany reluctantly awoke to her rooster's insistent crows. She needed to gather the eggs from the chickens, eat breakfast, and get to work. She had never realized how much she had done for her brother, until she had to do both of their jobs. A layer of dust covered her parlor furniture (they had once been her mother's prized possessions), and there were cobwebs in the kitchen. If only she could hire a girl to come and clean for her, but it would result in gossip that she could ill afford.

She trudged slowly through the mud, for it was raining. At least, she was wearing her own boots and pattens, to lift her feet out of the two inches of muck. When she arrived at the Astwell Palace servants' entrance, her cloak was soaked through, and most of the white powder had been washed from her face by the rain.

Would she be recognized?

She was half tempted to make her excuses to the house-keeper and return back to her cottage. But poor Clarissa had recently been abducted by the vile Lovelace, and Tiffany needed to know what happened next.

Standing in a puddle of mud of her own making, Tiffany took off her brother's cloak and her muddy boots. Luckily, there was nothing feminine about her secondhand leather shoes. A young maid came up to her. She was fresh-faced and pretty, not more than nineteen or twenty years old, with curly brown hair, a pert nose, and a sprinkling of freckles underneath bright blue eyes.

"I can clean those for you, Mr. Woodall," she said.

"That would be wonderful—thank you so very much," Tiffany said. "I am so sorry to put you to the extra work, Miss . . .?"

"Just Emily, sir," she said. "I'm a maid of all work, and I have yet to earn the right to be called by my surname."

"I am sure you shall soon, Emily," Tiffany said, slipping into her brother's embroidered shoes with a short heel. She had carried them underneath her cloak to keep them from getting ruined. "Thank you again."

Emily bobbed a curtsy, but her eyes were on another person in the room, Thomas. He was polishing the silver and looking quite as handsome as usual this morning. The first footman, however, did not seem to notice the maid of all work's eyes on him, or her apparent admiration. His attention and concern were on Miss Doddridge, who was coughing into a handker-chief. Her glorious golden hair looked stringy and greasy, like it was in need of a good washing. Her once-perfect cream-like complexion appeared almost gray in color.

"You should go back to bed, Sarah," Thomas told her. "You look as if you haven't slept all night."

Tiffany blushed for the young woman, presuming it entirely possible that she'd been engaged in other activities during the darkness.

Miss Doddridge opened her snuffbox and took a few sniffs. "I can't, Thomas. The duchess received a letter, and Lady Surrey is coming early to see her old friend before the rest of the party arrives. At least that's what she *says*." She paused to cough. "Lady Surrey will be here tomorrow, and the duchess needs me to help prepare for her arrival."

He handed her a small vial. "It's laudanum to help you sleep. Is there anything else that I can do for you?"

Tiffany didn't catch Miss Doddridge's reply, but she heard the young woman's coughs as she left the room. She'd lingered too long, listening to their conversation. Walking, she couldn't help but wonder if Thomas was ignorant of the maid's licentiousness and thievery. Too often love was blind, and when he finally opened his eyes, the young man was in for a most unpleasant surprise.

She arrived in the library with no further mishap. Choosing a chair near the fireplace, for her clothes were still a little damp, she opened *Clarissa* and prepared to face the nefarious Lovelace. As she rapidly read the paragraphs, Tiffany couldn't help but wish her heroine had a little less virtue and a little more gumption.

Her clothes were nearly dry when Thomas opened the door to the library for the Duchess of Beaufort. Despite Miss Doddridge's illness, she'd apparently dressed her mistress beautifully. The duchess wore a new wig that was so large and intricate, Tiffany couldn't keep her eyes off it. There were braids and curls, twists and whirls, and even a stuffed bird. Her day dress was made of Bengal pink muslin with vertical woven stripes. It had a rosier glow to it.

Tiffany closed her book and bowed. "May I be of assistance, Your Grace?"

The duchess held out a book. "I've never been much for reading, but I quite liked it."

Tiffany walked forward to take it from her. It was *The Two Mentors: A Modern Story*, the book that Miss Doddridge had taken from the library when the duke had caught her there flirting with Tiffany. The lady's maid had said that the book was for her mistress, but Tiffany had thought it was just a clever excuse to be in the library and to leave the room. Miss Doddridge must have actually given it to the duchess, and she had read it.

"I am delighted to hear it," she said with a surprised laugh.

"I should like another book like it."

"Oh yes," Tiffany said, and then added, "Your Grace, might I recommend *The Castle of Otranto?* It's a gothic story that will keep you reading late into the night."

The duchess inclined her head slightly in what was possibly a nod. Or perhaps, it was due to the fact that if she moved her head too much, the enormous wig on top of it would probably fly off. Then the elegant duchess stared at Tiffany without saying a word. Again, Tiffany wished that her brother's hat had covered her face better from the rain. She felt positively naked without the white powder that hid her face and freckles.

After a few moments, the duchess cleared her throat as if she expected something.

"Um—what would you like me to do, Your Grace?"

She rolled her eyes. "Give me the book you recommended."

"Oh!" Tiffany said. "I already put it in one of the guest rooms for your house party, but I can easily trade it for another."

"Do," the duchess said, and left the room.

Thomas closed the door behind her, and Tiffany felt like she could breathe again. Strolling over to the bookshelf, she selected, *The Expedition of Humphry Clinker,* simply because she thought the surname Clinker was very humorous.

Retracing her previous path up the stairs and to the large guest apartments, Tiffany walked gingerly so as to not step out of her shoes. She opened three doors before finding the room that had *The Castle of Otranto* and trading it for Mr. Clinker. She was about to leave the room, but she couldn't help pausing to marvel at its sumptuousness. The ceiling was two stories high, the bed's canopy brushing the top of it. The size of the room was larger than the main floor of her cottage. Wallpaper, intricate woodwork, and paintings adorned every wall. The room boasted two enormous fireplaces made from marble. Even the ceiling was adorned with gold. It was a room fit for royalty.

It was a room for aristocrats like Tess.

Tiffany had always known that their stations in life were different. That Tess's dresses were delicate and beautiful, whereas Tiffany's were serviceable. That Tess's home was twenty times the size of her father's vicarage at least. But when they were together, those differences had seemed to melt away. They had laughed at the same jokes and fancied the same village boys. They had sung together so many times. Tiffany's alto was the perfect contrast to Tess's floating soprano voice. They had gone to school together and shared the same bedroom. The same friends.

Tiffany had foolishly believed that she and Tess would always be friends, that the differences between them didn't matter—but she had been wrong. Tess had left for her first season and returned only a few months later engaged to a duke. Tiffany had been so excited to see her friend. To congratulate her on her upcoming marriage, but when she had arrived at Topham Castle, her dearest friend had acted ashamed of her. When Tiffany called her Tess, she corrected her. "My name is Lady Theresa, and you should address me as thus."

Stung, but still naive, Tiffany asked her friend about her fiancé and London, a city that had a mystical, magic draw for them both. Lady Theresa had answered curtly and then all but commanded Tiffany to leave. Her farewell words seared into Tiffany's heart. "We are no longer children, and we are no longer friends. You should seek company from those of your own class."

So why did Tess want to see her now, after almost three and twenty years? She couldn't understand it. Not only that, but Tess was also coming earlier than the other guests. Why?

But Tess had been right about at least one thing: they were not of the same class. Tiffany would never stay in a room such as this, but she didn't need to. Or even want to. She was content to have a cottage that was all her own.

Closing the door to the room, Tiffany saw Miss Doddridge leaning on the duke's valet's arm in a very familiar way. Her appearance was still haggard, but there was a feverish brightness to her countenance. The valet, whose name she had learned was Mr. Hickenlooper, was also red in the face.

This time it was Tiffany who coughed. The valet tried to pull away from Miss Doddridge, but her hold on his arm was too tight, as if she'd fall without his support.

"Miss Doddridge," Tiffany said. "The exact person I was hoping to find. The duchess asked for another book recommendation, and I am pleased to pass on this volume to you to give to Her Grace."

The lady's maid extended her arm to take the book. Tiffany could see snuff stains on the back of her hand.

"Of course, Mr. Woodall," she said with a flirtatious smile.

Tiffany returned the girl's stare. "I was wondering if either of you have seen my diamond pin? It went missing a couple of weeks ago, and I can't seem to find it anywhere."

Mr. Hickenlooper shook his head. "Can't say that I have, Woodall."

The lady's maid didn't answer, but there was a guilty flush of color in her cheeks. She lowered her eyes from Tiffany's. But Tiffany was not about to let her family heirloom go that easily.

"And you, Miss Doddridge?" she said. "Have you happened on my diamond pin?"

She slowly, almost seductively, raised her eyes back to Tiffany's. "I can't say that I have either, sir."

Tiffany cleared her throat. "I am afraid that it might have been stolen, and if I do not find it by tomorrow, I intend to inform not only the duke but also the constable of its theft."

"Sound idea," Mr. Hickenlooper said, and managed to disengage his arm from Miss Doddridge's.

The lady's maid teetered on her feet and then turned the other way, dropping the book before vomiting on the marble floor. The sound of her retching brought the maid named Emily. Tiffany's first instinct was to help the maids, but her half brother never would have. Gentlemen did not clean up messes. She had no choice but to return to the library, her own private sanctuary.

CHAPTER 11

Happily, it was not raining the next morning, but there were still many puddles to avoid. Her secondhand boots, however, had never looked better. Emily had done a capital job of not only cleaning the mud off them but also polishing them like new. Tiffany decided that she would wear her boots to walk to the palace every morning and then put on Uriah's too-large shoes. It kept his shoes in pristine condition and gave her many less blisters.

She half expected Uriah's diamond pin to be on her desk in the library, but it wasn't. She would give Miss Doddridge until the end of the day before she followed through with her threat to inform the duke of her suspicions.

The rest of the morning passed with many pages of *Clarissa* and shocking developments. If only the silly girl would attempt to escape the clutches of the villain!

Tiffany had spent so much time the previous evening embroidering flowers into the bodice of her dress that she hadn't taken any time to prepare her evening meal. She'd also slept late and skipped her breakfast. So, when two o'clock arrived, she was the first person to sit down for dinner. The other servants filed in and found their own seats. She noticed Emily sat on the very last seat at the woman's table. She must have been the lowest of consequence among the servants. Again, Tiffany noticed that Emily's bright blue eyes were on Thomas.

The first footman watched Miss Doddridge at the parallel table; his face full of concern, barely touching his food. She looked grayer and thinner than even the day before. Tiffany almost felt sorry for her. Bernard and Mr. Hickenlooper ate their meal as if nothing were amiss. Tiffany did as well, for she was positively famished.

Halfway through, Miss Doddridge started to cough. She covered her mouth with a handkerchief. As her coughing progressed, she stood up and left the room.

"You ought to call a doctor for Miss Doddridge, Mr. Ford," Thomas said.

The butler gave the first footman a haughty glare from the head of the table. "I hardly have time for that now. The Duchess of Surrey arrived just past noon."

Tess was in the same building as her. Tiffany's pulse quickened. She wondered when her old friend would ask to see her. Or perhaps Tess had already forgotten about her.

"Then I can go and fetch the doctor," Thomas said.

"You will not," Mr. Ford said. "You have work to do."

"If Miss Doddridge is still unwell in the morning," Mrs. Wheatley said, standing up at the head of the female table. "I will see that the doctor is called, but we can hardly deprive the duchess of her lady's maid when her guest has arrived."

Thomas did not speak again, nor did he eat another bite of his food. Tiffany did not share his romantic feelings for Miss Doddridge, but she too was concerned for the young woman. Whatever was ailing her was causing her to decline quickly. She hoped the maid would return the diamond pin and other stolen items. A clear conscience would only help her recovery.

Tiffany easily cleaned off her entire plate of Sussex pond pudding, boiled fowl, tongue, calves' head, and fruit. She set down her napkin on the table by her place setting. Standing, she turned to leave.

"Ah, Mr. Woodall," the butler said.

"Yes, Mr. Ford?" Tiffany said over her shoulder.

"Your sister's presence has been asked for this afternoon."

"Today?" she said in surprise. She assumed that Tess would spend the afternoon in her room, resting before dinner.

"Lady Surrey has specifically requested that your sister come at once."

"Oh. Very well then," Tiffany said. "I shall leave to fetch her."

She walked back through the sunken dining room and up the four stairs that led to the landing and servants' entrance. Removing her shoes, Tiffany pulled on her boots and laced them up. She was putting on her cloak when Mrs. Wheatley said, "What an honor for your sister, Mr. Woodall."

She nodded. "An honor indeed, ma'am."

It was an honor that Tiffany could happily have done without.

Her walk to Bristle Cottage was not nearly long enough. All Tiffany could think about was the Duchess of Beaufort's elaborate French wig. Tess would probably be wearing a similarly elegant wig with jewels and stuffed birds. Tiffany did not even own a simple wig (only a homemade hair cushion to make her coiffure appear larger). Her brother would never give her the money to purchase the false hair, and even if she were to purchase herself one now, wigs took many months to make.

Sighing, Tiffany opened the door to her cottage. She was going to appear unwigged, aged, and entirely provincial before her old friend. At least her dress was lovely, even if it was not quite finished. There was enough fancy stitching on the bodice to make it presentable, if not yet perfect. After Tess's visit, Tiffany would have plenty of time to add embroidery to the sleeves and the skirt.

If only she had a white wig of hair!

Tiffany might not have a wig, but she did have white hair powder. She could style her curls in a coiffure friseur and then use her brother's hair powder to dust it white. She would be nowhere near as stylish and elegant as Tess, but she would not need to be embarrassed by her appearance either.

Her brother's room was hot and stuffy, so she opened the window. The air outside was still warm and sticky, but there was a slight September breeze. She carefully took off Uriah's wig and clothes and placed them in his wardrobe.

Her shift was still on the floor from her mad dash that morning to get to work. Slipping it on, she sat down in front of her brother's mirror and combed her dark blonde hair and then added pomatum to the back of it so that it would keep its shape. As quickly as she could, she twisted each piece of front hair and put them in curling papers. She first pressed them with the iron and then allowed them to cool. Once cool, she untwisted the hair and then combed it out, creating an impressive halo of frizz around her face. Next, she placed the spearhead hair cushion at the back of her head, to give the hair a little lift. She then made buckle curls and a chignon, leaving a narrow piece of braided hair to fall down her back.

Once satisfied that she'd done her best with the hair crape and curls, she put on Uriah's plain linen peignoir to cover her shift. She picked up the cone mask with one hand and the hair powder with the other. The cone mask prevented the powder from getting into her eyes and face, but usually someone else applied the powder while the wearer held the cone. Attempting to do both, Tiffany covered her face with the cone and shook the powder on her head with her other hand. She removed the cone from her face, but she still couldn't see anything. There was white everywhere. Coughing, she inhaled the face powder in the air. Its flavor was not pleasant. She covered her mouth with her hand and took off the peignoir with the other. She used the cape to fan the white cloud out the window.

Tiffany fanned and coughed for several minutes. The white dust still hung in the air, but not as thickly as before. She heard a creak and she jumped.

Someone was in her house!

Had Miss Doddridge come to return the diamond pin directly to her?

Before she could react, the door to Uriah's room swung open, and Mr. Lathrop threw a bucket of water all over her perfectly crape-curled and powdered hair, drenching her shift.

"What in heaven's name?" she screeched at him.

Mr. Lathrop blinked but then averted his eyes from her. "I thought there was a fire. I saw the white smoke, and I heard you coughing."

Tiffany glanced down at her wet shift. It left little to the imagination. For the second time, she appeared before the bookseller in little more than her skin. Haphazardly covering her front with her cape, her anger replaced her embarrassment. Her hair was now dripping with water, and there was no time to dry it before she had to see Tess.

"As you can see, I am perfectly fine," she said with asperity. "Would you please stop trying to rescue me!"

"Very well," he said, his eyes still looking the opposite direction. "The next time I see you drowning in the lake or your cottage filled with smoke, I will simply walk by and leave you to your fate."

"Please do!"

Mr. Lathrop set down the empty bucket that belonged to her well, before touching his tricorn hat. "Good day to you, Miss Woodall."

He shut the door behind him before she could return the farewell. Not that she wanted him to have a good day. For once, she wished for the handsome bookseller to have a terrible day like her own.

She listened for the door to her cottage to close and watched Mr. Lathrop's upright figure walk down the road before she went to her own room and stripped off the wet shift. With a towel, she dried off her wet and pasty hair. Taking a fresh shift from her wardrobe, she put on her corset and panniers. She sat down in front of her much smaller mirror and tried to comb out the chunks of white paste that had once been powder. When she was finished, her hair was slicked back into a bun that was not at all flattering to her face.

Cursing Mr. Lathrop's interference again, she stepped into her gown and buttoned it up. It was so beautiful and soft. She regretted that she had to walk outside in it. It was the sort of dress that deserved a carriage. Putting on her ribbon-trimmed, Bergère straw hat (which blessedly covered a great deal of her hair), Tiffany tied the ribbon at her chin.

By the time she locked her cottage door, all of her anger had faded away, leaving only the sting of forgotten friendship.

CHAPTER 12

Even though Tiffany had been summoned to see the Duchess of Surrey, she was not foolish enough to go to the front entrance. She had learned her place, and she would not forget it again. Entering the servants' area, she saw Emily. Tiffany opened her mouth to greet the young woman but then remembered that Emily did not know her. The maid thought that she knew her half brother, Uriah.

"Excuse me, miss," Tiffany said. "I have been sent for by the Duchess of Surrey."

Emily's bright blue eyes widened at the sight of her. Tiffany internally cursed Tess, who was causing her to risk her life and livelihood for a whim. What if the maid recognized her? What if any of the other servants recognized her? She had to leave the servants' quarters as quickly as possible.

"This way, Miss Woodall," Emily said, pointing with her hand. The maid led her through the sunken dining room and back up to the hall where Mr. Ford's office was. The butler raised his beak-like nose at her and sniffed in disdain. Tiffany knew that she looked like a drowned fish.

"If you would be so good as to follow me," he said, but didn't wait for her answer before he started to walk away.

Tiffany was wearing her old boots, so she could easily keep up with his quick pace. Luckily, her beautiful new dress was long enough to cover them when it was down. She'd held the hem up on her walk to Astwell Palace, to keep the bottom of her dress clean.

Mr. Ford opened the door to a room that she had never been in before. It was a large crimson saloon with four fireplaces. A petite lady, dressed all in black, sat on the settee.

"Miss Woodall to see you, Your Grace," the butler droned.

Tiffany's heartbeat was bobbing in her throat as she stepped into the room and faced her old friend. Tess was just as beautiful as she had been over twenty years before. Her blue eyes were barely lined, and her face appeared as young as that of a woman of twenty. Her once-dark hair was covered by a moderate but tasteful white wig. And her figure was still trim, perfectly encased in a black silk gown that hugged her well-endowed chest and her narrow waist.

Tiffany felt like an overgrown beanpole beside the smaller woman. She curtsied and Tess gave her a small nod. A duchess did not curtsy to a commoner.

"That will be all, Mr. Ford," Tess said, her voice achingly familiar.

"Shall I bring some tea, Your Grace?"

Tess looked her in the eye. Tiffany slightly shook her head.

"No, thank you."

Tess did not sit down until the butler closed the door behind him. "Tiffany, you look as if you've fallen in a lake."

If they were younger, Tiffany would have recounted the story of the wig smoke with great humor, and they both would have laughed until they were in stitches. But she had no desire for the Duchess of Surrey to laugh at her now.

"At least I am clean," Tiffany said, and then added, "Your Grace."

Tess took a deep breath. "Why are you still standing?"

"I cannot sit until you invite me to do so, Your Grace."

She waved her hand. "There is no need for such formality between old friends like ourselves."

Tiffany sat down stiffly. "I presumed once to be familiar with you, Your Grace. I shall not do so again."

"Tiffany," Tess said, smiling, "surely, you have forgotten that terrible day. I know that I behaved abominably, but you were so happy then. You were engaged to Nathaniel."

Her old friend could not have hurt her more thoroughly if she had stabbed her with a dagger. Nathaniel was a wound that had never healed. Never closed.

"Yes, I was happy then. You were also engaged to your duke. Please accept my humble condolences for his passing, Your Grace."

"If you keep saying 'Your Grace,' I think I shall scream," Tess said with a little laugh. "Can we not be as we were? Must you be so formal and cold?"

"I am not who I was."

"I didn't hear about Nathaniel until years after it happened," she said, opening the old wound further. "I was heartbroken for you both to learn he drowned at sea. He was so young. So handsome and vibrant. I was so jealous of you."

"Of me?" Tiffany scoffed. "The poor, unwanted daughter of the vicar?"

"You," Tess said, her facial expression serious, "the girl who was engaged to a man that she loved and a man that loved her in return . . . I knew when the Duke of Surrey proposed that he was not only older than my father but that he also had a long-term mistress whom he loved, and that he had no intention of giving up for me."

"I'm so sorry."

"'Tis common enough in my class," she said with a humorless laugh, "for men to take mistresses before and during their marriages. Women can find lovers as well, but only after an indisputable heir and a spare have been born. As long as one is reasonably discreet and keeps up the pretense of fidelity in society."

For the first time, Tiffany put herself in Tess's place. She was privileged and spoiled, but she was also just as trapped by her birth as Tiffany was by her own. Tess had been given no control over her life or whom she married.

"I wish you had told me," Tiffany said in a voice barely above a whisper. "You used to tell me everything."

"As did you," she said. "But our relationship was already changing. You were so wrapped up in Nathaniel, and my mother was pressuring me to end our friendship. I thought a clean break was the kindest way to do it."

Tiffany shook her head. "There was nothing kind in the way you ended our friendship."

Before Tess could reply, the door opened, and the Duke of Beaufort strode into the room, his face wreathed in smiles. He reached out his hands to Tess.

"My dear duchess," he said, taking her hands and kissing each one. "I had no idea that you would arrive so early in the day, or I would have been waiting at the door for you."

"Like a footman?" Tess said, and with a giggle, she was transformed into the young woman who had once been Tiffany's dearest friend.

The duke laughed. It was a deep, pleasant sound. He released Tess's hands and gave Tiffany a bow. It was a stroke of civility that surprised her. The duke was entirely a gentleman.

"Miss Woodall," he said, taking her hand and bowing over it. He did not kiss it, for which she was grateful. "What a charming gown. I am so glad that you were able to visit us today."

Tiffany knew that she should thank the duke for the money for the dress, but she couldn't bear to admit her own penury in front of Tess. She'd been humbled enough already for a lifetime.

"Thank you, Your Grace," she said in a high, sweet voice. She wanted to sound different than she did when she spoke as Uriah.

The duke bestowed on them another ear-splitting smile. "I shall leave you two lovely ladies to your talk. I simply wished to welcome you to my home, Duchess."

He left the room, and Tiffany saw that Tess was blushing. She picked up a fan and began to wave it at herself. It reminded her forcibly of her own fanning of the hair powder. It was too much for Tiffany's composure. She started to laugh.

"What is it?" Tess asked.

"I am all wet because I used too much hair powder and I fanned it out the window. The local bookseller thought my cottage was on fire and threw a bucket of water on me."

Tess giggled again.

Tiffany covered her mouth with her hands, but she couldn't hold in her mirth. The harder she tried to stop laughing, the harder she laughed. Tess laughed too, and it felt like old times. Like nothing had changed between them.

"Well, as you say, at least you are clean," Tess said with another laugh. "Oh, Tiffany, I forgot how many scrapes you used to get into when we were girls."

Tiffany longed to protest that this scrape was not her fault, but she *had* used enough hair powder for a dozen wigs.

"How is your half brother?" Tess asked. She had remembered that Tiffany never claimed Uriah as a full brother. "I learned from the duke that you keep house for him."

"Yes," Tiffany said, sobered. "After Nathaniel died and then my father, there was really nowhere else for me to go, and Uriah took me in begrudgingly."

"You should have written to me."

Tiffany had thought about it at the time. She'd been willing to beg her old friend for a place in her household, even as a servant. But perhaps it was that same friendship that had stopped her. The change between them had been painful.

"How many children do you have?" Tiffany asked to change the subject.

"Two sons," Tess said. "Both are all grown now and living in London, if you can believe it. Osmond is very much like his late father and will be a very good duke. Theophilus has found his calling in the church."

Second sons were like daughters. They did not inherit very much; however, those of the aristocracy had connections and typically did not end up as lowly rectors, but as bishops. "Does he plan to be ordained?"

"He is not a member of the Church of England," she said, "but rather the Methodist religion. Theophilus intends to become a missionary."

Tiffany tried to keep the surprise from her face, but she'd always been abysmal at hiding her emotions. Another trait that her half brother had criticized her about.

"You seem surprised," Tess said with a smile. "I must admit that Theophilus shocked me as well when he told me of his conversion, but I have reconciled myself not only to his calling but to his faith. After the death of my husband, I was very low, and dearest Theophilus helped me find hope in his religion, and I am a changed woman. I am no longer that sinful, selfish creature that I have been my whole life, taking pleasure outside the bonds of marriage. I have repented and long to make amends for any wrongdoing I have done. Including my callous treatment of you, dear Tiffany. I came here specially to make reparations with you, my first friend. Please accept my heartfelt apology."

Part of Tiffany wanted to assure her old friend that all was forgiven, but in her heart it wasn't. So she said nothing.

Loud screams from outside the room broke their uncomfortable silence.

CHAPTER 13

Tiffany stood up and opened the door. There was no one in the hall, but she could still hear the loud sobs. Tiffany followed the noise to the servants' wing. Glancing behind her, she saw Tess walking in the other direction. She never had been one to deal with a mess. Unpleasantness was for servants and spinsters.

Mrs. Wheatley was sobbing and screaming in the middle of the narrow servants' hall, just outside her office. Without thinking, Tiffany went to her and touched her arm.

"Mrs. Wheatley, what is wrong?"

"She's dead!" the housekeeper sobbed.

"Who is dead?"

"Miss Doddridge is dead."

Tiffany's heart thudded painfully in her chest, her own shock nearly overcoming her. She felt guilty for threatening the girl the day before. Still, she managed to put a comforting arm around the housekeeper, who continued to cry. She would not have thought that Mrs. Wheatley would be so distraught after hearing how Miss Doddridge had blackmailed her.

"I should have stopped her. I should have watched her closer. I should have done more for her," Mrs. Wheatley said between racking sobs. "My poor, sweet Sarah."

"Where is she?" Tiffany asked.

The housekeeper sniffed. "She's in her room, Miss Woodall."

"And where is that?"

"In the attic with the other maids."

Tiffany patted the woman on the back. "There, there. I'm sure there was nothing that you could have done. Please take me to her, and we will care for her together."

Tiffany had helped many wives in her father's congregation prepare dead bodies for holy burial. Death did not frighten her. She took Mrs. Wheatley's arm and led the woman farther into the servants' quarters.

"Where is Thomas?" Mr. Ford yelled at Bernard. "The candlesticks are not on the dining room table yet, and I have measured your utensil settings, and they are subpar."

"Thomas went for the doctor," Bernard said, and for once the handsome young man did not smirk.

Mr. Ford's already red face turned a dark hue. "How—how dare he leave without my permission?"

The butler's outburst brought a new round of tears from the housekeeper. The other servants in the dining room and kitchen looked at them in surprise and concern.

"Mrs. Wheatley, what is the meaning of this?" Mr. Ford demanded.

She did not answer, but sobbed even louder. Emily brought the woman a freshly pressed handkerchief, which she used on her eyes and nose.

Monsieur Bonne came out from the kitchen, stirring a bowl. "Oh, *mon Dieu!* What has happened?"

Bernard shook his head. "It's about Sarah, innit?"

"Has something happened to Miss Doddridge?" Mr. Hickenlooper asked. His tone sounded almost hopeful, but perhaps, that was just his surprise.

Tiffany looked to Mrs. Wheatly to answer, but the house-keeper was not in a state to speak.

"I am afraid that the doctor is going to be too late to help her," Tiffany said. "Miss Doddridge has already passed away."

Monsieur Bonne dropped the bowl and the spoon he was holding. The mixture splattered on the floor. Two of the kitchen maids broke out in tears, out of sadness or surprise, Tiffany couldn't say. Bernard sat down in a chair, as if the news was too much to be born standing. Mr. Hickenlooper's eyes focused on the brass button on his uniform. He fiddled with it as if it were dirty, his eyes not meeting anyone else's.

Then Monsieur Bonne threw his arms around Mrs. Wheat-ley and spoke rapidly in French, presumably giving his condolences.

"Emily, if you'll come with us," Tiffany said, "we will need to clean and prepare her body for burial. Bernard, if you would be so good as to send the doctor to us when he arrives. I am sure that he will want to examine the body to determine the cause of death."

Tiffany gently pulled the housekeeper away from the chef and led her to the servants' staircase at the rear of the common room. They climbed three flights of stairs before they arrived in the maid's rooms in the attic. When they reached the top stair, Tiffany recognized the same putrid smell that had filled her cottage during her half brother's death. Mrs. Wheatley opened the third door, and the scent was so strong that Tiffany had to bring her handkerchief to her face to cover her nose. Miss Dod-dridge was not covered in her own refuse like Uriah had been. She was lying on the floor in her own vomit, beside her per-fectly made bed. The small bottle of laudanum, uncorked on her side table next to a half-empty glass of water.

It appeared that the young woman had been on her hands and knees close to the time of death. Her chamber pot was near her face and full of her sick. No doubt, she had used the bowl to catch the contents. It was all too similar to Uriah's death and made her stomach turn.

"Do you have any extra maid's clothing that I can change into?" Tiffany asked. Her task was not one to wear silk with. Mrs. Wheatley stood stock-still, but Emily nodded and took her to a room farther down the narrow hall. She even helped Tiffany take off her precious gown and put on a plain cotton one, with a white criss-crossing shawl across her chest and a matching white cotton cap.

They followed the smell back to the open door. Tiffany stepped closer to the body and gently turned the girl over. Miss Doddridge's green eyes were open, and her skin looked drawn and gray. As if she'd aged twenty years. Her resemblance to another person in the household was undeniable. Tiffany now had a shrewd idea what the secret was that Miss Doddridge had held over the housekeeper.

"Emily, why don't you go and get us more rags?" Tiffany said. "Mrs. Wheatley, are there any basins of water on this level of the house? I should like to clean Miss Doddridge up before the doctor and others arrive to see her."

Both ladies left the room, and Tiffany stepped to the window to fling it open. Any fresh air was welcome in the hot and confined space. There was little more inside it than a bed and a wardrobe. She went to the wardrobe to find fresh clothing for the lady's maid. She found a clean shift, but no additional corset. But she didn't think that they would need one. Miss Doddridge had lost a great deal of weight in a short time. Tiffany selected a beautiful blue dress with pheasants embroidered on the skirt. The last thing she needed was fresh stockings for her feet.

Opening the bottom drawer, Tiffany gasped. There were not any stockings there. The drawer was full of knickknacks. The painted rose snuffbox, rimmed with gold. A package full of French lace wrapped with a ribbon. The silver ring she'd seen the valet wear on his right hand. And a sparkle of light from her half brother's diamond cluster pin.

Miss Doddridge *had* stolen it.

Tiffany took the pin and tried to think of where to put it to keep it safe. Lifting her skirt, she attached it to the side of her chemise. She lowered the borrowed dress over it and opened the drawer further. She saw Thomas's pocket watch. Several silver spoons and one fork. And the candlestick that looked exactly like the one that had disappeared from the library.

The last item in the back was a coin pouch. Tiffany picked it up and opened it. It was near bursting, full of coins of all sizes. There had to be almost thirty pounds in there. A fortune for a maid. How had she gotten the money? And what had she planned to use it for? Tiffany pulled the strings tight and placed the bag in the drawer before closing it.

She found a pair of silk stockings, with a small hole in the toe, at the back of the wardrobe. Closing the wardrobe, she saw that Emily had returned with several rags and a bucket.

"Please set those down," Tiffany said. "And if you will take out the chamber pot and dispose of its contents, I will clean up the floor and Miss Doddridge."

Emily nodded and dutifully picked up the full chamber pot. Tiffany watched the poor girl dry-heave several times before she even left the room. Kneeling down carefully so that the material was behind her, she began to mop up the vomit with the rags and place them in the bucket. The color was overall a vivid green, but she recognized several chunks of food from their early dinner. There wasn't any blood or anything else suspicious in the vomit. Still, she kept a small sample of the sick in the glass from the side table, for the doctor to examine.

She had the floor mostly clean when Mrs. Wheatley returned with a basin of water. On her knees, Tiffany unbuttoned Miss Doddridge's dress, untied her corset, and pulled off her shift. She placed them all in a pile in the corner of the room, to be burned. She couldn't help wondering if Miss Doddridge had been using her charms to steal from the men of the household. If so, it appeared to have been a very effective strategy.

"If you will wash her," Tiffany said to the housekeeper, "then we can dress her."

Tiffany used the same water to clean her hands once Mrs. Wheatley was finished. They lifted Miss Doddridge onto the bed and dressed her. Emily returned, out of breath, and took the soiled clothing away, and the bucket of dirty rags. The air in the room was still rank when Doctor Hudson arrived. She was surprised to see that the doctor was a young man, not more than five and twenty, possibly less. He had closely set brown eyes, a long pointy nose, and a face covered in red spots.

"Is this how you found her?"

Tiffany waited for Mrs. Wheatley to answer, but the poor woman had begun to cry again.

"No," Tiffany said. "She was lying face down on the floor in her own sick. We have cleaned her up and changed her. The vomit has been disposed of except for the sample in this glass. There wasn't any blood in it, but I am sure if you would like to see the rest of it, Emily can show you."

He shook his head and turned pale. "That is not necessary, Mrs. . . . .?"

"Miss Woodall," she said. "I was here visiting when Mrs. Wheatley discovered the body."

"Very good of you to help," he said, and opened his black bag. He took out a small, cone-like instrument and pressed it against Miss Doddridge's unmoving chest. He listened to it for a few moments before taking out another instrument and placing it by her cheek. "Why was she taking laudanum?"

He pointed with his instrument to the uncorked bottle on the side table.

"I do not know."

Mrs. Wheatly sniffed. "To help her sleep. She wasn't feeling well this last week."

Dr. Hudson picked up the vial and brought it to his nose, breathing in deeply. He then poured the rest of the contents into a small bowl, then stirred it with a spoonlike instrument. "It smells and looks like normal laudanum, but the poison could have been in here."

Tiffany grabbed her chest with one hand. Her heart constricted in fear. "The, the p-p-poison?"

Mrs. Wheatley's face went white, and she looked as if she was going to faint. "No! No, it cannot be."

He held up the glass of sick. "I am afraid so. The bright color and general malodorous smell of the vomit lead me to believe that this young woman died from poisoning. Her jaw has become unhinged, which is caused by frequent and extreme vomiting. Another sign of foul play."

The housekeeper sat down on the edge of the bed. All of the blood was gone from her face. "Who would want to poison Sarah?"

Tiffany's hands flew to her own hot cheeks. "Are you sure, Doctor, that Miss Doddridge was poisoned? That it wasn't some natural malady?"

Mr. Hudson placed his instruments back into his black bag. "I am afraid, Miss Woodall, there was nothing natural about her death."

She thought of Uriah lying in his own sick. "But people with weak stomachs often vomit; and isn't some vomiting normal and good for the body?"

He handed her the glass of sick. "Not this color. Not this smell. This was caused by poison."

The bright green color and the smell of the vomit from the glass was making Tiffany feel sick. It was too similar to Uriah's the morning she had found him dead. That vomit was different than any other sick of her half brother's that she'd cleaned up. Those had not smelled pleasant, but that last malodorous one was acrid and foul.

Tiffany set the glass down on the side table and backed away from it in horror. "So, she was murdered?"

"Yes."

Mrs. Wheatley dropped her face into her hands and began to weep again.

Tiffany's head was spinning with realization. She wanted to cry like the housekeeper, but she had to know more. "By what poison?"

"I cannot say for certain which root or plant. I would guess something from the nightshade family."

She grabbed his arm. "How was it administered?"

The young doctor glanced down at her hand, and she removed it from his arm. He cleared his throat. "Ingested. Probably in her food and drink; or the laudanum."

Tiffany's stomach turned uncomfortably. Her half brother had been poisoned! But he hadn't had any laudanum. And why would anyone want to murder Uriah? It didn't make sense.

The only person who would have wanted to get rid of him was Miss Doddridge, who had stolen his diamond pin, but she was also dead.

"I suggest that you call in the constable. There is nothing more I can do for her." He put on his hat and then gloves. "I will see the butler for my fees."

Tiffany watched him leave the room and was frustrated that he was more concerned with his payment than he was that a young lady had been poisoned. She turned to look at Mrs. Wheatley, who took Miss Doddridge's limp hand and held it lightly.

"I wanted Sarah to have a better life," Mrs. Wheatley whispered. "She wasn't a good girl or a kind girl, but she didn't deserve to be poisoned."

"She didn't," Tiffany agreed. Neither had Uriah. Being a pompous prig was no reason to die. "Would you like me to have a footman fetch the constable?"

"Yes," she said. "And if you will please inform Mr. Ford what has transpired. He will need to speak to the duke about it. The duchess will expect Sarah to help her dress for dinner, but she will not be there. No one had a better knack for making the duchess look younger or prettier than Miss Doddridge."

Tiffany placed a hand on Mrs. Wheatley's shoulder. "Stay with her. I promise that I will do all that you have asked."

She was not even two steps from the attic rooms when she ran into Thomas. His face was a study of worry.

"How is Miss Doddridge?" he asked. "I saw the doctor leave. Is she better?"

No one had told him that the young lady was dead. This unpleasant task was now up to her. She touched his shoulder. "I am afraid that Miss Doddridge is no longer with us."

The tall man slumped to his knees on the stairs and began to cry. Tiffany's heart ached for him. She, too, had lost someone she loved. He buried his face into his hands.

"No. No. No."

If she'd known him better, she would have put her arm around him and attempted to comfort him. But Thomas did not know Tiffany; he only slightly knew her when she masqueraded as Uriah. And *he* was the one who had given Miss Doddridge the laudanum. Had he known of her unfaithfulness? Had she stolen more than just his heart?

With a shuddering breath, she passed by him. It took all three flights of stairs before she had regained her composure to talk to the butler. The blustering Mr. Ford was, for once, speechless, so Tiffany took charge. She ordered Bernard to go to Mapledown and fetch the constable, but he didn't move a step until Mr. Ford gave his nod of confirmation. Men rarely obeyed a woman.

There was nothing Tiffany could do except scrub her arms up to her elbows, change back into her dress, and wait for him to arrive. Emily helped Tiffany back into her silk gown and even offered to arrange her hair (which was now dry). For a maid of all work, Tiffany was surprised at how deftly the young girl arranged her curls. In fact, Tiffany thought that her hair had never looked better. She was so impressed by Emily's assistance that she sent her to help the duchess dress for dinner. Someone needed to wait on the duchess now, and Mrs. Wheatley was in no state to help anyone.

Poor thing.

Tiffany passed the housekeeper on her way to the stairs. She was still sitting next to Miss Doddridge's body, weeping.

Mrs. Wheatly stopped crying and looked up at Tiffany with red eyes. "Please tell your brother what has happened.

Mr. Woodall was fond of Sarah. I am sure he would like to attend her funeral."

Uriah.

He had been the first victim to die from poisoning.

"Of—of course," Tiffany stammered. "I am sure he will be devastated by the news and wish to p-pay her every respect."

"Always a gentleman," the housekeeper said, starting to cry again.

Tiffany gave the woman a quick curtsy and all but ran to the stairs. Once the door to the attic had closed behind her, she lifted up the side of her dress to see her chemise. The diamond cluster pin was still there. Letting her skirt back down, she began to walk slowly down each stair with dawning realization.

Whoever had killed Uriah still thought that he was alive.

The poisoner thought that Tiffany was him.

Would they try to kill Uriah again?

Tiffany touched her own throat, feeling her frantic pulse. She had to find out who the murderer was and stop them before *she* was the next victim.

CHAPTER 14

It was odd to sit in the servants' common room dressed as a woman. Not that she minded wearing a dress, but she was used to playing her role as Uriah there. She had to keep reminding herself that while Uriah might have known the servants' names and positions, Miss Woodall did not. Thinking of her half brother brought another wave of grief. Perhaps if she had called Doctor Hudson and the constable at *his* death, she could have prevented the murder of Miss Doddridge. Guilt settled over her head and shoulders like a cloak.

She had to find out who had done this terrible thing. Not only to protect herself but because she owed it to Uriah. Despite being disagreeable and closefisted with money, he'd taken her in and given her a home when she had no other. He hadn't been kind or pleasant or considerate, but she hadn't starved. And she knew for certain that he would never have buried *her* in the back garden under the crack willow.

The French cook brought her a cup of tea with extra sugar; it helped a little—until she remembered that it could be poisoned. Setting it down, Tiffany could not help but wonder who had poisoned both Uriah and the young lady's maid. And why?

What was to be gained by *her* death? Would one of the other women at the servants' table become the new lady's maid, or would the Duchess of Beaufort hire a fashionable French one?

Killing a person for their position seemed extreme, but advancement among servants was slow, and their wages were paltry. A lady's maid was called by her surname instead of her given name. She had the greatest status of a female in the servants' quarters, after the housekeeper. She also had the privilege of receiving any of the duchess's castoffs, from her beautiful gowns to her old gloves. A clever woman could make quite a side business by selling those items discreetly. And if the bag of coins was anything to go by, Miss Doddridge was probably hawking stolen items as well.

Tiffany wondered if the beautiful little snuffbox with the painted roses was stolen or given to Miss Doddridge. She wouldn't know unless she spoke to the duchess herself.

There was also the fact that Miss Doddridge had been blackmailing her aunt, Mrs. Wheatley. The housekeeper truly seemed stricken by the girl's death, but it could all be an act. Mrs. Wheatley had the most to lose if Miss Doddridge had allowed her tongue to run. A woman of Mrs. Wheatley's age and position would have a very difficult time finding a new place; especially without a reference. She would go back to being a lower servant, with greater hours and smaller pay.

Then there were Miss Doddridge's three lovers: Bernard, Thomas, and Mr. Hickenlooper. Had they all known that she was playing them false? Perhaps Miss Doddridge had even more lovers that Tiffany was not aware of—possibly even Uriah. The very thought made her skin crawl.

Could jealously have been the motivation for poisoning?

Miss Doddridge was in possession of Mr. Hickenlooper's ring. If it had been a gift, was there an understanding between them? In some households, marriages between the servants were allowed; but since there were no other married servants in the duke's employ, Tiffany couldn't help but surmise that relationships between servants was forbidden here. Mrs. Wheatley was not married. The title of "Mrs." was merely an honorary one given to her for her position as housekeeper.

The housekeeper had been civil to her when she was dressed as Uriah, but she'd known about the thefts, including that of her brother's missing diamond cluster pin. Mr. Ford had been almost genial with her at dinner, compared to his treatment of the other male servants. But as she knew all too well, smiles could be deceiving. The footmen were too busy goggling at the girls to pay Tiffany/Uriah much attention at meals. Thomas had shown her to the library on her first day. He had looked at her suspiciously, but then again, she had been behaving erratically. Opening doors to rooms that she should not have been in. Had he also known of the missing items? Had he thought that Uriah was involved?

As the librarian, no one worked beneath Uriah, or really above him, save his employer. None of the servants would have been qualified to fill his place at his death. They were not gentle-born, nor had they attended university. The murderer hadn't killed him for his position but might have killed him for his knowledge. Not his familiarity with Ancient Greek or Roman languages, but because he knew of someone's indiscretion. She wished that Uriah had told her who it was and what they had done, that night not so long ago when he'd said someone at the palace needed to repent.

Had the knowledge been worth killing for?

Had Miss Doddridge been involved somehow?

"Miss Woodall," Emily said, "Constable Lathrop is here."

Tiffany turned to see Mr. Lathrop's strong figure framed by the afternoon sun. She knocked over her teacup in surprise, and it shattered on the porcelain tiled floor. Mr. Lathrop frowned at her. Embarrassed, Tiffany stooped to pick up the large pieces of the teacup. At least it was just a basic cup for servants and not a fancy bone china piece of a set.

Would he be the one who arrested her if her masquerade was discovered? Was burying your half brother in the back garden a hanging offense? Or would she be sent to a prison?

"I am so sorry," she said as she placed the broken pieces on the saucer and set it on the table nearest to her.

No one answered her. Mr. Ford looked stricken, and Mrs. Wheatley was still sobbing. The cook, Monsieur Bonne, had already returned to his kitchen, along with the other servants who had gone back to their work.

"Miss Woodall," Mr. Lathrop said, "I didn't expect to see you here."

No doubt because he had drenched her with a bucket of water not a few hours before. "I was visiting the Duchess of Surrey when Miss Doddridge's body was discovered."

He nodded.

She waited for someone to offer to take him to see the deceased, but no one else did. "Why don't you follow me upstairs, and I shall show you to Miss Doddridge's room, sir."

Mr. Lathrop gestured with a gloved hand for her to lead. With a deep breath, she set off up the first flight of stairs.

"You seemed shocked to learn that I was the constable," he said in a low tone, his eyes full of accusation.

Did he think that she disapproved of him being the constable? That was not at all the case. She was simply alarmed to see a man that she liked more than a confirmed spinster should.

"I was surprised," she admitted.

"You are not the only one," he said. "When my father died and the Duke of Beaufort appointed me as constable in his place, nearly everyone in Mapledown was shocked and angry. Mr. Shirley even complained to his bishop that a man of color could not be trusted to uphold the law. But the duke was adamant, and because he is so much respected, I was allowed to keep my post."

"It now makes sense why you keep trying to rescue me despite it not being needed," Tiffany said with a wink.

"Or wanted," he said with a smile that warmed her insides. "Do you often come to the aid of damsels in distress?"

Mr. Lathrop laughed and the sound echoed on the stairs. "Rarely. And after my last two failures, I do not think I will make a habit of it."

Tiffany laughed and then he joined her. It felt as if the tension in the air disappeared like the dew before the sun. The last time that she had laughed with a gentleman had been Nathaniel. Uriah had not tolerated levity.

She sobered when she remembered the seriousness of his visit. Also, she began to lack breath when they reached the third staircase. "I—I will tell you what I saw. Once—once I catch my breath."

He took her elbow and helped her up the rest of the stairs. Mr. Lathrop was trying to help her (again), but he obviously didn't know that his touch would make it even harder for her to breathe. His fingers held her arm firmly; there was nothing romantic about it. So why did she feel like her whole body was responding to him? Her pulse quickened. Heat pooled in her belly. And when she felt his warm breath on her ear, she shivered in delight.

When he released her elbow at the top of the stairs, Tiffany regained her composure. The smell of the sick had not fully dissipated, and she recalled why she was there.

"I was drinking tea with the Duchess of Surrey," she began, "when we heard screams from the hall. I went out to investigate and found Mrs. Wheatley very upset in the servants' wing. She told me that Miss Doddridge was dead. Mrs. Wheatley, Emily, and myself came upstairs to see if we could help in anyway. But Mrs. Wheatley was correct, Miss Doddridge was dead. Emily and I cleaned up the mess and her body. The doctor arrived shortly after and examined both the bottle of laudanum and the stomach contents. Doctor Hudson suggested that she had been poisoned and that we should call you."

Tiffany opened the door to Miss Doddridge's room. The smell was strongest there, and the glass sample still sat on the side table next to the empty bottle of laudanum. Miss Doddridge looked peaceful on the bed. Mr. Lathrop's face paled at the sight of her.

"You seem very calm around the dead."

She felt the blood rush to her cheeks. "My father was a vicar. I often helped prepare bodies for burial. I am not squeamish about the dead. It's the living that are truly dangerous."

He gave her a curt nod of agreement. "Was her body warm or cold when you found her?"

Tiffany had to think for a minute. "It was still warm."

"Then she hadn't been dead for very long," he said. "Was there anything else suspicious that I should know of?"

She bit her lip. How much should she share with him? She could hardly explain that she'd seen Miss Doddridge in a compromising position with both footmen (at different times). Miss Woodall didn't visit the palace; Uriah worked there. She also couldn't tell him her suspicions about the lady's maid's involvement with Mr. Hickenlooper either, without Mr. Lathrop assuming her source of information was her half brother. He would probably wish to speak to him, which would be disastrous for her. He might find out that Uriah was dead. And she didn't intend to tell him about Miss Doddridge's blackmailing the housekeeper—information *Tiffany* wouldn't have known.

"When we were dressing Miss Doddridge, I went through her drawers, looking for the correct articles of clothing, and I found these," Tiffany said, opening the bottom drawer.

Mr. Lathrop stooped down next to her, and she breathed in his lovely scent of leather and paper. He picked up the candlestick. "This isn't a candlestick for a servant. It's made of gold."

She nodded without saying a word. She would let Mr. Lathrop come to his own conclusions without betraying her own masquerade or her half brother's death.

He picked up the ring and then the pocket watch, before setting them back into the drawer. Pulling out the drawer, he held up the bag of coins. "This is more money than I would have thought a servant would have."

"It's much more than I have."

He stood up with the drawer in his hand. "Best take these items to the butler for identification of ownership and give the coins to her family."

Mr. Lathrop walked to the door of the room.

"Do you need her body for any further examination?"

He shook his head. "I won't know more than the doctor. I'll tell Mr. Ford to send for the grave diggers, and Mr. Shirley to prepare for her burial and funeral."

"Very good."

Tiffany followed him out of the room, and when they reached the stairs, he offered her his free arm. She felt chills as she placed her fingers lightly on his strong forearm. Forgetting her purpose for the second time. Forgetting everything but the feel of his arm and the pleasure she found in his presence. For the first time that day, she wished that there were more than three flights of stairs. She could have walked down a dozen with him.

When they reached the common room in the servants' quarters, she released his arm, and he took the drawer with two hands.

"Mr. Ford and Mrs. Wheatley," he said, "would you please help me identify the contents of this drawer?"

Mr. Lathrop held up the candlestick.

"That belongs in the library," Mr. Ford said.

Mr. Lathrop set it on the table and took out the rose snuffbox and the French lace.

"The lace belongs to the duchess," Mrs. Wheatley said with another bout of tears. "But the snuffbox was a gift to Miss Doddridge."

"I saw the Duchess of Beaufort give it to her a fortnight ago," Thomas added.

The constable nodded and took out the silver spoons and fork.

"The kitchens," the butler said. "I can't believe we had a thief in our midst. Well, she got what she deserved, then."

Next, Mr. Lathrop held up the pocket watch.

"That was mine," Thomas said. "But it wasn't stolen. I gave it to Miss Doddridge. We were engaged to be married."

"And did you give her this silver ring?" Mr. Lathrop asked, holding the band between two fingers.

Thomas shook his head mournfully. Tiffany's heart went out to the young man. She glanced at Mr. Hickenlooper and waited for him to claim the ring, but he didn't. After a few more moments of silence, Mr. Lathrop placed the ring back in the drawer.

"I trust, Mr. Ford, that you will see these back to their original owners?" Mr. Lathrop said. "And the money to her family?"

"Of course," the butler said.

"Also, if you would see that Miss Doddridge's body receives a proper burial."

"You can't leave the body here, Constable," the butler insisted. "Her Grace is throwing a house party. It would be most unseemly."

"Then send it to her family," Mr. Lathrop said.

Mrs. Wheatley shook her head. "I don't think that is wise. Perhaps, for a little more money the rector would be willing to keep the body at his house until the funeral?"

"I've never known Mr. Shirley to turn down a fee," Mr. Lathrop said sardonically. "I will leave you to your grief, but I will return after the funeral and expect to speak to every servant in the house."

Mr. Ford stood and bowed to Mr. Lathrop, who inclined his head.

"Miss Woodall, may I escort you home on my way to the village?" Mr. Lathrop asked. "It's growing dark."

Tiffany suppressed her urge to smile at a most inopportune time. "Please—and thank you."

CHAPTER 15

Mr. Lathrop gestured for her to go first through the door. They walked together in silence until they were nearly halfway around the lake.

"The water is so beautiful at night," he said.

"Do you walk around it often?"

"In the summertime I do," Mr. Lathrop said. "I find the lake to be peaceful, but only once have I found a nymph."

Tiffany was grateful that the sun was setting and that it was dark enough that she hoped Mr. Lathrop couldn't see her blush, but she rallied her wits enough for a response. "Did the nymph turn into a tree when you caught her?"

"No," he said, stopping and looking her in the eyes. "She turned into a beautiful and angry woman."

He had called her beautiful again. She forced herself to start walking once more. If she gazed at him any longer, she would have thrown herself into his arms.

"Then you've learned your lesson," she said breathlessly. "Nymphs don't like to be caught."

"I believe they prefer the chase."

They reached Bristle Cottage much too soon. Mr. Lathrop touched his tricorn hat, as if to continue walking.

"Would you like to come in for some tea?" she asked.

"I don't think your brother would appreciate my visit."

"He's not here."

Mr. Lathrop blinked.

Tiffany hurried on, "He had plans to eat his supper with Mr. Shirley. It would only be you and I in the cottage. I'm afraid that I don't have a meal prepared, but we could share some bread and butter. It isn't much, and I don't blame you if you'd rather go home."

"I should be pleased to stay," he said, then swallowed.

Maybe he was as nervous as she was. Tiffany opened the door to the cottage and took off her hat and shawl. Mr. Lathrop handed her his black hat and gloves and his coat, which was cut short in the front but had tails in the back. She hung them on the hooks by the door.

"Would you like to sit in the parlor, while I prepare the tea?" she asked.

"I'd rather come with you to the kitchen and help you, if I may."

Help me.

Uriah had never once offered to help her. Tiffany assented, and while she poured the water into the kettle, Mr. Lathrop started the fire. She stooped down next to him to place the kettle over the flames. He turned to look at her. Their faces were only an inch apart.

"Miss Woodall," he began.

"Tiffany," she interrupted. "Please call me Tiffany."

He smiled and she felt warm all over. "And you can call me Sam."

"Samuel?"

"Samir," he whispered. "But the English do not like foreign names, so my father called me Sam."

"I think Samir is a very handsome name," she said, the warmth spreading up through her legs. She could no longer meet the intensity of his gaze, and she glanced down to see that her hem was on fire. The heat was not a feeling, but a flame.

Before she could react, Samir had grabbed the teapot and emptied its contents on the bottom of her new silk gown. He stood up and stamped out the remaining fire with his boot. She hoped the diamond pin attached to her shift was unscathed. Offering his hand, he helped her to her feet.

"Thank you," she said.

"I have finally rescued you," he said, smiling. "Why don't you sit down at the table? I'll make the tea."

Breathless, Tiffany took her bread and butter to the table. She watched Samir refill the kettle and stoke the fire. A man had never waited on her before. Not even Nathaniel. Samir then took the seat next to hers. Tiffany's hand shook a little as she sliced and buttered the bread.

She handed it to him. "It's not much."

"Your friendship is the feast."

As she bit into her own slice, Tiffany couldn't have agreed with him more.

Samir boiled more water for tea and even poured her a cup. "Were you able to finish *The Castle of Otranto?*"

"Yes!" she said, setting down her slice of bread on the plate. "It was so exciting! I was so relieved that Isabella was not forced to marry her father-in-law. And I was quite desolated when Matilda was stabbed. Poor girl."

"What about poor Conrad?" he asked, leaning across the table toward her. "He was killed by a falling helmet from the sky on his wedding day."

Tiffany wrinkled her nose. "Yes, that was very odd and a little sad. But he was already sickly to begin with, so he didn't have long to live anyway."

Samir laughed, a warm, rich sound. "Did you enjoy reading the novel?"

"It was like being transported to another world, another life, entirely," she said. "I loved it so much that I read *The Old English Baron* and *The Two Mentors* as well. And I liked them even better than Otranto."

He shook his head. "Oh no."

"Oh yes," she said with a laugh. "The hero, Theodore, seemed equally happy to have Matilda or Isabella to wife, as if there wasn't a difference between them."

"It was a difficult choice between two beautiful young maidens," Samir said, shrugging his broad shoulders. "Luckily, Matilda was stabbed by her father, Manfred, and then the decision was made for him."

Tiffany snorted. "If only there had been a second mysteriously falling helmet to kill Manfred, the entire story would have been perfect."

Samir lifted his teacup as if to toast. "To mysteriously falling helmets."

Tiffany lifted her glass and gently clinked it against his. "To mysteriously falling helmets."

They both sipped their hot tea and laughed together. Tiffany felt a lovely kinship between them. She could have talked books with him all night.

CHAPTER 16

She was nearly dressed as Uriah, with the diamond pin on her lapel, when there was a loud knock on the door to her cottage. Tiffany grabbed the wig and pulled it over her hair before answering the door. It was Emily from Astwell Palace.

The maid's bright blue eyes widened and her mouth fell open. "You look so different without face powder, Mr. Woodall."

Blast.

Tiffany cleared her throat and said in a low tone, "Is there something that I can help you with, Emily?"

"Not you, sir," she said, shaking her head. "Mr. Shirley has requested that your sister come and help him with the final preparations of the burial of Miss Doddridge. The service is to be held in the afternoon today. Mrs. Wheatley sent me to ask you."

The rector was a great blunderbuss! Still, she could hardly refuse him or Mrs. Wheatley without causing a fuss that could endanger her masquerade.

"Of course," Tiffany said. "I shall see that my sister goes at once to help prepare for the funeral. I shall not come to the palace today, but I will see you and Mrs. Wheatley at the funeral this afternoon."

"Very good, sir," Emily said, bobbing a curtsy. "I shall let Mrs. Wheatley know not to expect you for dinner today."

"Good day," Tiffany said in a higher tone than she'd meant to.

Emily's sharp eyes looked at her so closely that Tiffany closed the door. If only she could close the maid's suspicions as easily. She traipsed back up the stairs to Uriah's room and took off the wig and then each article of men's clothing. At least she had not yet painted her face or attached the itchy black circular patches on her cheeks. She returned to her own bedchamber to pull on her darkest dress. It was a deep gray. She didn't own a black dress, but she put on a black bonnet that covered nearly all of her hair, and gloves and a shawl in respect for the dead. No matter what Miss Doddridge's sins were, no one deserved to die in their own sick.

Tiffany placed Uriah's face powders and paints in a bag before strolling slowly to the village. She was in no rush to see the rector. But eventually her steps led her to the rectory. She knocked smartly on the door. One of the rector's many dour-faced daughters answered it. The young woman looked to be around sixteen or seventeen years old. She had ghostly pale skin, dark eyes, and nearly black hair pulled back tightly in a bun. Her hairstyle did nothing to soften the sharp lines of her cheeks and jaw. Tiffany tried smiling at her, but the young woman's expression remained grim.

"Miss Shirley, I am here to help with Miss Doddridge's burial."

"This way, Miss Woodall," she said in a flat voice. "I am relieved that you have come. My father does not wish for me to touch the harlot."

Tiffany stumbled as Miss Shirley said that ugly word. Whatever Miss Doddridge's personal choices, she was more than her worst mistakes. Tiffany hated how the world demeaned women, especially fallen ones.

"I do not mind touching her," Tiffany said. "I have always believed that it is best to leave the judgment to God and to show mercy to our fellow creatures, as Jesus Christ shows us by his infinite atonement."

Her speech was met with a scowl. Apparently, Miss Shirley followed her father's way of thinking and believed that all of the villagers would be burning in hellfire. Tiffany followed the stiff young woman through a parlor and kitchen that were scrubbed clean. The furniture was sparse and austere; even the curtains were black. Miss Shirley led her to a small room off the kitchen, where Miss Doddridge already lay in a coffin. The deceased was still wearing the clothing that Tiffany had selected for her the day before, but her hair needed tidying and her hands to be placed in a position of prayer.

"Might I have a comb and some hairpins?"

Miss Shirley did not immediately answer, and Tiffany was afraid that the young woman would not give her hairpins to a harlot. But either mercy or charity finally took over, for she agreed to go and fetch some. Miss Shirley closed the door behind her, as if to keep the taint of Miss Doddridge to the one room.

Tiffany took off her gloves—she only had one pair and could not afford to spoil them. Miss Doddridge's mouth hung agape because her jaw was still protruding and dislocated. Tiffany did not wish to harm the body, but she also wanted the young woman to look her best for her viewing before the funeral. Resolved, she placed one hand on the cold forehead and her other on the jaw, pushing until she heard a click. Once Sarah's jaw was back in place and her mouth able to close, Tiffany took a ribbon from the dress and placed it around her chin, tying it above her forehead, to keep the lips closed.

If only the poor girl had kept her lips closed during her life, she might still be alive. Either the young maid had tangled with a bad man, or she'd blackmailed the wrong person. Tiffany wished she knew how Miss Doddridge fit into it all and what Uriah had known about her. Or how well he'd known her.

The rector's daughter returned with a comb and two hair-pins. She placed them on a side table and left the room again without a word. Tiffany was careful not to move the ribbon that held the chin, as she slowly combed through Miss Doddridge's hair. Gently lifting the head, Tiffany arranged it into coiffure chenille, a large bump in the front and curls in the back. The next thing she needed to do was to make Miss Doddridge's face look more natural. She opened the bag she'd brought with Uriah's powders and paints. The white face powder made Miss Doddridge look pale and not the sickly yellowish-green color of poisoning. Tiffany added a little rouge to her cheeks and a touch of red to her lips. Last, she added some purple powder to her eyelids. Miss Doddridge did not look as beautiful as she had the first time that Tiffany had seen her, but she did look presentable. Pretty enough to catch the attention of all the male upper servants at the palace.

All Sarah needed was some flowers to hold in her hands.

Tiffany put the cosmetics back into her bag and pulled the hairs out of the comb before placing it on the table. She left the house through the kitchen door and released the hairs into the wind. She hoped that a bird would find them and use them for its nest. It came as no surprise to Tiffany that no flowers grew near the rectory; such a frivolous beauty would not have been tolerated.

She wound her way down toward the river. On its bank were several varieties of wildflowers. Tiffany picked sprays of white, blue, and yellow. She tied them together with a little bit of twine that she had in her bag and made her way back to the rectory. She did not knock, but walked through the kitchen door and back to the room with the body. Carefully placing the flowers in Miss Doddridge's hands, she brought them together as if the young woman was in prayer.

The door opened and Tiffany startled. It was Mr. Shirley, and he was smiling at her with his yellow teeth bared.

"Miss Woodall, I can see already that you will make a capital rector's wife," he said, pointing to the coffin. "I have never seen a prettier corpse."

"I wanted to give her the sort of farewell that I would wish for," Tiffany whispered reverently. The sort of farewell she should have given her own half brother. "It is a pity that servants do not have their own homes for the viewing and the funeral processions to leave from."

"You are all Christian charity, Miss Woodall," Mr. Shirley said. "Particularly to those that are the least deserving."

"Aren't we all the least deserving and in need of mercy?"

"God knows the feelings of our hearts and the thoughts of our heads," he said. "But it is your heart that I wish to know."

He couldn't.

He wouldn't.

Not even the rector would propose over a dead body.

"Miss Woodall, I have strived to be patient, but in the face of death I cannot but realize that our lives are short and that waiting is wrong."

"Our lives are short," she said, because that was the only part that she agreed with.

"Then say that you will be my wife and the mother of my children," he said, again attempting a ghoulish smile.

"I am flattered by your proposal—" Tiffany began, but before she could finish refusing him, Miss Shirley opened the door to the little room and ushered Mrs. Wheatley in. The small room was overcrowded with a coffin and three people.

"Miss Woodall has done a work of miracles," Mr. Shirley said.

Mrs. Wheatley sniffed loudly before nodding. "Aye, she has. Sarah looks beautiful."

"Will the duke be paying for the funeral, or . . .?"

Tiffany let out an indignant huff. The rector wanted his fee even before the funeral started. The man had absolutely no proper feelings.

"I will be paying for it," Mrs. Wheatley said, and pulled out her purse. "And extra, since you were so kind as to take the body for the night."

Mr. Shirley held out his hand, and the housekeeper placed the coins into his waxy palm. His skeletal fingers closed tightly around the money.

"I shall go change into my cassock," he said, bowing to them and then leaving the room.

The funeral was still several hours away. The rector was probably just looking for an excuse to count the money and leave the room. Tiffany looked from Mrs. Wheatley's tear-stained face to the already soaked handkerchief in her hand. Guilt and grief were two sides of the same coin; but how much guilt did the housekeeper possess?

"I am so sorry for your loss."

A solitary tear slid out of Mrs. Wheatley's eye and made a trail down her face. "I should have called for the doctor sooner."

"Why didn't you?" Tiffany asked in a gentle voice.

The housekeeper sniffed again. "I thought I knew what was causing her malady, and I didn't think that calling a doctor would help."

Miss Doddridge had been vomiting—an early sign of pregnancy—and she and Mrs. Wheatley had caught the young woman in the act of lovemaking with Bernard. "You thought she was with child?"

Mrs. Wheatley let out a loud sob as she nodded.

"And you didn't want to call for the doctor or a midwife for fear that Miss Doddridge's condition would be discovered and that she would be dismissed."

The older woman wiped at her wet eyes with her damp handkerchief. "Miss Woodall, I beg of you, please do not speak a word of this. My niece's reputation is already damaged. There is nothing to be gained by sullying her character further."

Tiffany placed a comforting hand on the woman's arm. "No, there is not, and I would be the last one to cast a stone at your daughter."

Mrs. Wheatley flinched away, looking like a frightened rabbit. "How did you know?"

"She has your eyes, and Uriah told me that Miss Doddridge was blackmailing you," she said quietly, studying every move, every sound the housekeeper made. For she knew personally how desperate a person could be when they were about to lose their place and their home. "It was not hard to guess that the connection between you was closer than aunt and niece."

"Do you want money for your silence?"

"No, no," Tiffany said, holding up her hands. "I simply want justice for Miss Doddridge and wish to understand the motivations for why someone would wish to poison her. And I promise you that I will never speak of your connection to Miss Doddridge again, but I would like to know who her father is and if he knows of her existence."

"He's long gone," Mrs. Wheatley said. "His name was Jonas Hill, and he was an undergardener at the palace over twenty years ago. When he found out that I was with child, he left for the sea. He didn't want to be forced by the parish to marry me. Once he'd gone, I didn't know what to do, so I confided to my sister about my situation. She was already married to a tenant farmer and with a family of her own. She agreed to take my child for a yearly sum and give her a respectable name."

"How did Miss Doddridge learn the truth?"

The older woman covered her eyes with her hands. "I don't know. I don't know. My sister might have told her before she died. She might have guessed on her own."

"Was Miss Doddridge asking you for money to keep silent?"

"Yes," Mrs. Wheatley said. "And for favors. If I had caught any other servant in the same way that I had caught her with Bernard, they would have been dismissed. She used the knowledge as leverage over me to keep silent about her thefts."

"Then you knew silverware and candlesticks were going missing," she said. "And when I asked you about my half brother's diamond pin, you knew she had taken it."

The housekeeper fell to her knees and held her hands together beseechingly. "Please, Miss Woodall. I know that I have sinned greatly, but I have worked for over twenty years to remedy my mistakes. I used my influence with the duchess to get Sarah her position two years ago. I tried to love Sarah. I did my best to hide her mistakes, but she didn't want my love. She wanted my money."

Tiffany held out her hand. "Let me help you up. There is no need for you to grovel before me. I gave Uriah his diamond pin back, and he won't say another word about it."

Mrs. Wheatley placed her cold hand in Tiffany's and allowed herself to be pulled to standing. "Thank you."

"I believe you," Tiffany said, "and I have no desire to see you lose your place that you have worked so hard for. What did Miss Doddridge plan to do with the money?"

"She wanted to pose as a lady in Bath or Tunbridge Wells and find a rich gentleman to marry."

It was not a terrible plan. Miss Doddridge was very pretty and she'd had the duchess's old gowns; with enough money, she might have even pulled it off.

"If a rich gentleman was her ambition, why did she dally with the footmen and the valets?"

"Money," Mrs. Wheatley said flatly. "She was exchanging her favors for money and trinkets. She told me that she would have enough coins by the end of the summer to leave. It was only a few months away, and I thought that I could keep paying her until she left. If she did marry a rich gentleman, I assumed that I would be safe. She wouldn't want her husband, or anyone, to know who I was, or what I was."

There was no reason for Mrs. Wheatley to murder her daughter, *if* she was really planning to leave. The housekeeper had also explained why Mr. Hickenlooper's ring was in Miss Doddridge's drawer. "Thomas said that he was engaged to Sarah. From what little I saw of him, his affections appeared to be sincere."

"They may have been," she said. "Sarah's were not. She had no intention of marrying a servant. I believe she agreed to the engagement so that he would give her his pocket watch and part of his pay. She might also have been trying to use his intimacy with the Duchess of Beaufort to her advantage."

Her last sentence caught Tiffany by surprise. She had not known that the duchess and the footman were intimate. Public knowledge of their romantic indiscretion could be quite damaging to the duchess's reputation. Miss Doddridge might have learned about it from Thomas; servants did not always have the choice to refuse such liaisons. But could Uriah have known?

"One last question," Tiffany said. "Did Sarah have any enemies on the staff? Perhaps other female servants? Anyone who would want her dead."

Mrs. Wheatley closed her eyes tightly and then shook her head. "I cannot think of anyone in particular. Sarah ignored the lower servants, and they in turn ignored her."

Tiffany patted the older woman on the shoulder. "I shall leave you to say your goodbyes alone."

She had placed her hand on the doorknob, when she heard Mrs. Wheatley ask, "How do I know that my secrets are safe with you?"

"Because I, too, have secrets."

CHAPTER 17

The church bells rang the death knell. It was almost time for the funeral. Retracing her early path, Tiffany was dressed as Uriah. All that a man was expected to wear for mourning was a black hatband, but Tiffany had worn her half brother's darkest blue suit for the service. She'd arrived in front of the rectory too late for the viewing. The servants from Astwell Palace began to sing a hymn. The church bells were still ringing, and combined with Mrs. Wheatley's loud weeping, it gave a somber tone to the mournful proceedings.

Thomas, Bernard, and two other young men from Astwell Palace that Tiffany did not know carried the coffin out of the rectory and made the short walk to the church graveyard adjacent to it. Their expressions were solemn. Mrs. Wheatley was the first person behind the coffin, still holding her soaked handkerchief and making a great show of her grief. She was followed by the other maids, all dressed in their black livery, then the rest of the male servants with black hatbands. Tiffany took up the rear.

Mr. Shirley met them at the gates, and the procession entered the church; all of them took seats in the back of the building. Tiffany slid into her brother's bench in the middle. The closer pews belonged to the prominent families in the neighborhood, none of which were attending the funeral. Tiffany felt like a lone island and wished that there were others near her to share the rector's stare.

For once, Mr. Shirley kept his sermon brief and only implied that Miss Doddridge's soul was going to experience eternal torment. At least that was what he said in English, what he intoned at the end in Latin was probably far worse.

Tiffany was the last to leave the church. She watched the pall bearers lift the coffin and carry it to the already dug hole in the graveyard. They gently set it down into the earth. Tears fell freely down Thomas's handsome face. He did not attempt to stem his sorrow. As with Mrs. Wheatley, Tiffany was unsure if his emotions were caused by guilt or grief. Had the poison been in the laudanum? If so, had he put it there? Then how had Uriah died? Emily came up to him and gave him a handkerchief. He nodded his thanks, apparently too overcome to speak.

Unfortunately, Mr. Shirley gave another small service over the grave. Luckily, Tiffany was too far away to hear what he had to say.

After the rector's prayer, she watched Mr. Hickenlooper walk toward the grave, but when he was close enough to see inside the hole, he paled and turned around. Raising his own handkerchief to his mouth, he left in a hurry, brushing shoulders with Bernard on his way out. Bernard emitted an exasperated "Ha" and dusted off his shoulder, as if his coat had been dirtied by the valet's touching it. He swaggered to the hole and peered in. Placing his hand in his pocket, he pulled out the rose-painted snuffbox that had been in the drawer. Tiffany thought that he was going to put it in the grave as a remembrance for her, but instead, he flicked it open and snorted it. Closing the snuffbox, he left the churchyard without a word.

Neither man had behaved naturally near the grave.

More men and women came forward. She recognized them as servants from the palace, but she did not know their names. None of them lingered over the open hole, but simply walked by with their heads lowered in respect. The last person in the line was Mr. Lathrop. She had not even known that he was there, which was probably good, because he distracted her. He stood in front of the grave for several minutes. Perhaps, like her, he was thinking about who had killed Miss Doddridge.

He turned, and his searing eyes met Tiffany's. It was as if there was an invisible connection between them. For a moment, she thought that he could see right through her disguise, but then he cast his eyes down and left.

Tiffany hadn't meant to be the last person in the graveyard, and she didn't want another tête-à-tête with Mr. Shirley. She touched her brother's tricorn hat. "Good day, Rector."

"Woodall," he said with a nod.

As she walked slowly back home, Tiffany admitted to herself that she was no closer to discovering who had harmed Miss Doddridge and Uriah, or how. But she wasn't about to give up. There were many more pages to read in this story.

CHAPTER 18

The servants' dining room was nearly silent when she entered it, save for the sound of silverware scraping against china. Despite Miss Doddridge's funeral only having taken place the day before, everyone had returned to their work as if nothing had happened. Only the somber mood in the room betrayed that a death had recently occurred.

"Mr. Woodall, I thought that you were not coming," Mr. Ford said. His lined face looked older, wearier.

Tiffany sat across from Mr. Hickenlooper, whose plate was nearly clean. "I was distracted by my work. I hope that I haven't inconvenienced anyone."

"Of course not," the butler said.

She glanced at Mrs. Wheatley, who sat at the head of the female servants' table. Her face was a little red, but there weren't any recent signs of tears. She wore her usual dark dress and housekeeper's apron and mobcap.

Tiffany hesitated before scooping up for herself some potatoes, roasted mutton, swan with currant jelly sauce, a slice of bread, and vegetables. All of the dishes had already been served from, and she doubted the murderer would be daring enough to kill an entire staff. Besides, she'd grown lazy about cooking herself supper at her cottage, so she tried to eat a large dinner to make up for it. Stealing a glance at the footmen, she saw Bernard was back to his usual self. He was making eyes at a woman, who had to be ten years his senior, with dark red hair and a nice figure, even in a maid's uniform. The older woman returned his smiles. He was quick to find a new victim of his charms.

Thomas's eyes were focused firmly on his half-eaten plate. His entire countenance was downcast. He didn't need to be wearing black to be entirely mournful. Tiffany had been right in assuming that his feelings for Miss Doddridge were sincere. And her eyes were not the only ones on the handsome footman. Emily, from the end of the female table, watched his every movement. Her blue eyes were full of concern, full of love.

Tiffany had never known the feeling of love unrequited, but she was sure it was a painful one. Perhaps as painful as a love lost.

Could Emily have poisoned Miss Doddridge? Her room was near to the room of the deceased lady's maid. And since Sarah's death, Emily had not only assumed her position as lady's maid, but she'd also comforted Thomas. Perhaps with Miss Doddridge gone, she might even gain his affections.

Was jealously a strong enough motive for murder?

Love?

Tiffany chewed on her mutton and her thoughts. She was the last person to leave the table. On her way back to the library, she saw Bernard and the redhead sneak into a room. Happily, it was not located near her beloved library. She was able to return to her favorite chair, and pulled out *Clarissa*.

She was so engrossed that she did not hear the door to the library open.

"Well, Uriah, it has been a long time," Tess said.

Tiffany gulped. If anyone could see through her disguise, it would be her former best friend. The one who had come up with the idea for the lark of Tiffany masquerading as her half brother all those years ago.

She got to her feet and executed a stiff bow. "Your Grace."

Tess walked closer and held out her delicate hand to Tiffany. Did she expect Tiffany to kiss it?

Oh dear!

Tess expected *Uriah* to kiss her hand. Awkwardly, Tiffany took the proffered hand and gave it a brief brush with her lips. She gulped. Backing away from Tess, Tiffany cleared her throat.

"Is there anything I can assist you with, Your Grace?"

Tess tittered. "Oh, Uriah, you are still so formal. Were we not friends once? So very long ago."

"I am honored that you considered me a friend."

"I don't know how I could have endured my childhood without you and Tiffany," she said with a friendly smile bordering on flirtatious. "And I cannot endure another meal with only the duke and the duchess to speak to. The rest of the house party does not arrive until tomorrow, so you and Tiffany must come to dinner and keep me company."

"We would not wish to presume on our employer's good graces."

"Catharine doesn't mind, and Francis would do anything to please me," Tess said confidently.

The old Tess was used to having her own way, and it would seem that age had not changed that about her friend. Tiffany would not be able to get out of the dinner.

"I'm afraid that I have a prior engagement with Mr. Shirley," Tiffany said. "But my sister would be delighted to make one of your party."

"Fie, sir," Tess said, swatting at Tiffany's arm flirtatiously. "Uriah Woodall, you must put the man off. You haven't seen me in over twenty years. Surely, this fellow will understand that you cannot offend the Duke of Beaufort when he condescends to include you in a dinner party."

"I am a dull companion," Tiffany said, desperate not to be committed as two people in the same place at the same time. "You and my sister would have a much better time without me."

Tess stuck out her chin in a pouty manner. "La, sir! Nothing you say could be as dull as another night of Francis discussing his favorite hunters, or listening to Catharine tell me for the hundredth time that she has a snuffbox to match each of her gowns. Especially since I have already endured an entire morning of her showing me each box in her collection. I cannot wait until the rest of the party arrives!"

Tiffany thought it odd that Tess called the Duchess of Beaufort by her given name. She had always supposed that duchesses were called "duchess" by those of similar rank. But it would be confusing to have two women in the same household both calling each other "duchess." Still, she couldn't comprehend calling the Duchess of Beaufort *Catharine*. She was too formidable of a person to have a common name.

"Please, Your Grace," Tiffany said, "I do not feel at ease in the company of my betters. Please allow me to keep my previous obligation."

Tess put her hand on Tiffany's arm, and Tiffany blushed with embarrassment. What would Tess think if she knew that she'd been flirting with a woman instead of a man?

"How you have changed, Uriah," she said. "You used to think that you were equal to anyone's company. Besides, Francis is your third or fourth cousin once removed. You should not feel ill at ease in his company. There is not a more affable man alive than the duke."

Tiffany's heart was beating like the sound of thunder. She stepped back from Tess. This was not working.

"If you wish it, I will be there. But perhaps my sister should stay at home. She has not a gown fitting for such an occasion, Your Grace. I wouldn't wish for her to be embarrassed by the differences of our stations."

"I would lend her one of mine," Tess said, the pouty look back on her face. "But she is so tall like you, nearly half of her calves would be showing. Mayhap, Catharine wouldn't mind lending Tiffany a gown and the matching snuffbox? They both have such tall, statuesque figures."

"Tiffany couldn't, wouldn't, shouldn't wear one of the duchess's gowns," she said, talking about herself in the third person. "It would be most improper."

"Fie, sir. No more excuses," Tess said with a little laugh. "Send Tiffany over early, and I will ensure that she is dressed the equal to any duchess."

Tongue-tied and out of excuses, all Tiffany could do was nod.

"Four o'clock then," Tess said, wreathed in smiles, and walked to the door.

She stood in front of it until Tiffany realized that *she* was supposed to open it. Tiffany learned that duchesses didn't touch doorknobs. They just made life difficult for their oldest friends.

CHAPTER 19

The hem in the front of her silk gown was ruined, but as long as Tiffany purchased some material for a matching petticoat, she could gather the undamaged material and let the underskirt be seen. She'd only worn the dress once, and she wasn't even finished with the embroidery on the sleeves. If it hadn't been for Mr. Lathrop's—no, *Samir's*—quick thinking, she would have lost the entire dress and possibly been burned by the flames.

She couldn't help but believe that the accident was also slightly his fault—if he hadn't distracted her, she wouldn't have started her gown on fire.

A smile formed on her lips. It always did when she thought of Samir Lathrop. There was so much that she didn't know about him, and she longed to know everything, from the first page of his life to the most recent chapter. She was certain that his life story would be as fascinating to her as he was.

Shaking her head, Tiffany forced herself to focus. She could not wear her silk dress to the palace, so she would have to wear one of her plain ones. It wouldn't matter, since she was changing her raiment when she got there. But how was she possibly going to be two people in the same place? It was impossible. If only she had not tried to make so many excuses to Tess, she might have been able to send a note (with herself) that she was ill. But during the disastrous interview with Tess as *Uriah*, she hadn't mentioned that she was unwell, only uncomfortable. And knowing Tess, she would probably have already procured a gown for Tiffany from the Duchess of Beaufort, whose temperament was anything but calm. Tiffany/Uriah didn't wish to earn her ire.

She couldn't be two places at once, but she could be two people in one night. Tiffany donned a dull blue wool dress and packed a satchel with Uriah's wig, clothing, face powder, and velvet patches. She went over her plan as she walked to Astwell Palace. She would allow herself to be gowned and attend dinner. Then she could change into Uriah's clothes, to drink the after-dinner coffee. Then she should excuse herself and put the borrowed gown back on and wear it for the rest of the party before changing back into her own clothes and trudging back home. Her stomach turned, and her overly large dinner was coming back to haunt her. The plan was anything but perfect; it was fraught with risk. There were so many chances of being caught, but since she couldn't think of anything else to do, she continued walking forward.

At least dressed as herself, she didn't have to worry about anyone trying to poison her at dinner.

Tiffany went to the servants' entrance as she was used to. She could have hardly walked through the main doors of a palace in a homespun wool gown. Even so, her hands shook as she curtsied to the housekeeper.

"I have been invited to dinner."

"A gown has been prepared for you in one of the guest rooms, and Emily will help you dress," Mrs. Wheatley said with a painful smile. "This way, Miss Woodall."

She followed the housekeeper out into the main hall. They walked up the grand staircase to the guest rooms that Tiffany had placed books in. Mrs. Wheatley held open the door for her. Emily was waiting in the room. On the vanity was an assortment of beauty products that looked like a fancy tea setting, including a little silver teapot. She couldn't help but wonder what all of those tins, bottles, brushes, and metal tongs were for. And if any of those powders or potions could be used for poisoning. But Tiffany supposed that she would find out when Emily put them on her, and it would be the perfect opportunity to question her about Thomas.

"Thank you," Tiffany said.

The housekeeper bowed to her and then left the room, leaving her alone with Emily.

"It is kind of you to help me today."

"'Tis my job, Miss Woodall," Emily said, and put a hand on Tiffany's shawl, as if to take it off.

Tiffany flinched. "I am not used to someone else undressing me."

Emily smiled. "Aye, me neither. But aristocratic ladies don't even know how to pull up their own stockings."

A laugh bubbled up from Tiffany. "I shall be terribly out of place at dinner. I don't think anyone has ever pulled up my stockings for me before. Why don't I take off my own dress and you can assist me with the new one?"

"Whatever you like, Miss Woodall."

"Tiffany," she said. If she wanted Emily to confide in her, she would have to feel comfortable with her. A kinship with her.

"I couldn't."

"I assure you that there is nothing special about me that would preclude you from using my Christian name, Emily," she said. "My brother and I have been living in genteel poverty for almost my entire adult life."

"But you were born a lady."

"I was born a woman, just like yourself."

"Very well, I'll call you Miss Tiffany."

"I sound more like a debutante than a confirmed spinster," Tiffany said, slipping out of her gown and pulling off her thick stockings. She stood in only her chemise, corset, and panniers. Emily then untied her panniers and replaced them with a pair of padded ones that made Tiffany's hips look twice as wide. Then she added a padding in the back for a false rump.

"Do you mind if I tighten your corset?" the young maid asked. "I don't think the dress will fit 'round your middle if I don't."

For a moment, Tiffany thought that her not very dainty waist would finally be in her favor. She could hardly be expected to wear a gown that did not close, but alas, Emily's arms were strong and she pulled Tiffany's corset tight enough that her middle looked half its usual size.

"Do you like being the duchess's lady's maid?" Tiffany squeaked out. Breathing and speaking were both nearly impossible with her corset tied this tightly.

One side of Emily's mouth quirked up into a half smile. "I like it well enough. But there's no guarantee I'll keep the position. Mrs. Wheatley is unhappy that I was sent above other female servants that have worked here longer. And the duchess says that she wants a French lady, but then hints that if I am satisfactory, she might keep me."

"I-I didn't mean to cause any strife when I sent you that day, Emily," Tiffany managed to choke out. "I simply noticed that you were very skillful, and thought that you would do the job well."

"And I thank ye for it," Emily said. "You might have changed my life forever. Such an opportunity doesn't come along in every girl's lifetime."

Tiffany smiled. "I hope that the duchess does keep you."

"Aye, so do I," she said. "I'm less moody than Miss Doddridge, and I plan to work twice as hard to convince Her Grace to let me stay."

"I take it that you were not fond of Miss Doddridge."

Emily was hanging up Tiffany's woolen dress. "She was a right nasty piece of work."

"Did all the maids dislike her?"

"I dunno," Emily said, closing the door to the wardrobe. "Now, if you'll take a seat on the stool, I will apply your face powder and arrange your hair."

Tiffany waddled like a duck to the stool in front of the vanity and carefully sat down on it. Her wide panniers and false rump made the entire process a precarious one. She planned to continue her questioning of Emily, but one could hardly speak while their chin was in the tight grasp of another. Emily applied some sort of liquid to her face before dusting the powder on her. She darkened both Tiffany's eyelashes and eyelids. Then she applied the rouge and an alkanet root paste on her lips. Looking in the mirror, Tiffany did not recognize herself. The person in the reflection looked like an aristocrat, not a poor relation.

Emily took out Tiffany's hairpins and began to comb out her curls to make a large, crape frizzy halo around her face.

"I noticed at the funeral that you are quite close to Thomas," Tiffany began. "The poor young man, he seems to be taking Miss Doddridge's death quite hard."

A scowl formed on Emily's face, and her blue eyes narrowed. "He was always too good for the likes of her. He's well shot of her, in my opinion. A girl like her would only give him heartache."

"But a girl like you . . . would not?"

The maid didn't immediately answer, but yanked out a snarl in Tiffany's dark blonde hair. Tiffany had to close her lips not to yelp in pain and protest. But she probably deserved it for asking such a personal question.

"He can like who he likes," Emily said, pulling Tiffany's hair again roughly and using the comb to make it puff up like a cloud over her head.

Tiffany watched the maid's reaction closely as she said, "I heard that the duchess is quite fond of Thomas."

Emily wrinkled her nose, and the expression of disgust on her face was impossible to disguise. But was she disgusted with the footman or the duchess?

Or both?

Tiffany took a quick breath before she continued. "I daresay the Duchess of Beaufort was not happy about Thomas's relationship with Miss Doddridge."

The maid gritted her teeth but continued to style Tiffany's hair. "I couldn't say, miss. I wasn't her maid then, but I do know that Her Grace is relieved to see him out of the clutches of that *harpy*."

Tiffany winced at that word—or maybe at Emily's rough handling. Looking in the mirror, she was amazed how the maid had managed to make her hair stay in place with only a few ribbons. She was talented with her fingers. Then Emily arranged a few curls at the base of Tiffany's neck. She handed her a cone-like instrument.

"If you'll cover your face, Miss Tiffany," she said, while protecting Tiffany's dress with a delicate white peignoir hemmed with ruffles.

Tiffany placed the cone over her face and felt Emily sprinkle hair powder on her head.

"You can take it off now."

She did and sneezed. Emily laughed. Tiffany did too. The maid then helped her into the gown, which she was (unfortunately) able to button all the way up. Tiffany stole another glance in the mirror and was astonished by her transformation. She looked younger, prettier, and had a great deal more of a bosom than usual.

"Emily, you're a witch."

"What?" the maid said aghast.

Tiffany held up her hands. "Oh no. I meant it as a compliment. You've quite transformed me into someone else. Someone better."

Emily shook her head. "You were already perfect."

Blinking, Tiffany thought that the girl was giving her false flattery. But the sincerity on Emily's face could not be mistaken.

Tiffany gave a laugh. "Thank you. But I am so very far from perfect. I'm nothing but an old spinster."

"You are kind when you don't have to be. When you don't need to be. There is no greater perfection."

A warmth spread through Tiffany's chest. She had been trying to gain Emily's confidence with her questions, and instead, Emily had gained hers.

"I am about to ruin your high opinion of me," Tiffany said. "I am going to put on my own silk stockings and heels. No proper lady would do that."

Emily giggled and handed Tiffany the pair of silk stockings. They were so smooth that it felt like touching water. Tiffany stooped down to pull on her stocking and toppled off the stool to the floor with a loud thud.

"Are you alright, Miss Tiffany?"

Tiffany felt sore, but all she could do was laugh at her own clumsiness from the floor. "Perhaps this is why duchesses don't put on their own stockings."

Emily smiled and shook her head.

Tiffany slipped on the other stocking and accepted Emily's hand to help her to standing.

"Why don't I put on your heels," Emily said. "Just to be safe."

Tiffany laughed again. "Thank you. That is probably for the best."

She stuck out her foot, and Emily slipped the delicately heeled shoe on it. The shoe was as intricately and beautifully embroidered as the dress, if a little bit snug. When she put out her other foot, she couldn't help but feel like a princess—no, a queen. If only she could have enjoyed this dinner party with her old friend instead of having to try to be two people in one night.

"I'll take you to the parlor, where you'll wait for the rest of the party," Emily said, bobbing a curtsy and opening the door to the room. It was as if Emily had transformed into a different person. Into a servant. Her posture was erect and her eyes downcast. "This way, Miss Woodall."

Tiffany tried giving her a reassuring smile, but Emily's countenance did not change. She did not speak another word until they reached the door to the parlor. "I'll be waiting this evening to help you undress, Miss Woodall. Please let me know if you require anything else."

"Nothing at all," Tiffany said, and squeezed Emily's arm as she passed. "You've been brilliant."

Chapter 20

Tiffany grew more and more nervous as the minutes passed without anyone entering the room. She knew that she was not the typical guest. She was of a lower rank and therefore could be kept waiting as long as the aristocracy wished. But it did nothing to help her nerves. She kept practicing her excuses for Uriah being late. When Thomas opened the door for Tess to come in, her excuses all spilled right out of her in a jumble. "Uriah will be arriving later. He couldn't break his previous engagement. I hope you are not at all offended."

"Disappointed, not offended," Tess said with a flick of her fan. "Fie! He is so fun to tease! The poor man takes everything so seriously."

"And you do not?"

Tess smiled as she sat down on a settee and spread out her gown. "No. But I am trying to take things more seriously now that I have found my Methodist faith. My son felt that I was too inclined to levity and licentiousness, but I have assured him that is the case no longer. I will do no more than flirt with a gentleman unless I'm married to him."

Tiffany did not think of herself as a prude, but she'd never heard a woman speak so openly about her affairs.

"La! I have shocked you, dear Tiffany," Tess said. "But these little affairs are quite common among the upper class. We do not marry for love, you see, so we are forced to find it outside of our marriage."

"I hope you have found love," Tiffany said. "You deserve to find love."

Tess's mocking smile faded. "I did. I had for nearly fifteen years. But I cannot find solace in his arms anymore."

A familiar sadness filled her soul. She knew from Nathaniel how painful it was to lose someone that you loved. "I'm so sorry to hear about his death."

A solitary tear slid down her cheek, and she shook her head. "He is not dead. He is married to someone else. But I must give him up now, despite our mutual feelings. My new faith demands it."

Tiffany did not know what to say and was saved an answer by Mr. Ford opening the door for the Duke and Duchess of Beaufort. She stood and curtsied to them both.

The duke smiled at her warmly. "Ah, Miss Woodall, what a delight it is that you were able to join us tonight."

He then walked over to Tess and took her hand and kissed it. "Duchess, you look more dazzling every time that I see you."

Tess tapped his arm with her fan. "A lady of my age never refuses a compliment."

"But where is Mr. Woodall?" he asked. "Are we not to enjoy his company also this evening?"

Tiffany felt the blood rush to her face, and inexplicably her corset seemed to tighten. "He had a previous engagement, but he means to join us later in the evening."

"Excellent," the duke said, and offered one arm to his wife and the other to Tess. He escorted them out of the room, and

Tiffany followed behind them like a servant. He led them to a dining room decorated in celestial blue that was positively sumptuous in size and decor. Three crystal chandeliers glittered from the ceiling. The table was oblong and could have seated as many as thirty, but only five chairs and place settings were there. The duke led his wife to the head of the table and helped her into her chair, then escorted Tess to the seat on his right side. There were two place settings left: one next to Tess and one across from her. Tiffany did not know where she was supposed to sit, so she stood awkwardly by the door.

The duke pushed in Tess's chair and then came over to Tiffany and offered his arm to her. "My dear Miss Woodall, if you'll allow me to escort you."

She had not expected such condescension or consideration. As if she were a woman of rank, and not the spinster sister of his librarian. Gingerly, she placed her fingers on his white coat, which was so fine that she thought it might tear if she touched it too roughly. He led her to the opposite side of the table from Tess and surprised her again by holding the chair for her and pushing it in.

Tiffany stole a glance at the duchess, who was staring at her, a look of revulsion on her countenance. Was it because Tiffany was wearing one of her gowns? Or did she find something so appalling about Tiffany's person or appearance that she could not help but scowl.

Mr. Ford directed Bernard and Thomas, and the many courses of dinner began. Tiffany wished that she didn't know that the palace contained a murderer, so she could properly enjoy the delicate and expensive feast before her. She watched intently to make sure that she was not the first to partake of any food. Bernard served his tureens with a smirk on his face. As if he knew something the others did not. Thomas had the air of someone attending a funeral. He gave Tiffany a small smile as he served her the sixth course, but he was positively frigid as he dished out the swan on Tess and the duke's plates. The first footman was the stiffest near the Duchess of Beaufort, refusing to meet her imploring eyes during any of the courses. Mr. Ford watched over the entire proceedings like a judge at court and was quick to refill any glass of wine that fell below half full.

Everything on the table was a culinary delight. Some were savory, like the ox cheeks and the calves' heads in ragout. Others were sweet, like the currant jelly on the fowl, the cakes, and the dessert of fruit and damson cheese. Every bite felt delicate.

The conversation at dinner was minimal. The oblong table was simply too large for proper conversation, unless they wished to yell at each other from each end. Even her view of Tess was obscured by a large silver figurine of a tiger that sat in the middle of the table. But Tiffany didn't mind at all. She was more than content to focus on the feast in front of her. It wasn't until the duchess stood that Tiffany's stomach dropped. The duchess was signaling that it was time for the ladies to leave the room. Tess also stood, and Tiffany managed to get to her feet and waddle behind them to the door.

Mr. Ford held open the door to yet another beautiful room, and the duchess and Tess entered it.

Tiffany stopped at the entrance. "I will join you in a moment if I may, Your Graces. I need to—"

Tess laughed. "I think we both know what you need to do. Go on, Tiffany."

If only she had to pee and not pretend to be Uriah. Tiffany retraced her steps back to the guest room where Emily had helped her into the exquisite gown that she was wearing. Her fingers shook as she unbuttoned the tiny pearls. Carefully stepping out of the dress, Tiffany laid it on the bed and stripped off the stockings and heels. She was unable to loosen the corset, so she took the strips of cloth from her satchel and bound her chest over the top of it. If she thought she couldn't breathe before, she really couldn't get a deep breath now. She quickly put on Uriah's clothing and plopped his wig over her beautifully powdered hair.

Her gaze roamed the room and she saw a pitcher, basin, and a cloth. She dipped the cloth into the water and gently washed the dark powder from her eyes. As an extra precaution, she powdered her face a second time before adding the three velvet black patches on her cheek. Glancing in the mirror, she was satisfied that she no longer looked like a woman. She hurried back to the room where the two duchesses and now the duke were sitting.

Thomas stood outside the door and opened it for her.

"Uriah!" Tess cried. "I am so pleased that you made it. You must come and take a seat next to me."

Tiffany swept her best bow yet and then sat down on the settee next to Tess. "Where is my sister? Is she not here?"

Tess patted her mid-thigh with her hand. Tiffany flinched and nearly jumped up to standing.

"She'll be back shortly, I assure you. Sometimes ladies need a few minutes to take care of nature."

Tiffany knew that she was blushing, but she supposed that Uriah would have been red-faced as well at the mention of anything to do with "nature."

"We are both greatly honored by your invitation, Your Grace," Tiffany said, looking at the Duchess of Beaufort.

"I'm always happy to accommodate a guest," she said in a clipped tone. "And I have been quite pleased with the new novels you've purchased."

"Novels!" Tess said, her mouth wide. "Uriah, you have shocked me to my toes. I would have thought you would've disapproved of them."

He had.

Tiffany bit her lip and then cleared her throat. "The duchess requested the latest and most interesting books for her guests; I could have hardly provided her with sermons."

Tess crowed with laughter, and the duchess even smiled.

"I do not know if our guests will get to read the novels," the duke said, winking at his wife. "Catharine seems to have claimed them all for herself."

"I have enjoyed them more than I can say," the duchess said. "There is something so delicious about being scared. I have rarely been better entertained for hours by the most accomplished performers of plays."

"Praise indeed," the duke agreed.

"Perhaps I should go look for Tiffany," Tess said, flipping her fan. "I fear that she must have gotten herself lost."

Tiffany scrambled to her feet. "Allow me to, Your Grace."

"Very good, Uriah," she said, and squeezed her hand. "But don't be gone too long."

Tiffany nodded and pulled her hand away from Tess's. She couldn't make her way to the door fast enough. Passing through it, she all but ran back to the guest room. Unbuttoning her coat and chevron patterned waistcoat, she quickly cast them off. Pulled off her breaches and stepped back into the gown. She nimbly buttoned up the front of it and took off Uriah's wig. Tiffany straightened a few curls and darkened her eyelids again before leaving the room.

At the bottom of the stairs, she ran into Emily, who curtsied to her.

"Hello, Emily."

"You ought to take off the patches, Miss Tiffany," Emily said, "if you don't wish to be recognized."

Gasping for air, Tiffany raised a hand to her cheek and felt the three velvet circular patches. She tried to breathe, but there was no air in her lungs. She'd been caught in her masquerade. She could lose her cottage. She could go to prison. Tiffany was entirely at the mercy of Emily.

Emily stepped closer to her and gently pulled off the three velvet patches. "Mr. Woodall never once spoke to me. Nor even spared me so much as a glance. I knew there was something different from the first day that you arrived and couldn't find the library."

"And you didn't say anything?"

She shook her head. "Who would have believed me? And besides, you have been kinder to me than anyone else in the palace."

"It would appear that your kindness to me greatly exceeds anything that I have done for you."

"You'd better not keep them waiting any longer."

Tiffany nodded and rushed back to the parlor. Her nerves were in shreds before Thomas even opened the door.

"Ah, Tiffany," Tess said in her usual bright voice. "You've found your way back, but now we have lost Mr. Woodall."

Tiffany grasped together her shaking hands as she made her way across the room to sit near Tess. "I'm afraid that my brother is not feeling well and has decided to go home."

"Poor Uriah," Tess said with a giggle. "I'm afraid that I scared him off with my flirting."

"Oh no," Tiffany said. "Uriah has a long history of stomach complaints. He was very glad to see you again after so long. He said that you hadn't altered in the least."

"Perhaps he is the flirt!" Tess said with another giggle.

"The duchess has been blessed with youthful looks," the duke agreed about Tess. His wife, the other duchess, simply fanned herself, with a look of boredom on her face.

"I'm feeling quite languid tonight," the Duchess of Beaufort said. "And I am in need of entertainment. Miss Woodall, do you play?"

Tiffany said, "No" at the same moment that Tess said, "Yes."

Tess placed her hand on Tiffany's arm. "Don't be modest— you play beautifully. You were by far the most accomplished student on the harpsichord at our school, and she has the voice of an angel. Truly."

Squirming in her seat, Tiffany felt herself flush. "I'm afraid that I have not had the means nor the opportunity to play since school, and I am sure that any performance of mine would not entertain the company in the least."

"Fie!" Tess said with a pout. "I'm sure you've sung in the last twenty years."

The funny thing was that she hadn't. Singing had always brought Tiffany joy, but there had been precious little to be happy about in her adult life. She'd had no instrument to prac- tice on, and Uriah hadn't liked the sound of "her screeching," as he called it, while she baked or cleaned. Tiffany couldn't help but think that music and the arts were another privilege of the aristocracy. Could Tess really have no idea what Tiffany's life was like?

"A pity," the other duchess said with a yawn.

"Perhaps a game of cards?" the duke suggested.

Whist was agreed on, and Thomas brought in a card table. Tess and Tiffany were partners against the Duke and the Duch- ess of Beaufort. They played for only small stakes, but even then,

Tiffany knew that she had to win. If she didn't, she would not be able to eat a morning or evening meal. Gambling with one's food money was hardly a sound choice, but Tiffany did not know what else to do.

Tess, as ever, seemed oblivious to why the duke would set such low stakes, and complained that it ruined the fun. She smiled broadly when she did well and pouted when she lost a hand. It was as if Tess was still the same spoiled girl from their childhood who had always gotten her own way.

When the duchess yawned several times in a row, Tiffany stood and made her excuses. Happy to escape with her meager winnings.

Emily was waiting in the guestroom when Tiffany arrived. She helped her undress without a word and took the beautiful gown, the silk stockings, and the delicate heels back. It had only been Tiffany's for the night. Tiffany slid on her other dress and noticed that all of Uriah's clothing that she'd left strewn across the room was neatly packed into her satchel. On top of Uriah's wig sat the three small, circular velvet patches.

"Would you like me to explain?"

The maid shook her head. "I need to go help the duchess undress for the evening, Miss Tiffany. I wish you a pleasant walk home."

"Thank you again for all that you have done for me this evening," Tiffany said. "I am in your debt, and if you need anything, please, let me know."

Emily opened the door for her, and Tiffany found her way out of the house through the servants' quarters. It was quite dark outside. The only light was the moon shining on the lake. She saw the small ripples in the water chasing each other, but never touching. It was lovely but also frightening. Somewhere in the palace lurked a murderer. She clutched her throat with one hand.

"Miss Woodall," Thomas said from the door. "Has a carriage been called to take you home?"

Tiffany turned back to see his tall form illuminated by the candlelight inside the palace. She shook her head. "No, but it is not a far walk. Less than a mile."

"But you have no light."

Tiffany shrugged her shoulders a little. "I should have thought to bring a lantern with me."

Thomas held up a hand. "One moment, Miss Woodall. I'll fetch a lantern and accompany you home."

Truthfully, she was glad for both the light and the company on her walk back to the cottage. Thomas held the lantern high so that she could easily see the path in front of them.

"It is good of you to walk me home."

He shook his head slightly. "It is the least that I could do. They should have called you a carriage. You were a guest."

"Alas, spinsters are afforded very little consideration, I'm afraid," Tiffany said with a smile.

Thomas returned it. "Footmen aren't either."

She briefly placed her hand on his arm. "I am so sorry for your loss. My brother said that you were particularly attached to Miss Doddridge. It must be a very difficult time for you."

He sniffed and nodded. He didn't say anything, but Tiffany knew all too well that words could not adequately express the pain of losing the person that you loved.

"It must have been equally hard to discover that she was not the woman that you thought she was," Tiffany said, and watched his face for a reaction.

Thomas shook his head. "I should have known earlier. I was warned by—by someone that Sarah was not faithful to me, but I thought they were lying. Disparaging her on purpose."

Tiffany regretted having to ask the next question, but she needed to understand his motives. "Did you learn of her unfaithfulness before or after her untimely demise?"

He turned his head away from her and walked several steps before speaking. "Miss Woodall, I do not think that is any of your business."

She did not blame him for snubbing her impertinent question. Still, she had to know the answer. "I can't help but wonder if Miss Doddridge's behavior was the cause of her death."

Stopping mid-step, he positively glared at her. "I do not like what you are insinuating. I would never have harmed the woman that I loved, no matter what she did. And if I'd known, I would have stopped anyone else who tried to."

Tiffany gave a small nod. "I'm sure the *duchess* is sad to lose such an excellent lady's maid."

He quickened his pace. "I would not know, ma'am."

The expression on his face suggested quite the opposite.

When she reached the door to her cottage, Thomas held up the lantern so that she could unlock it, and waited for her to go inside before leaving. Despite her cruel questioning, he was truly a gentleman.

As she lit her candle, she had to admit to herself that she was no closer to catching her half brother and Miss Doddridge's murderer. All of the upper servants seemed to have reasons to kill Uriah or Sarah, or both. They all had something to hide. Including herself.

CHAPTER 21

Sunday was no longer a day of peace for Tiffany. Trudging on her way to the church, she wished that she could attend a different sermon at another chapel. One without a rector that proposed marriage over dead bodies. Despite her father's cold manner at home, his sermons had always brought her hope and renewal each week. She'd also loved the way the light spilled through the stained-glass windows and the beautiful pictures and sculptures of her Savior. Alas, she felt no warmth as the Mapledown church loomed before her.

"Miss Woodall, you look very well this morning," Samir said.

Tiffany smiled in response. She'd spent a good part of the previous night hemming up the burnt part of the dress and was happy to be wearing such a lovely gown to church. Happier even that Samir thought she looked well in it.

"Almost as handsome as you look this morning, Mr. Lathrop," she said, noticing that Samir had not called her by her given name in public. It would have caused unnecessary and unwanted gossip for them both. She as a single lady and he as a man of color.

Samir's brown eyes smiled at the corners as he offered her his arm. Tiffany did not hesitate to take it. She loved standing close to him, for he smelled of paper and cinnamon spice.

"How is your investigation coming, Constable?"

The brightness that had been present in his countenance dimmed. He shook his head slightly. "I'm afraid very poorly, Miss Woodall. I know neither the poison nor the means in which it was administered . . . I have spoken to Mr. Canning, the apothecary, and he swears that he has not sold any night-shade plants to any of the palace staff or to the villagers. The poison must have been acquired outside of Mapledown, which hardly narrows down my search."

"Did you question the doctor?"

"Doctor Hudson had no additional light to shed on the murder," he admitted. "The only thing that he was certain of was that she was poisoned, because of the color and smell of the vomit, in addition to her dislocated jaw. I went and spoke to the palace chef, Monsieur Bonne, but he assured me that all of the servants were dished out their meals from the same bowls and tureens. Something that Mr. Ford and Mrs. Wheatley also concurred with. It seems highly unlikely that she was poisoned during meals, or some of the other servants would have been affected by it. And the doctor had already disposed of the laudanum. He said that he didn't think that it had contained the poison, but he couldn't be entirely certain from his examination of it."

"Then you have no leads?"

"None."

Tiffany exhaled slowly. It seemed like an impossible puzzle. They did not know the means or the motive of the murder. Any hope of justice for Miss Doddridge and Uriah was beginning to slip away. And every breath she took could be her last. The murderer could strike again, and this time would kill her instead of her half brother.

Samir opened the door to the church for her, and Tiffany reluctantly let go of his arm. She missed his warmth and presence immediately. Walking to her pew, she felt Mr. Shirley's beady eyes on her. She carefully averted her gaze from his shiny forehead and his frizzy toupee extension that added volume to the front of his hair. She wished that Samir sat in front of her so that she might surreptitiously study him. The view of Mr. Shirley's fourteen children all in black was enough to throw her into the dismals.

At the end of his sermon, Mr. Shirley cleared his throat. Tiffany was ready for him to pray.

"It is with great delight," he said, "that I publish the banns of marriage between myself, Mr. Washington Shirley of Mapledown, and Miss Tiffany Woodall of Mapledown. This is the first time of asking. If any of you know cause or just impediment why these two persons should not be joined together in Holy Matrimony, ye are to declare it."

What in the heavens?

Tiffany's mouth fell open, and she felt as if she was going to be sick. Every eye in the church turned to stare at her. Some smiling, some disapproving, and one accusing—Samir's acorn-brown eyes. She longed to stand up and protest her own banns, but it would cause just the sort of stir that would ensure her masquerade was revealed. Instead, she looked from face to face, pleading in her mind for someone to protest. The only lady in the room who appeared more stricken by the announcement than herself was Widow Davies. She looked to be around fifty, the same age as the rector, and her hair was snowy white (not from powder). She wore unrelieved black and had four grown-up sons, who sat next to her in a row, from tallest to shortest.

After the shortest and longest pause of Tiffany's life, Mr. Shirley continued to the prayer. He then paraded down the

middle aisle like a bride and eagerly addressed all of his parti-
tioners at the door, accepting their congratulations on his
upcoming marriage. Tiffany forced herself to her feet. She did
not want to be the last person out of the church, for then Mr.
Shirley would offer to walk her home, and she did not think that
she could keep her temper for that long a distance.

She walked down the aisle, but Samir stood before her and
the door.

"I thought that I knew you, Miss Woodall," he whispered.
"It appears that I do not."

Tiffany longed to touch his arm and assure him that it had all
been some great mistake. But before her mind and body could
decide on the correct action, he'd turned on his heel and left her
standing alone. Trudging to the door, again she was the last to leave.

Mr. Shirley held out his waxy hand to her, but she could not
take it.

"Your reading of the banns took me by surprise," she said. "I
did not think that everything was settled between us."

"You said that you were flattered to receive my proposal," he
said with a yellow-toothed smile. "As much as I appreciate your
modesty, I admit that I have grown weary of the wait. Besides
you have two more weeks of the banns being read to reconcile
yourself to the idea of marriage."

She nodded and walked away without another word. She had
two more weeks. At the end, she would have to reveal her masquerade or be married. Either way, she would lose Bristle Cottage.

Tiffany had a fortnight to somehow find a way out of this
fix, for she would rather be buried next to Uriah, underneath
the crack willow, than be married to Mr. Shirley.

Chapter 22

Monday morning came, and Tiffany was no closer to coming up with a plan to keep her beloved cottage and her position as librarian. At first, she'd only come to the palace so that Uriah's absence would not be missed. Now she came every day because she loved it—loved every single thing about being a librarian. She adored organizing, classifying, cataloguing, purchasing, and—most of all—reading the books. There could be no greater profession in the world than that of a librarian, a position reserved (like so many) only for males.

Her mood was not improved by the ending of *Clarissa*. It seemed that women in fiction only died. They did not rescue themselves or chart their own course. Even in novels, it seemed as if men had all the power. Even the authority to read the banns without a lady's express permission.

Tiffany was early to the servants' two o'clock dinner and found Bernard leaning suggestively over the older redhead. She laughed, but they parted when Mr. Ford entered the room. From his jacket pocket, Bernard took out the rose-painted snuffbox and sniffed a pinch before standing by his seat at the servants' table. As far as she could tell, he seemed to show no remorse at his lover's death. Instead, he'd taken one of her possessions and used it as his own. For all of his good looks, he was a most unpleasant young man.

She took her place at the head of the table by Mr. Ford, but couldn't help casting a glance down at Emily, sitting at the bottom of the women's table. So far, the young maid had not spoken of Tiffany's masquerade. Tiffany hoped that she never would; however, such knowledge was dangerous. Emily could accidentally share it without any malintent. Fear of Emily or herself slipping up, and of the possible addition of poison to her meal, took all the joy out of Monsieur Bonne's lovely dinner. The food for the servants wasn't as delicate as the courses served to the duke and duchess, but it was still delicious and much heartier.

Glancing at Thomas, she saw the grief on his handsome face. There were circles underneath his eyes and a slackness to his jaw. He said nothing and ate barely more. Her gaze was not the only one that watched him with concern. Emily's darted to his face between every bite, and Mrs. Wheatley gave him several motherly looks of concern from her table. Tiffany was relieved to know that the footman had people within the house to care for him.

Returning to the library, Tiffany spent a rather unfruitful afternoon. She tried to organize the natural science section of the library, but her mind was muddled with her own problems. How could she get out of an engagement that she'd never entered into in the first place? How long could she possibly keep up the masquerade of being both her brother and herself? And what were the consequences under the law for not reporting his death nor assuring him a church burial? She cringed when she thought of Samir coming to arrest her. Any good opinion he had of her would be buried with Uriah.

She was also no closer to discovering Uriah's and Miss Doddridge's murderer. Mrs. Wheatley and Thomas both appeared grief-stricken and guilty. Emily knew how to keep secrets. Bernard was callus enough to poison his lover. That left Mr. Hickenlooper, with whom Tiffany had never even held a conversation. Perhaps she could befriend him? She sat across from him at dinner, although they had never spoken.

Leaving the library, Tiffany saw Tess and the duchess, both arrayed all in white like angels, and the newly arrived members of the house party: three gentlemen and two more ladies. They paraded past her in their enormous coiffures, jewels, and elaborate costumes, not even acknowledging her existence, as if Tiffany were no more than a statue or a piece of furniture.

Tess's eyes met her own for an infinitesimal moment but then turned back to her companion. She slipped her arm through his and tapped him with her fan flirtatiously. "Did you hear the latest on-dit about the crown prince, Lord Talgarth?"

"Is it true?" her elegant companion asked. He was by far the handsomest man of the party, with broad shoulders and excellent calves. His clothing was beautifully tailored, and he wore no face powder or cosmetics at all. His features were so pleasing that he didn't need to hide behind makeup. Lord Talgarth must be Tess's married lover.

"Yes!" Tess said with a giggle, and passed by Tiffany without giving any sign of their former relationship.

Tiffany tried to assure herself that it was because she was dressed as Uriah. Surely, her old friend would not have snubbed her if she'd known? But a sharp pain in her chest reminded Tiffany that Tess had done this before and would probably do it again. For all of her protestations of friendship, Tess belonged to a different class. A higher class than Tiffany's. And she would not demean herself in front of her lover and the other aristocrats by acknowledging a connection with a librarian or a spinster.

The Duchess of Beaufort was the last person to walk in front of Tiffany. She did not address her either, but she stopped directly in front of her. Taking out her snuffbox, she flipped it open and took such small pinches that Tiffany couldn't even see them on her delicate hand. The duchess sniffed into one nostril and then the other.

She snapped her snuffbox closed. "Come, Thomas—Lady Adkins has requested your assistance."

Thomas gave Tiffany a glance of sympathy as he walked by, as if he too knew what it was like to be treated like he was less than human. Tiffany's heart ached for the handsome young man. To be stolen from your home and taken to a new country in order to be put on display like some sort of animal. It was not right. It was not just. Especially since the footman was still mourning the woman he'd thought he was going to marry. He should have been given some time to mourn. But servants weren't given the privilege of grief.

If the footman and the duchess were indeed intimate, she was certain that Thomas was no longer happy in the arrangement. If he ever had been.

Tiffany could not escape the palace fast enough. She practically ran through the servants' quarters to the outside.

The smell that met her nose was awful.

She stepped around the bush to see Bernard vomiting violently. He was on his hands and knees, and his body kept spasming after the sick ceased to pour from his mouth.

"I'll go fetch help."

Tiffany reentered the palace. The only person she saw was Monsieur Bonne, and her French was not good enough to converse with him. She ran through the servants' quarters until she saw Mr. Ford.

"Sir, Bernard is violently ill outside," she said. "He is in need of medical assistance."

Mr. Ford's red face paled to a puce. "You don't think he's been—?"

The butler did not need to finish the sentence. Tiffany knew what word he was looking for: *poisoned*.

The very word made her stomach roil. It so easily could have been her. "His symptoms are similar to Miss Doddridge's."

He nodded and then brushed past her. He yelled for the maids to prepare to clean up the mess. "Where is Thomas? Someone needs to go for the doctor."

Following behind him, Tiffany knew the answer before Emily told him.

"He's with the duchess and her party, sir."

"The addlepate," Mr. Ford cursed. "Mr. Hickenlooper! Mr. Hickenlooper!"

The small valet opened a door and came out to the main servants' quarters. "Mr. Ford?"

"You need to fetch Doctor Hudson at once."

Mr. Hickenlooper stood up taller, tipping his head back a little in a vain attempt for greater height. "I am a valet, sir. Such a task is beneath my position. Send someone else."

The butler's face was back to the usual dark red. He grabbed Mr. Hickenlooper's lapels and nearly lifted the small man off the ground.

"I am in charge here, and I did not ask for your opinion, sir," Mr. Ford said, spitting in the man's face. "Now, go and fetch the doctor."

Mr. Hickenlooper smoothed his jacket lapels and lifted his head erect until it was slightly leaning back. "Very good, Mr. Ford."

The valet put on his hat and left Astwell Palace with his plummeting dignity. Tiffany quickly trailed behind him. She didn't want this opportunity to speak one on one with the valet to slip away. Since he was a short man, he had short legs, and he wasn't twenty feet away from the palace before Tiffany caught up with him.

"A bad business that," she said, tipping her hat to the valet.

Mr. Hickenlooper stiffened. "I would have gladly fetched the doctor for any servant but Bernard Coram. That man is a disgrace to the service."

Tiffany highly doubted that the valet would have been more willing to fetch the doctor for anyone, but she let that pass. She was here to weasel the truth out of him, so she'd allow him to retain any false dignity he thought he could maintain.

"He's certainly one with the maids."

"Not just the maids, if you know what I mean," Mr. Hickenlooper said, his eyebrows raised.

She did not have to feign the surprise on her face. Was Bernard bedding one of the guests? The thought was not as outlandish when Tiffany remembered what Tess had said about aristocrats finding love outside of their arranged marriages. She'd foolishly supposed that Tess had meant with those of their own class, but obviously that was not the case, because she suspected an intimate relationship between the Duchess of Beaufort and Thomas.

"I catch your meaning, sir," she said, slowing her pace to match his. "But I thought that he was romantically entangled with the late Miss Doddridge."

Mr. Hickenlooper grimaced. "Miss Doddridge was not romantically entangled with anyone. She had no heart, and she got what was coming to her."

Tiffany's mouth fell agape. She'd assumed that Mr. Hickenlooper had given his ring for Miss Doddridge's favors. Had the lady's maid stolen his ring like she'd stolen the silverware?

"I must confess, Mr. Hickenlooper, that I once saw her on your arm," she said. "I supposed that the two of you might be, shall we say, more than acquaintances?"

He stopped walking. "You insult me with your insinuations. I would never keep company with the likes of her."

Turning to look back at him, she said, "Then why did she have your ring?"

Mr. Hickenlooper's cheeks puffed out like a chipmunk, and his face was as red as an apple. "That is none of your concern."

The valet tried to walk by Tiffany, but she held out her arm. "I wonder if the constable will think that it is none of *his* concern?"

Mr. Hickenlooper stepped back. "The ring had nothing to do with her death."

"Then why was it in her possession?" Tiffany asked. "You can confide it to me, or you can apprise the constable. But I promise, if you tell me, I will not breathe a word of it to another soul."

The valet breathed in and out several times. "The harpy was blackmailing me."

"Miss Doddridge?"

"Yes!" he spat out. His face was the color of a bright red tomato. He looked both angry and embarrassed. "She followed me and saw . . . something; she threatened to tell the duke. It'd have gotten me sacked. I gave her the ring in exchange for her silence. But I swear to God that I never harmed her. I never even laid a hand on her. It was she that grabbed my arm and draped herself all over me. I wanted nothing to do with a woman of her ilk."

The way he said "woman" made Tiffany think that he was not interested in their sex at all. Tiffany had a pretty good idea what Miss Doddridge had held over the small valet. If Mr. Hickenlooper preferred the company of men, she did not blame him for wishing for secrecy. Such an accusation would send him to prison. Possibly, death. Uriah had once told her that there were over two hundred capital crimes in English law, and that might be one of them.

She nodded her head. "You have my word that I will not mention it again."

Mr. Hickenlooper passed by Tiffany. "Why do you even care? Were you in love with the girl?"

Tiffany shook her head. "I only wish to see her receive justice."

"She has received justice," he said, and continued walking without another word to her.

Tiffany couldn't help but agree, as she unlocked her cottage, that justice had found its way to Miss Doddridge. She'd blackmailed two servants. She'd stolen from her employers. And she'd lied to Thomas.

But as far as she knew, Uriah hadn't deserved to die.

What was the connection between her half brother, Miss Doddridge, and Bernard? The relationship between Miss Doddridge and Bernard was clear enough to her, but how did Uriah fit in? Was he another of Sarah's lovers? Yet he had claimed that his diamond pin was stolen, not traded for sexual favors. The only thing that all three people had in common was that they worked at Astwell Palace, for the Duke and Duchess of Beaufort. Could their deaths have something to do with the ducal family?

All she knew for sure was that whoever had killed her brother still thought he was alive. And eventually, they would come for her.

CHAPTER 23

When Tiffany arrived at Astwell Palace the next morning, there was no sign of Bernard's illness from the day before. The servants' dining room smelled as if it had been recently scrubbed with lemon soap. She was surprised when she saw Samir standing in the middle of the room between the two long tables, an angry and disheveled Bernard on one side of him and the French chef on the other. He had both of his arms out, as if to keep the two men from reaching each other. Bernard's skin looked pale, tinged with green. His forehead was sweaty and his eyes watery.

"I tell you, Lathrop," Bernard yelled, pointing at Monsieur Bonne, "I've been poisoned, and that man prepares all of my food. No one else could have done it, and I want justice for myself and Miss Doddridge."

"*Moi*, I would never harm any young woman," Monsieur Bonne said with a thick French accent, touching his chest.

"Calm down, Mr. Coram," Samir said, grabbing hold of both of the footman's arms. "You have no evidence—nothing but his word against yours."

Bernard wormed away from Samir and spat on the newly scrubbed tile floors. "But I'm a bloody Englishman, and my word is worth twice as much as any French frog's."

"I did not do anything," Monsieur Bonne said, his voice high and on the border of hysteria. "I swear. I simply cook."

Samir held up his arms. "Mr. Coram, I cannot act without proper evidence. I can assure you that I will do all within my power to discover who poisoned you."

Bernard pointed accusingly at Monsieur Bonne. "The foreigner should be arrested—or at the very least sent back to France. England should be for the English."

Tiffany sucked in a breath. It wasn't the first time that she'd seen violence and insults slung against those who were from a different country or had a different skin color.

"I should have known that you would side with a foreigner," Bernard continued to yell. "You bleedin' dark-skinned Indian."

Samir winced at those hateful words.

She could no longer stay silent. "That is quite enough, Bernard. You are embarrassing yourself and all of Astwell Palace. I demand you apologize to Mr. Lathrop immediately."

"Or what?"

Tiffany was shorter and smaller than Bernard, but she was not afraid of him. She was so angry that her hands were shaking. Pulling off her glove, she slapped him across the face with it. "Or I will give you the thrashing that your father should have given you long ago and teach you some respect."

Mrs. Wheatley rushed between Tiffany and Bernard. "There will be no violence, or we will all lose our positions. Bernard, you have clearly yet to recover from your ailment. I suggest that you go and stay at your father's cottage, until you are quite yourself again. I shall make your excuses to Mr. Ford."

"I can't bugger off in the middle of the duchess's house party."

"I assure you that Monsieur Bonne, as our chef, is far more important to the success of the party than a mere second footman," the housekeeper said. "Go at once, and don't come back until I send for you."

Bernard's face was the picture of resentment as he grabbed his hat, shoved it on his head, and left the kitchen, slamming the door behind him.

Monsieur Bonne released several shuttering breaths. "That was, as you say, most unpleasant."

Mrs. Wheatley passed by Samir and put an arm around Monsieur Bonne's shoulders. "Most unpleasant. Bernard always is. Come, let me make you some tea, Monsieur. You look as if you need some. We can't have you falling ill before dinner. Lady Surrey is looking forward to your calves' tongue especially."

Tiffany watched Mrs. Wheatley guide Monsieur Bonne to the other side of the dining room and up the four stairs to the kitchen. It felt like she was left all alone with Samir, even though there were other people nearby.

"I don't understand you, Woodall," Samir said. "Why did you defend me to him?"

Uriah would not have. He would have agreed with Bernard's hate and prejudice, blaming foreigners for what was wrong in his own country, treating people who were different from him as evil or even criminal. Tiffany could not think of one reason why Uriah would have stepped in.

"Whatever the reason," Samir said with a small bow, "I thank you for it."

"You should not need to thank someone for treating you as an equal," Tiffany said gruffly. "You're just as much an Englishman as he is."

"Even though I was born in India?"

"You live here. You work here. You serve as our constable," she said. "Where you were born does not matter."

Samir studied her closely. Too closely. His eyes widened, as if in recognition. Tiffany should not have stood so close to him. She should not have let her face show how much she cared.

"Good day, Lathrop," she said, and continued on to the library.

Once she closed the door, she leaned back against it and sighed deeply. She felt like a witch in a noose. The rope was tightening around her neck every day.

Chapter 24

Stumbling into her cottage, Tiffany stepped out of Uriah's too-large boots. She collapsed in a chair, emotionally and physically spent. She didn't have the energy or the interest to cook herself supper. There was not even leftover bread for her to eat. The kitchen was bare. She had not gone to the shops. How she wished that she could hire a local girl to clean the house and cook her dinner. She could almost afford it after her next quarter's pay. If only she didn't have to pretend to be Uriah and herself. But she was foolish to even think of it. It was only a matter of time before her masquerade was found out and she lost her cottage.

These dismal thoughts followed her up the stairs to Uriah's room, where she undressed. Her hands were so shaky that she knocked the container of face powder off the vanity when she put the wig on its stand. Stooping down to pick it back up, she saw that the wretched bottle had rolled behind the wardrobe. Standing back up, she used the rest of her strength to pull one side of the wardrobe forward. She got back on her knees to grab the bottle and saw that right next to it was an elegant snuffbox, painted like a peacock with a rainbow of blue feathers. She hadn't known that Uriah had his own snuffbox. Snuff was another expense that they hadn't been able to afford. Her half brother had only been able to indulge in the habit when other people offered to share some of theirs.

Picking up the snuffbox, she brought it closer to her eyes. This was no common trinket. The golden swirls and hinges appeared to be made of real gold. There was no way that her half brother could have ever afforded to purchase it. The little box was worth more than Uriah made in a year working for the duke.

Had he stolen it?

Had Miss Doddridge known as well? She'd inferred that she knew he took snuff.

There was also the possibility that someone had given it to him. Something that Tess had said came back into her mind. Tess had complained that the Duchess of Beaufort bragged that she had a snuffbox to match each of her gowns. Had she given one of her many snuffboxes to Uriah? And why?

Opening the box, Tiffany touched the mixture. It was dry and smelled like a sweet floral rose perfume.

The rose-painted snuffbox!

Miss Doddridge had been carrying the rose snuffbox and partaking of its contents. And she had died from poisoning. Bernard took the snuffbox after her death and started snorting the snuff. Within a few days, he began to vomit like she had. But he had not died. Perhaps he'd taken less of the mixture? Or his larger male body required more of the poison, to kill?

Good heavens!

This was the poison.

Uriah, Miss Sarah Doddridge, and Bernard had all been taking the snuff, and they all had been sick.

She bit her lower lip. This ruled out Bernard as a suspect.

She didn't think that he was clever enough, or brave enough, to partially poison himself to throw off suspicion. Both Emily and Mrs. Wheatley would have had access to Miss Doddridge's room and the snuffbox, for their own accommodations were also in the attic. And Thomas was romantically close to Miss Doddridge; he might also have had an opportunity to add the poison.

What to do next? She needed to get the rose-painted snuffbox from Astwell Palace and compare it to the contents in Uriah's snuffbox, to see if they were the same. Only then could she be certain that the snuffbox was the carrier of the poison. And if so, then she knew the means by which both Uriah and Miss Doddridge had been killed.

CHAPTER 25

Tiffany was not exactly certain how she was going to retrieve the rose snuffbox the next morning. What excuse could she use to enter the male servants' quarters in the basement? She did not sleep at the palace. And if she made it to the basement without someone seeing her, would she need to search every room before she found Bernard's? That would take a great deal of time and increase the chances of her being caught. It was even possible that Bernard had it on his person when he'd left for his parents' cottage.

She went first to the library, to take off her too-large boots. They would give her away with their noise. Opening the door, she peeked down the hall both ways. It was empty. Walking quickly in her stockings, she made her way to the door that led to the common room and the servants' staircase. She was breathing heavy as she reached the bottom of the stairs that led to the male servants' rooms.

Tiffany opened a door to a narrow hall and a long line of doors on both sides.

Think.

Mr. Ford's room would probably be one of the first rooms on either side of the door. Like the assigned seating of the table, Mr. Hickenlooper's room would be next, followed by Thomas's.

The fourth room would belong to the second footman, Bernard. Taking a chance, Tiffany opened the door on the left. It was cramped and nearly bare. There were two beds and a basin on a table between them. She quietly closed the door and tried the one across the hall. It was twice the size of the other and had a wardrobe, a chair, and a fine coverlet on the bed. She assumed that it was the butler's room.

Closing the door, she counted three handles down and opened the fourth. The bed had not been made, and the wardrobe doors hung open. She stepped into the room and closed the door. She rifled through the already opened wardrobe but found little more than a night shirt and a second livery in a pale shade of blue. The drawers were empty, and she found nothing beneath the bed or in the basin of water. All that was left in the room was the bed itself. Distastefully, she lifted the sheets and coverlet: nothing. She picked up the pillow, and underneath it was the rose snuffbox.

Tiffany didn't hesitate. She grabbed it and stuffed it into her jacket pocket. Returning to the door, she ascertained that no one was in the male servants' hall. She ran to the door that led to the stairs. Breathless, she ascended as quickly as her stocking feet would allow. Her foot touched the marble on the ground floor.

"Mr. Woodall, can I help you?" Mr. Ford asked with a bow. He was standing in the common room.

She shook her head and tried to catch her breath. "Only delivering a book for the duchess," Tiffany lied.

Mr. Ford huffed. "Are you unaware, Mr. Woodall, that you are only to give the duchess items on a silver tray?"

"I was, sir."

"Never again insult her by giving something from your own hand, Mr. Woodall," he said. "No matter your birth, in Astwell Palace you are a servant and should behave as such."

Tiffany nodded her head. "I will. Thank you, Mr. Ford, for informing me."

Without giving the butler a chance to respond (and to notice her stocking feet), Tiffany continued walking to the library. She didn't feel safe until she had closed the doors, leaving her alone with the wonderful books. Making her way to her desk, she sat down and pulled out the rose snuffbox. She placed it next to Uriah's peacock one. They were similar in size, shape, and quality. She opened Uriah's first and caught a whiff of the lovely rose. Then she opened Bernard's snuffbox—it also had the same perfume.

She compared the contents of both snuffboxes. As far as she could tell, they looked relatively similar in color and texture. The only difference was that Uriah's snuff was dry, and Bernard's was wet. Tiffany was not much acquainted with snuff. Her father had thought it a disgusting habit for men or women and discouraged it in his parish.

As far as Tiffany was aware, Uriah had never taken snuff regularly before now. It would have been an additional expense that their genteel poverty could not have afforded. But if he was given the snuffbox and contents by the duchess, Tiffany believed that he would have used it. He longed more than anything to be treated like a gentleman. Seen as a gentleman.

Could the Duchess of Beaufort have poisoned Uriah? Surely, he was beneath her notice. Uriah was incredibly egotistical, and his condescending manner would have annoyed a saint—but enough to murder him?

Or was it something he'd seen or found out? Had he been referring to the duchess as the person at the palace who needed to repent? Her intimacy with Thomas?

And why would the duchess want to murder her own lady's maid? Right before hosting a house party?

Unless Miss Doddridge had also known about the indiscretion and had to be silenced before she could talk. Or maybe the older woman was jealous that he preferred the pretty young lady's maid?

Or was it something else entirely?

Tiffany scratched her head and slumped back in her chair. A memory of Miss Doddridge floated into her mind. The lady's maid had thrown herself at Tiffany/Uriah and she'd been saved from an awkward scene by the arrival of the duke. She wracked her mind for his words, but she couldn't remember them. She'd been too shocked by both Miss Doddridge's and the duke's arrival. But she did recall their meaning. He'd hinted that the lady's maid was free with her favors. If one of the guests were enjoying Bernard's company, could the duke have been bedding Miss Doddridge? If so, perhaps that was a strong enough reason for the duchess to poison her lady's maid. She had the means, the motive, and the opportunity. What could be more natural than giving her faithful servant a pretty trinket?

Was Bernard another target or an unexpected victim? As far as Tiffany knew, the Duchess of Beaufort hadn't given him the snuffbox; he'd taken it from Miss Doddridge's belongings. Tiffany couldn't help but feel that Bernard might have deserved his terrible experience for robbing the dead.

Sighing, Tiffany was getting a head of herself. She didn't know for sure that either snuffbox was poisoned. She needed to talk to someone who did. The only person in Mapledown with that sort of knowledge would be the apothecary.

★　★　★

Tiffany left Astwell Palace after dinner and trudged back to her cottage to change her clothes from men's breeches to a woman's dress. The walk to the village was considerably cooler without Uriah's wig and with a little bit of air coming up her skirts. She circumvented the rectory and church, passing by Samir's bookshop. She couldn't help but peek in at him. He was sitting in a chair, reading a book. She longed to know the name of the book, so she could read it too, and then they could have given their own opinions about it. It would be a pleasure to speak to him again about the characters and the settings. She was sure that he would have a different perspective but that he would consider hers.

He had always treated her with respect.

Regretfully, she continued walking down the main street until she reached the last shop. Mr. Canning's apothecary. She opened the door and felt as if she had stepped into another world. One wall was filled with bottles of all shapes and sizes on shelves. The ceiling was covered with drying herbs and plants that hung so low they brushed her hair. On one wall, there was a fireplace on which a large cauldron was bubbling. The smell was pungent and acrid. A man stood, stirring it. He looked like a wizened wizard. His hair was long and white in the back, and his beard was just as long in the front. He wore a red cap and gave her a smile; he was missing several teeth.

"Miss Woodall, is it?"

"Yes," Tiffany said, growing accustomed to the many smells and the smoky room. "Mr. Canning, I was wondering if I could ask you a question."

"You just did."

Tiffany laughed. "True. I was hoping to ask you a question about snuff."

He let go of his hold on the spoon in the cauldron and limped over to the counter. "Miss Woodall, questions don't feed my family."

"Perhaps I could buy some tooth powder, and then you could answer my question."

Mr. Canning gave her another toothless grin before picking a bottle of white powder off the shelf behind him. He plunked it on the counter. She hoped that the powder wouldn't rot her own teeth out.

"Two farthings."

Tiffany fished the coins out of her reticule and counted them into his wrinkled palm. Mr. Canning pocketed them.

"Now fer yer question."

She took the two snuffboxes out of her reticule and placed them on the counter by the bottle of powder.

Mr. Canning whistled. "I could give you a good price for either of these beauties."

"I'm not interested in selling them," Tiffany said, "but in discovering their contents."

With one wrinkled hand, he opened the rose snuffbox. He brought it to his bulbous nose and took a long whiff.

"Expensive stuff. Pure and perfumed. That's from a London tobacconist, I reckon."

"And the other."

Mr. Canning opened Uriah's peacock snuffbox. "This one hasn't been taken care of."

"Because it's dry?"

"Yes," he said, stroking his long white beard. "No true snuff user would ever allow their mixture to dry out. It ruins the snuff."

"Are they the same mixture, do you believe?"

Mr. Canning sighed. "Looks like it."

He took a pinch of both and placed them on the back of his hand before snorting them.

It felt like Tiffany's throat closed. Would such a small amount hurt the older man?

"Yes, they're the same."

"I-I should have told you before you partook," she said breathlessly. "I believe that the snuff might be poisoned."

Mr. Canning shook his head. "There are hundreds of varieties of snuff, but they consist of three basic types: rapé, a coarsely grated Swedish snuff; Scotch snuff, which is dry powdered and unflavored; and Maccaboy, which is what this one is. Maccaboy is moist and highly scented. It's impossible for me to say if it's poisoned, Miss Woodall, for I don't recognize the ingredients in it."

"You can't tell?"

He lifted the rose snuffbox to her face. "I can tell that it was soaked in some sort of floral oil, but that's it. It don't smell like the typical lavender oil, which is what most folks use to keep their snuff moist."

Tiffany took a deep breath, and she agreed. It didn't smell like lavender, but it did smell sweet, as the scent from a flower. She remembered what Doctor Hudson had said. "I believe it might be from the nightshade family of plants."

He shook his head. "That don't narrow it too much, Miss Woodall. It could be nightshade itself, hemlock, belladonna, or mandrake; and even common vegetables, like tomatoes, eggplant, potatoes, and peppers, are a part of the nightshade family."

"But it smells sweet, like a rose or an apple."

Mr. Canning snapped the snuffbox closed; and with it, their discussion. "Would you be needing any other powders or cures today, miss?"

"Do you mix snuff at your shop?"

"That I do," he said, "but naught this fancy. I soak my leaves in either cinnamon or almond oil."

Tiffany closed Uriah's snuffbox and placed both boxes back into her reticule. "Thank you for your help, Mr. Canning."

"Don't forget your tooth powder," he called.

She turned back to pick up the bottle from the counter.

"Be careful, Miss Woodall," Mr. Canning said, touching the side of his bulbous nose with a long finger. "Whoever could afford this sort is not someone you'll want to tangle with."

Tiffany nodded and thanked him. The last thing that she wanted to do was tangle with the Duchess of Beaufort. She walked back past Samir's shop. She should have gone in and confessed the whole to him, but she couldn't convict the duchess without condemning herself.

CHAPTER 26

There was no other choice. Tiffany had to leave Mapledown. Not literally, but she had to shed her true identity. She could no longer masquerade as both herself and Uriah. It was becoming impossible to be two persons. If she stayed as herself, she would lose her cottage and find herself married to the rector. If she stayed as Uriah, she would keep her cottage and her beloved library, and never have to worry about Mr. Shirley's unwanted attentions.

If the duchess struck again with her poison, Tiffany could expose her safely as Uriah. And now that she knew how the poison had been administered, she should be safe enough from Her Grace. *Hopefully.*

It wasn't a perfect plan.

Tiffany loved being a woman, but she could think of no other scheme to save herself except to sacrifice her identity.

How to get rid of herself?

She would have to be called away to nurse some relative or other. Spinsters were supposed to care for sick relatives and attend to any other unpleasant task that no one else wanted to do, for they were seen as economically worthless. A burden. Tiffany needed to be "sent away" far enough that no one in the town would be able to visit without great cost. The city would also need to be large enough that no one could be presumed to find her if they were looking. She couldn't say that she was visiting relatives. Tess would know that Tiffany had no other family than Uriah. She would have to go visit Mrs. Coates, Nathaniel's widowed mother, who had moved to Manchester to live with her other son after Nathaniel's death.

Manchester was a large city to get lost in. It was also industrial, so she needn't worry about Tess or any fashionable person looking for her there. Not that she thought that her old friend really intended to renew their friendship. Tiffany could seemingly disappear there with relative anonymity. Now all she needed to do was remove any evidence of herself from the cottage and her bedchamber.

Packing her shifts and dresses, Tiffany felt as if she was stripping away a part of herself. The last thing that she placed into Uriah's old trunk was the silk gown from the duke. She hadn't finished the embroidery on the skirt yet, but the bodice and sleeves were complete and beautiful. The gown reminded her of Samir. He'd saved it with his quick thinking, but now their friendship would be over. Like everyone else, he would believe that she had gone.

She closed her eyes and, for a moment, pretended to wear the silk dress and to marry Samir. *Tiffany Lathrop.* It was a lovely name. Samir leaned forward and placed his lips on hers, and she melted in his strong arms, relishing his intoxicating smell of tobacco and books.

The top of the trunk fell closed with a loud snap, waking Tiffany from her fantasy. She knew now, when there was no hope, that she loved Samir. It was different from her love for Nathaniel, but no less strong.

No less beautiful.

No less doomed.

Samir was the constable of Mapledown, and she'd buried her brother and stolen his identity. She didn't even know if Samir returned her feelings. He had only ever expressed his friendship. He'd also said she was beautiful, but that was hardly a declaration of his intentions. She really was a silly old spinster.

Heaving the trunk over her shoulder, Tiffany climbed the ladder up to the attic and stuffed the trunk in as far as it would go. She shimmied back down and went to the parlor, to Uriah's old writing desk. She took out a fresh sheet of paper. She needed to write to Mr. Shirley and irrevocably end any understanding between them (real or imaginary).

Dear Mr. Shirley,

I am conscious of the great honor that you have bestowed on me with your offer of marriage. But while I am flattered, I never accepted your hand. In fact, it is impossible for me to marry you now or ever.

I am leaving Mapledown for Manchester City, where I will be taking care of Mrs. Coates. She is the mother of the man to whom I was once engaged to marry. She is getting on in years and is no longer able to walk. In another life, I would have been her daughter, and since she had no other daughter, I will now act as one by taking care of her.

I do not know if or when I will ever return to live in Mapledown. Mrs. Coates's own mother lived to be ninety-three, and it is possible that she will also live that long. I intend to remain with her until the very end.

I wish you all happiness in finding another union and in the care of your children and parish.

Sincerely,

Tiffany Woodall

She set down the quill and sighed. It was such a relief to know that she was no longer entangled with Mr. Shirley, but the cost of her freedom had come high. Painfully high. Pouring a little sand on the letter, she let the ink dry before blowing it off. She folded it and put wax on the seal.

Now all she had to do was deliver it to the rectory, and she would be entirely free of the rector. Steeling herself, Tiffany put on Uriah's tricorn hat and full-skirted coat. She held the letter in her hand the whole walk to Mapledown, inexplicably afraid that it would disappear if she didn't. She knocked on the rectory door. Miss Shirley, the eldest daughter, answered it.

"Mr. Woodall, may I help you?"

"I have a letter for your father from my sister," Tiffany said, holding it out to her.

Miss Shirley didn't take it. Instead, she opened the door further. "I am sure Father would want you to give it to him yourself."

"I shouldn't wish to disturb the rector," she said quickly. "If you would just give this to him."

Miss Shirley then smiled at Tiffany. Her smile was not as frightening as her father's, but it still had a skeletal look to it. It did nothing to soften her austere face. "You could never be a disturbance, Mr. Woodall. My father has greatly missed your visits, and so have I."

Tiffany gulped. Miss Shirley could not be much above sixteen, and she was looking at Uriah as a prospective husband. He was three times her age. From her own experience, Tiffany knew that eligible gentlemen were hard to come by in a small town, particularly if you were born the daughter of a clergyman and had little or no money. Your birth was too high for the local tradesmen's sons and too low for the local nobility and gentry.

Perhaps Miss Shirley was hoping that her youth would make her attractive to Uriah. Tiffany couldn't think that she was attracted to Uriah (or Tiffany), but rather, drawn to the fact that her half brother had a gentlemen's position and a home of his own.

"Let me take your coat and hat," she insisted.

"Very well," Tiffany said, handing the items to her. "Please lead the way."

"Anything you ask, sir," she said with another alarming smile.

The young woman led her through the house that was much too quiet to be the home of fourteen children. She opened the door to the rector's study and library. His frizzy toupee was off, and his balding head reflected the setting sun.

"Father, Mr. Woodall to see you," Miss Shirley said with a bow. She gave Tiffany one more smile before leaving the room.

Mr. Shirley put on his hairpiece. "You caught me unprepared, Woodall. But I have missed our discussions of late. Please, do be seated. There is no need for ceremony between colleagues."

"The Duchess of Surrey has requested my company at Astwell Palace," Tiffany said, and it wasn't a lie. She took a seat in a wingback chair and tucked one ankle behind the other.

The rector bared his teeth. "What a valuable connection. I look forward to making her acquaintance."

Tiffany held her letter out to him. Mr. Shirley looked surprised, but he took it.

"What's this?"

"It's from my sister," Tiffany said, standing. "I will allow you to read it in privacy."

The rector waved his hand. "Sit back down. You've only arrived. And we are very nearly family. I can read a letter in front of you."

She held her breath as he broke the seal and opened the letter. His already thin face seemed to tighten and grimace at every sentence.

"I must speak to her before she leaves," he said. "I am sure that I can change her mind."

Tiffany shook her head. "I am afraid that you are too late. She left this afternoon."

"She has already left? How? Where?" Mr. Shirley demanded. "For I did not see her take the coach from Mapledown."

She should have thought of this before now. *How* had Tiffany left? Scrambling for an answer, she choked out, "She took the coach from Bardsley."

It was the town closest to Mapledown.

Mr. Shirley crumpled the letter in his hand, his usually waxy face now red. "She has made a fool of me! The banns have already been read."

Tiffany folded her hands together in her lap. "It is unfortunate, but the banns have to be read three times before a marriage. I am sure this is not the first time that a couple have resolved not to marry after the banns have been read."

He got to his feet, huffing. "I am the rector of this parish. I cannot lose the respect of my congregation and become a laughingstock in the community. You will simply have to go after your sister and bring her back to Mapledown."

Tiffany also stood and held up both of her hands. "Shirley, my sister has made her decision. I suggest that if you would like to save your reputation, you find another woman as quickly as possible and marry her."

Mr. Shirley fumed, his hairpiece askew. "You are the man of your house. Why did you not force her to do as you wished?"

"A woman of forty knows her own mind," Tiffany said gruffly. "No man needs to make it for her . . . Nothing good can come of the continuation of this conversation. I bid you adieu."

She left the room and nearly escaped the house before she was accosted again by Miss Shirley.

"Going so soon, Mr. Woodall?" she said. "Might I tempt you to stay with some cake?"

"Offer the loaf to someone your own age, child," Tiffany said, putting on her hat and finally leaving the rectory.

She hoped to never step foot again in that house.

CHAPTER 27

Tiffany awoke with a jolt from a nightmare. She sat up and realized that she was in Uriah's bed. At least the mattress had been replaced since he died there, but she would have rather not slept in the room. She had little choice, though. Uriah had slept there, and she was now him. Also, it was the largest bedchamber and faced the road—superior in every way to her own. The villagers would expect her to sleep there.

It was silly, but she missed her smaller, cozier chamber. Peeking through the curtains, she realized that it was almost dawn. The cottage needed to be swept, and she really ought to make bread this morning or she would have nothing to eat for supper all week. Wearing Uriah's old nightshirt, she rolled up the sleeves and first prepared the bread. It could rise while she cleaned the cottage from top to bottom.

Tiffany grabbed and twisted the dough in her hands. She used to pretend that it was her half brother's face, but the face she longed to pound now was the Duchess of Beaufort's. The audacity of the woman to murder her own servants and continue on as if nothing were amiss. As if they weren't even people with their own lives and secrets.

She dropped the dough back on the table. Miss Doddridge had been blackmailing two other people. Had she also tried to blackmail the duchess? As her lady's maid she would have had more access to her mistress's secrets than anyone else. She would have known where she went and when. She would probably also have known who shared her bed. Miss Doddridge would have had a wealth of information that the duchess did not want her husband or the greater world to know. If only Tiffany could discover what Miss Doddridge knew, then perhaps she could prove that the duchess had killed not only her but also Uriah.

Picking up the dough and kneading it, Tiffany thought about her half brother. It didn't make any sense for the duchess to poison him. Unless . . . he had been one of her lovers. No, that thought was too ridiculous to be considered. Uriah was not young or handsome or agreeable.

She put the dough in a wooden bowl and covered it with a cloth before scrubbing the kitchen. She swept the main floor and went upstairs to fetch the linens. If she was fast, she could wash them and put them out to dry before she needed to leave for the palace. She fetched water from the well and then scrubbed and scrubbed until her hands were red and raw. She hung up the sheets and then went into the kitchen to shape the loaves and put them into tins. There would be barely enough time for a second prove before she needed to get them into the open range.

Dashing up the stairs, Tiffany gave herself a sponge bath before binding her breasts. She put on her shirt and then ran back down the stairs to put the bread into the oven. Brushing her hand against the metal side of the range, she cried out in pain. There would be a blister. But Tiffany didn't have time for a burn this morning. She needed to be dressed and on her way to Astwell already. Perhaps now that she had gotten rid of her alternate (real) identity, she could hire a maid of all work. Trying to take care of the cottage in the mornings and evenings, and work as a librarian during the day, was running her ragged.

She sat down in front of the vanity and for a moment thought that she'd already put on her face powder, but it was flour on her nose. She quickly applied the face powder, lip color, rouge, and eye powder. Placing the velvet patches precisely, she next put on Uriah's long matching waistcoat; a brocade coat with a high collar, trimmed with braid; and velvet knee breeches. Her hand throbbed with pain as she tied the cravat and pulled up her stockings to button. The last thing she needed for her transformation was the wig. She placed it on her head. It was as itchy as ever. She would need to send it back to the wigmaker soon for a good boiling to get rid of all the small bugs.

Locking the front door, Tiffany remembered that she still had bread in the oven. She left the door open and rushed back to the kitchen. Grabbing cloths, she pulled out the two loaves, which looked a deep brown. They were a little overbaked, but still edible. She poured the remaining water in her bucket on the stove, for she couldn't leave a fire burning and she couldn't wait for it to die down.

By the time she reached Astwell Palace, Tiffany was exhausted, ornery, and the burn on her hand had swollen to a blister the size of a guinea. She went straight to the library without speaking to any other servants. But it was impossible to focus with her hand feeling like it was on fire. She needed to put something on it to take away the sting, or she would never accomplish anything.

Leaving the library, she wandered back to the servants' quarters. She walked past the empty hall to the dining room. She was surprised to see Bernard had returned, and with him, Samir.

The pain she felt in her chest was nearly as torturous as the burn on her hand. She would never see him as herself again.

"Mr. Lathrop, I am surprised to see you here," she said. "And Bernard, are you quite recovered?"

He stood up taller. "I am indeed, Mr. Woodall—thank you for asking. My stepmother's pudding fixed me right up."

"Here he is," Mrs. Wheatley said from behind her.

Tiffany turned to see Mrs. Wheatley and Thomas walking together. The expression on both of their faces was fearful. Something was happening.

"Mr. Thomas Montague, on behalf of the crown," Samir started, "I arrest you for the murder of Miss Sarah Doddridge and the attempted poisoning of Mr. Bernard Coram. You will be held in custody until a trial can be arranged by the court of assizes."

"But I didn't—I wouldn't—" Thomas started to say.

"Where is the warrant?" Tiffany demanded.

Samir pulled a folded paper from his jacket pocket. He unfolded it and showed them all. It was a warrant for Mr. Montague, signed by Sir Walter Abney, the justice of the peace. Tiffany had seen the man at church. He lived on an estate called Maplehurst, north of Mapledown. Uriah had tried to befriend him, but Sir Walter Abney was a baronet and did not care to associate with a lowly gentleman, even if his birth was better than Sir Walter's, whose tradesman grandfather had purchased his title.

"I am so sorry," Samir said, folding the paper back up and placing it back in his pocket.

He truly did look sorry, but Mr. Coram appeared smug and satisfied. Of course, the footman had gone to the justice of the peace after Samir had refused to arrest Monsieur Bonne. Had he tried to get the chef arrested again? Or was he simply using the opportunity to implicate Thomas and take his place as the first footman? She believed Bernard capable of any type of chicanery.

"This is nothing more than ignorance and prejudice," Tiffany hissed. "There is absolutely no proof that Thomas had anything to do with either poisoning. He is simply being arrested because he is African. You must not do it, Sam—sir."

"I have to, Mr. Woodall," Samir said. "More servants than just Bernard saw Mr. Thomas Montague giving Miss Doddridge a vial before her death. His story has already been corroborated by Mr. Ford and Miss Whitney."

She had also seen him give a bottle to her. She turned to the footman. "What was in the vial?"

"Laudanum, sir, to help her sleep."

Tiffany shook her head so vehemently that she worried that Uriah's wig would slip. "But Doctor Hudson didn't know for sure that there was poison in the laudanum. It's only conjecture."

"Mr. Woodall, I appreciate your assistance," Thomas said, "but there is no good in defying the law. I will pack my bag, if I may, and go with Mr. Lathrop to Mapledown Jail."

"Of course," he said.

"I shall prepare a basket of food for you," Mrs. Wheatley said. "Bernard, it appears that we are again without a footman. Please report to Mr. Ford at once."

The smirk on Bernard's face fell a little as he left the room. Tiffany watched Thomas go down the hall and to the stairs that led to the basement and the male servants' rooms. Samir didn't follow him. He clearly trusted him not to run. Mrs. Wheatley bustled past them both to the kitchen, calling for Monsieur Bonne. Leaving Tiffany alone with Samir.

"Why are you arresting an innocent man?" Tiffany asked in a whisper.

"Sir Walter Abney opposed my becoming constable because I am half Indian. If I do not fulfill my duty as his deputy and fulfill this warrant, someone else will. And he believes that the poisoning was caused by something added to the laudanum."

"Appeal to the duke," she insisted. "Surely, as a man of color, you understand what it is like to be discriminated against?"

He shook his head. "I have already spoken to the Duke of Beaufort this morning. He believes that it is best not to aggravate Sir Walter at this time. Mr. Montague will get a fair trial, and if he is innocent, as you believe, we must trust that a jury will set him at liberty."

"I do not trust a judge or a jury," Tiffany said. "There is no justice for people like him or like—" She had been about to say "me" but caught herself. As a woman, she held no voice in the law. But dressed as a white man, Uriah would receive a fair trial. "Yourself."

"I will do my best to make Mr. Montague as comfortable as possible while I continue to search for any evidence of the true culprit," he said. "It will have to be indisputable if we hope to overturn these charges."

Tiffany nodded. Of course, it wasn't enough to prove that Thomas didn't do it. Samir would have to prove that someone else did. And no one would believe a bookseller's or a librarian's word over a duchess's. They would need her to confess—or they would have to catch her in the act of the crime. But how?

"I will do anything in my power to assist you."

Samir eyed her curiously, but then gave her a half bow. "You surprise me. But I appreciate the help and your concern, Mr. Woodall."

Tiffany recalled her burned hand and followed Mrs. Wheatley into the kitchen. Monsieur Bonne had a large basket on the center table, and it was filled with breads, savories, fruits, and spirits.

"What can I help you with, Mr. Woodall?" the housekeeper asked.

Without saying a word, Tiffany held out her burned hand.

"Bless me!" she exclaimed. "That's a right terrible burn. Monsieur Bonne get Mr. Woodall some cold butter to put on it."

The French chef did as he was asked, and the butter took some of the sting away. But it couldn't take away the sting of watching Thomas and Mr. Lathrop leave together. From the window, she saw that they walked side by side on the path, as equals, but one was going to jail.

CHAPTER 28

Samir's words kept replaying in her head that night: they would need indisputable proof to overturn the charges against Mr. Thomas Montague. She had to tell Samir about the snuffboxes and the poisoned mixture. But how could she word it carefully enough that he did not discover that Uriah *had* died of poisoning. A small, nervous part of her wished to tell Samir the whole truth. She would be trusting her life in his hands.

There were no other hands that she could trust more, but still she hesitated. How could his admiration or growing affection withstand the knowledge of Tiffany's duplicity? She pictured his handsome face changing from one of kindness to repugnance. Not that she could blame him; she was not altogether sure how she would have responded to learning that he had buried someone in his back garden.

She managed to get a few fitful hours of rest before the morning. As she ate her crusty bread and soft-boiled egg, Tiffany decided that she would tell Samir everything. Thomas deserved no less than a constable in full possession of the facts.

Everything seemed to slow that morning. Even putting on her clothes and makeup, she felt as if she were in a book, languishing in the middle pages before the climax. When she reached Samir's bookshop, her heart was racing. She could feel the sweat pouring down the back of her neck underneath the wig. She had never felt more nervous in all of her life. It took all her courage and resolution to open the door. The bell rang that was attached to it.

"Be with you in a minute," Samir's voice called from the backroom.

Tiffany strolled into the shop and pretended to gaze at the pamphlets until one caught her attention: *The Female Husband: Or, the Surprising History of Mrs. Mary, Alias Mr. George Hamilton, Who Was Convicted of Having Married a Young Woman of Wells and Lived with Her As Her Husband. Taken from Her Own Mouth Since Her Confinement.* It was only eight pages long, but it was enough to make her feel sick with fear. Mary Hamilton had dressed as a man and been charged with fraud for marrying a woman. Tiffany hadn't married another woman while dressing as a man, but she wondered if she, too, would face the same charges. She'd also not reported her own brother's murder.

She read the sentencing:

> *The he or she prisoner at the bar is an uncommon, notorious cheat, and we, the Court, do sentence her, or him, whichever he or she may be, to be imprisoned six months, and during that time to be whipped in the towns of Taunton, Glastonbury, Wells, and Shepton Mallet.*

The illustration showed a bare-breasted woman in breeches being whipped on a scaffold. Her hands crossed her own chest as if to cover it. Would she, Tiffany, be subjected to the same indignities? Would she spend six months in prison? She didn't even know where the closest prison was. Would there be a separate one for females, or would she be tossed in with the men, some of whom would be convicted rapists and murderers? The local jail, where Thomas was confined, was only for short-term stays, before sentencing or for minor infractions of the law. Her infraction would not be considered minor.

Her whole body shuddered.

"Mr. Woodall?"

Tiffany jumped. She turned to look at Samir and did not even have to pretend to frown like Uriah. Opening the satchel that she carried, she took out the two snuffboxes: one peacock blue and the other rose red.

"What are these?"

She cleared her throat. Her earlier resolution fled. She could not, would not, tell Samir the truth. She couldn't bear to be stripped half naked in the main square and whipped.

"I wish to tell you something in confidence," she began in a gruff voice. She pointed to the blue snuffbox with the painted peacock. "The Duchess of Beaufort gave me that snuffbox, and when I partook of the mixture, it made me violently ill. I ceased taking it, and as you can see, it has dried out. I thought perhaps that it did not agree with my constitution; however, my sister found this rose snuffbox in the possession of Miss Doddridge when she died. The symptoms and the vomiting were the same. It did not raise my suspicion until I saw Bernard in possession of this same rose snuffbox, and then—"

"He was poisoned by it," Samir finished.

"Exactly," Tiffany said. "I cannot say whether the Duchess of Beaufort gave this snuffbox to Miss Doddridge, as Mrs. Wheatley and Thomas suggested, but you can see by the gold filigree that it must have been a very expensive trinket. One quite beyond the pay of a lady's maid."

Samir's beautiful brown eyes widened. "Are you accusing the Duchess of Beaufort of poisoning not only yourself but her lady's maid?"

Her situation was tenuous, she couldn't bring attention to herself. "I do not wish to accuse anyone, sir. But I do think it would be wise for you to ascertain from the duchess if she did indeed give this rose snuffbox to Miss Doddridge."

"And if she did?"

"You might even ask her to give you the rest of her bottle. Are you a snuff taker, sir?"

"No," he said, his lip curling in what appeared to be disgust.

Tiffany was no admirer of the habit either. "Typically, the batch is kept in a jar and only small amounts put in the snuffbox. You could have it examined by a professional to see if it is indeed poisonous."

"I cannot accuse the Duchess of Beaufort of poisoning her maid."

"Perhaps it was an accident," she lied. "Perhaps the duchess is unaware that the contents of the jar have spoiled in some way."

Samir picked up a snuffbox in each of his hands and weighed them like the scales of justice. "Are you absolutely certain, Mr. Woodall, that the poison was administered through snuff?"

"Mostly," she said, exhaling. "I know of no other method that would successfully poison Miss Doddridge and Bernard without more servants becoming ill."

"And why did you not bring this to my attention before now," Samir asked suspiciously.

Tiffany took a deep breath. "Honestly, I only realized a couple of days ago that there was any coincidence between my own stomach ills and Miss Doddridge's death. Like yourself, I did not want to act unless I was sure. But if it is true that the snuff contained the poison, the law and Sir Walter Abney must absolve Thomas of all charges."

He must have believed her excuses, for he nodded his head slightly. "I suppose I will have to go and ask for an appointment with the Duchess of Beaufort. Would you like to accompany me, Mr. Woodall?"

"Yes," she said. "I should already be at the library this morning."

"I meant to the interview."

Tiffany gulped. "I should be happy to, sir, if you think I can be of any assistance. I only request that you do not show her my blue snuffbox, nor introduce my own difficulties to the discussion. The Duke and Duchess of Beaufort are my employers, and I cannot afford to offend them."

Samir handed her back the blue snuffbox and pocketed the rose one. "Very well, Mr. Woodall," he said, gesturing to the door. "Shall we?"

The invisible noose around her neck tightened so much that she could barely breathe. The imaginary scaffold beneath her feet was beginning to shake, as if it could collapse at any moment.

CHAPTER 29

A long walk with Samir should have been a dream come true for Tiffany. Instead it was an awkward length of silence. She could tell that he did not know what to make of her, or Uriah—whoever he thought she was. A part of her still longed to confess to him the whole terrible truth, but fear kept her silent.

They passed by the lake and the exact spot where Samir had first noticed her. Where he'd tried to rescue her from drowning when she was washing. The night that she'd buried Uriah. It had only been a few weeks ago, but if felt like her life hadn't started until then. She'd felt more emotions in the last few weeks, more freedom, than she had felt in the last twenty years. She regretted nothing. Not one glance or one word with Samir. Nor one moment spent in his company.

"It is good of you to take an interest in Mr. Montague," Samir said.

Tiffany looked down at her too-large boots that were precariously flopping as she walked. "He is a good, kind young man, and he does not deserve his fate."

"Do any of us?"

These four little words stopped her in her shoes. She wanted to answer both yes and no. She thought of Miss Doddridge and her blackmailing. Clearing her throat to speak lower, she said, "Sometimes people get what they deserve, and other times people don't deserve the hand that they're dealt."

"True, sir," he said. "Some of us are born dukes, and others are born booksellers."

"Or librarians," Tiffany said with a little smile.

Samir blinked, and Tiffany wiped the smile off her face. She must have looked more like herself when she smiled. She would have to remember not to in his company. Not that she foresaw spending much time with Samir; a friendship between them now would be impossible. Every time she thought about telling him the truth, the illustration of Mary Hamilton being whipped, and bare from the waist up, entered her mind. She closed her mouth so tightly that it pinched.

"Congratulations on your sister's engagement to Mr. Shirley," Samir said. "I wish her every happiness."

He didn't know that "Tiffany" had left.

"I am afraid that there was a slight misunderstanding between the good rector and my sister."

"A misunderstanding?" Samir said, his next step bringing him closer to her.

She took a deep breath. "Tiffany felt that it would be better for all parties if she were to leave for a little while."

"She's gone! Where?" Samir asked, an urgency to his tone.

"Manchester," she said. "She is going to care for a Mrs. Coates there."

"A relation?"

"Uh, no. Not really. Mrs. Coates is the mother of the man that she was once betrothed to. He was a sailor and he died at sea many years ago."

"For how long will she be gone?"

"Indefinitely," she whispered.

Samir continued to walk, increasing his speed.

They did not speak again until they reached the servants' entrance of the palace. Samir pointed with his hand for Tiffany to enter first. The servants' dining room was empty this late in the morning. Tiffany wandered through it on the way to Mr. Ford's office. She knocked smartly on the door. The red-faced butler yelled, "Come in!"

She opened the door and Samir followed her inside the tiny little room, with barely more than a desk and chair, where the larger man sat.

"Mr. Woodall, Constable Lathrop," he said, his thick brows raised. "What can I help you with this morning?"

Tiffany looked at Samir.

He blinked several times. "Mr. Ford, I know that it is quite untoward, but I was hoping for a few minutes of the Duchess of Beaufort's time today."

"Regarding?"

Samir blinked again. "Miss Doddridge's death and a possible lead that may assist Mr. Montague's case."

"And what, pray, do you think that a *duchess* has to do with the death of a servant?" Mr. Ford said in a quelling voice that made Tiffany quake in her boots.

"Nothing," Samir said quickly. "We were only hoping to ask her some questions regarding her snuffboxes. It will only take a few moments, but it may be enough to save a man's life."

The butler breathed in deeply, his large nostrils flaring. He pulled open a drawer in his desk and took out a paper with the Beaufort crest printed on the top in gold. Pointing to the pot of ink and quill on the desk, he said, "You may write her a note, but I cannot guarantee that Her Grace will deign to see you."

Samir picked up the quill and dipped it into the black ink:

Your Grace,
As constable of Mapledown, I request your assistance in the inves-
tigation of the death of Miss Doddridge and the accusation against
Mr. Thomas Montague. I believe he is innocent. I have a few
questions that I should like to ask you at any time convenient.

"Tell her that you'll be waiting in the library," Tiffany interjected.

He nodded and added one more sentence:

I will await your pleasure in the library.
Yours ever,
Mr. Sam Lathrop

Mr. Ford poured a little sand on the letter and then folded it in half before placing it on a silver tray. "I will see that it is delivered to Her Grace."

"Thank you, sir," Samir said.

"Thank you, Mr. Ford," Tiffany echoed, and left the room first.

She headed to the library, hearing Samir's firm footsteps behind her. Opening the door to the large room, she felt the familiar joy of being surrounded by so many books—so many worlds that could be opened by simply turning a page.

"Mr. Lathrop, please make yourself comfortable," she said. "You may be here all morning and afternoon."

Samir nodded. "I shall find myself a book, then."

"Let me know if you need anything."

"You are too kind, Mr. Woodall," he said, again looking at her so closely that she felt he could see through her skin.

Tiffany retreated to her desk and favorite chair. She pulled out her cataloging and made a list of the different classifications that she wished to be included together. She decided to organize the books within their subjects by the author's last name, followed by the title should the author have multiple books on the same subject or if there were multiple authors with the same last name. This order, she believed, would make the finding and organizing of books efficient and easy.

Glancing up every few minutes, she saw Samir reading the first volume of *Clarissa*, which she had left out. How lovely it would be if they could discuss their opinions of the writing and the story. She longed to confer with him about the villainous Lovelace and the tragic fate of the heroine.

It was almost time for dinner when Mr. Ford opened the door. Both Tiffany and Samir quickly got to their feet. Tiffany did a little too quickly, and her left foot stepped right out of her boot. She stooped down to put the shoe back on and saw the duchess's feet walk into the room. The pair of slippers she wore were silk, with tulips and leaves embroidered around them. Tiffany's eyes moved up her gown, again a symphony of lace and pattern and texture. So beautiful. The Duchess of Beaufort's face was heavily made up, and her lips were pursed to the side in a pouty expression. The wig she wore today was twice the height of her head and had as many ribbons as a shop.

Samir bowed deeply to her, and Tiffany bent forward. Emily entered the room like a quiet mouse behind the duchess. Mr. Ford shut the door, and Emily remained beside it.

"Mr. Lathrop," the duchess said in a bored, cold voice, "you have requested to see me regarding something to do with Thomas's innocence."

"Thank you for coming, Your Grace," he said, bowing again. "Won't you be seated?"

"I do not mean to stay that long," she said.

"Of course, of course," Samir said, pulling the rose snuffbox from his pocket. "Do you recognize this snuffbox, Your Grace?"

"Yes."

Tiffany inhaled a breath so quickly that she coughed.

"It was found in the possession of Miss Doddridge when she died," he continued. "Did you give it to her?"

"I might have," the duchess said with a flick of her fan. "I don't keep a list of my trinkets."

"It is only that several stolen items were found in Miss Doddridge's bedchamber, and I am trying to ascertain if this item was a gift or a theft."

Had Thomas lied for Sarah when he said the duchess had given it to her?

There was a pregnant pause before the duchess brought the fan in her hand to her face and covered the lower half of it. "A gift, I suppose. Is that all?"

"No, Your Grace," Samir said, stepping forward. "I fear that perhaps the snuff has spoiled and may have caused Miss Doddridge's death and Bernard's illness."

She snapped her fan closed.

"Are you accusing me of something, Constable?" she asked, her words like knives.

Samir held up his hands. "No, no. No, Your Grace. Mr. Woodall and I are only worried for your health and safety. If the mixture is poisonous, we do not wish to see you harmed in any way."

"Emily," the duchess said, waving her fan as if to hurry her servant.

The maid ran forward.

"Go and fetch the jar of snuff that is on my dressing room table and give it to the constable."

Emily gave a deep curtsy. "At once, Your Grace."

The duchess turned as if to go. Samir rushed forward to open the door for her.

"One last thing," Tiffany said.

The Duchess of Beaufort stopped walking and glared over her shoulder.

Tiffany took a quick breath, before she asked, "Where did you purchase the snuff?"

The lady shrugged her elegant shoulders.

"In Mapledown or in London?" Tiffany pressed.

"Mr. Woodall, you should address me as, Your Grace," she said. "I am not your friend, like the Duchess of Surrey. And for your information, a duchess does not purchase anything. Others procure things for her."

Tiffany lowered her head. "I am sorry if I spoke out of turn, Your Grace. Please forgive my impudence."

"London," she said, and left the room.

Samir shut the door behind her, and they both let out a loud sigh.

Tiffany pointed to him and laughed. "I guess I am not the only one who is relieved the interview is over."

He smiled. "Her Grace is not quite as welcoming as the duke."

"No," Tiffany agreed, shaking her head, "but she did give us some valuable information."

"The duchess *did* give Miss Doddridge the snuffbox."

"And the snuff was purchased in London."

"When the servant returns with the jar," he said, "I will take it to Mr. Canning, the apothecary, to examine."

"Don't bother."

"Excuse me?"

She shrugged her shoulders. "I already took both snuffboxes to him to examine, and he said that he could not recognize the oil that the leaves were soaked in. Doctor Hudson thought it was a plant from the nightshade family, but Mr. Canning could not identify which one."

Samir sighed again. "I suppose I could make a trip to Bardsley today and ask the apothecary there. He might know more about it."

"Is there a rush?"

"The assizes judge only comes to Mapledown twice a year. Unfortunately for us, he is in town this week. Mr. Thomas Montague's trial is to be held tomorrow at ten o'clock in the morning," he said. "If I am to try to acquit him, I will have to have proof by then."

Emily opened the door to the room and held out the jar of snuff on a silver tray to Samir. He took it.

"Thank you," he said.

"Anything to help Thomas," Emily said. "Has he any hope?"

"I believe he is innocent, miss," Samir said. "And I will do everything in my power to prove it."

"You are a good man, Constable," she said.

Tiffany could not have agreed with her more.

"Good day, Mr. Woodall, miss," he said, and tipped his hat to them.

Tiffany watched them both leave the library. She would be late again to work tomorrow, for there was no way that she was missing that trial.

CHAPTER 30

It was hard to have faith in a law that didn't recognize the rights of women. At least as a man, Thomas Montague had more rights than her. But he was also African, the people that the English had enslaved. Would he receive justice at the hands of his oppressors? Tiffany couldn't think it very likely. She tossed and turned most of the night.

In the morning, she applied extra white face powder to the dark bruises underneath her eyes. It didn't help her appearance much. Still, she dressed in Uriah's finest suit and tried to shake the louses out of his wig before she put it on. Her walk into town this morning was even more sobering than it had been the day before.

Again, she could feel a phantom noose encircling her neck, ever tightening.

She had done all that she could do. Hadn't she? She had protested his arrest. She'd risked compromising her own disguise to show Samir the snuffboxes, and she'd been with him when he met with the duchess. There was nothing more that she could do.

Tiffany took a seat in the back of the dimly lit room of the sessions house. The ceiling was low, and in the air, she could smell human urine and smoke. Nearly every bench that lined the room was full of men and women eager to witness the proceedings. On the front row, she saw Samir sitting next to Thomas. They were both dressed in their church clothes. They looked handsome and not at all criminal. On the row behind them sat Mr. Shirley and the awful Sir Walter Abney, who watched the room through his small, round quizzing glass. It hung from his short, double-breasted burgundy waistcoat, attached to a chain on his belly.

Mr. Ford and Bernard were on the third row, and several other male servants, grooms, or gardeners from Astwell Palace that she had seen in the dining room, but she didn't know their names. The remaining rows were filled with townsfolk.

The church bells struck ten o'clock. One of the rector's many children must have rung them. The door to the stifling room opened, and a man, wearing a white wig that was so long it reached his waist, walked in. He was dressed in black robes, and his painted white face wore a sneer.

"Please stand for His Honor, Judge Phineas Faulkner," Sir Walter Abney yelled.

Samir got to his feet, and Thomas did as well. The rest of the room scrambled to standing. Tiffany was one of the last to rise. She watched the judge parade to the front of the room, in great stateliness, before stepping up to the raised platform and sitting at the table.

On his right, also on an elevated platform, were two rows of benches. On them sat twelve men: the jurors. She recognized Doctor Hudson, Mr. Canning, and the shop clerk Mr. Wesley, as well as the butcher, the carrier, the farrier, the clothier, the candlemaker, the baker, the miller, the weaver, and the tanner. All white men.

The assizes judge picked up a gavel that had been set on it and pounded against the wood three times. She winced every time it struck.

"You may be seated," he said in a high, pinched voice.

The sound of scuffling benches and people sitting down filled the room. Tiffany was relieved to sit down herself. The reek of the room was making her feel ill.

"We are here today because Mr. Thomas Montague is accused of the horrid crime of murder and also of poisoning a fellow servant," Judge Faulkner squeaked out.

Tiffany heard murmurs from the crowd and wished she could hear what they were saying. She hoped that they had come with an open mind.

"But first, I would like to go over the law," the judge said. "In 1752, the Murder Act was passed in Parliament, and it states that the punishment for a convicted murder is hanging."

Several men nodded. Tiffany gasped.

"However, hanging is not the end of their sentence. The murderer's corpse is sent to the sheriff or constable, to be put in the gibbet and suspended thirty feet in the air. There it will be displayed as it decays, a visible deterrent to prevent any future murders in your parish."

Tiffany grabbed her handkerchief and brought it up to her mouth. She felt like she was going to be sick. But other members of the audience cheered, clapped, and stomped their feet in bloody approval.

"Sir Walter Abney," Judge Faulkner continued in his high voice, "you signed the warrant for Mr. Thomas Montague's arrest. Please share the evidence that brought you to this conclusion."

He waddled to the front of the room like an overdressed peacock. "If it please your honor, I should like to call Mr. Coram to speak."

The judge nodded. "Come to the front."

Bernard stood, clasping his hands together, and stood by the table where the judge sat, facing the jury. His expression was somber.

"Mr. Bernard Coram is a footman at Astwell Palace and knows intimately about Mr. Thomas Montague's behaviors," Sir Walter continued.

"What behaviors?" the judge asked.

"Mr. Montague tried to court Miss Doddridge—" Bernard began.

"A white woman?" Judge Faulkner interjected.

Bernard nodded. "When she refused him, he poisoned her laudanum."

The crowd exploded in taunts and jeers at Thomas. Tiffany held her breath, waiting for violence to erupt.

The judge picked up his gavel again and slammed it down so many times that Tiffany lost count.

"Here. Here! There will be order in my court!" Judge Faulkner screeched.

The townsfolk quieted, but Tiffany could still hear their whispers, and the expressions on their faces were murderous.

Samir stood up and bowed to the judge and then to the jury. He held up several papers in his hand. "Thank you, Your Honor and esteemed jurors. Dr. Hudson of the jury has already examined the laudanum and did not think that it contained the poison. And as to Mr. Coram's other accusation, I have statements from the housekeeper and several of the maids that say that Miss Doddridge not only accepted Mr. Thomas Montague's courtship but encouraged it."

Judge Faulkner shook his head. "Disgusting. The Bible clearly says that God created everything after its own kind. It is the divine order of His creation. An African should only marry an African; and an Englishman, an Englishwoman."

Tiffany ached for Samir. He was the son of an Englishman and an Indian woman. The judge was acting like they were different species entirely, instead of all children of the Lord. All human beings with the right to life and liberty.

Samir winced but showed no other sign of anger. "Be that as it may, interracial marriage is not the crime that is being judged today. We are here to find the murderer of Miss Sarah Doddridge, a person that Mr. Thomas Montague held in such esteem that he offered her his heart and hand in marriage. He would never have harmed her."

The miller, who was also a juror, cupped his mouth and yelled, "Boo!"

His fellow jurors stomped their feet and echoed his "Boos."

"What about me?" Bernard jeered. "That bloody African poisoned me just because I had a little sport with his filly. And right willing she was."

Both the crowd and the jurors responded with catcalls and jeers.

"Is it true that Mr. Montague was given the position of first footman over you, Mr. Coram?" Samir continued.

"Yes," Bernard grunted.

Samir turned from the judge to the jury, and then to the rowdy crowd. "In my opinion, this case should be dismissed. Mr. Coram has no evidence and has based his accusations on nothing but jealousy of a rival servant. It would appear that Mr. Coram wanted Mr. Montague's betrothed, and now he wants Mr. Montague's position by accusing him of murder."

A rotten apple core hit Bernard on the cheek and then clattered to the floor.

The judge stood up, gavel in hand. "That is enough. Sir Walter Abney, do you have any other proof of Mr. Montague's guilt, beyond your witness?"

Sir Walter Abney dropped his quizzing glass and shook his head.

"Mr. Lathrop, as constable," Judge Faulkner said, pointing his gavel at Samir, "do you have any further evidence to influence the jury's decision and my sentencing on this case?"

"I do, Your Honor," Samir said, and picked the jar of snuff up from the floor. He opened the lid and set it on the table in front of the judge. Next, he took the rose snuffbox out of his pocket and held it up before the crowd. "Mr. Coram, do you recognize this snuffbox?"

The second footman's face went white.

"I think it is safe to say, based on the expression you are wearing, that you do?"

"Yes," Bernard said tersely.

"To whom did it belong?"

"Miss Doddridge."

Tiffany heard the soft hum of many whispers.

"Yes," Samir said, opening the snuffbox with a flick of his thumb. "It was found in her bedchamber after she died. How did it end up in your possession, sir?"

This time the courtroom was completely silent. Tiffany could hear herself breathing in and out.

"I don't have to answer that, do I?" Bernard said, turning to the judge in supplication. "They're both bleedin' dark-skinned foreigners."

"Answer the question, Mr. Coram."

He looked down at his hands. "I took it after she died. She didn't have a need for it anymore."

"Did you also partake of the snuff that was inside it?" Samir asked, holding the snuffbox out to Bernard.

"I might have."

"Did you have any poisoning symptoms before you started to inhale the decease's snuff?"

"I dunno."

"But I do," Samir said, closing the snuffbox with a snap. "Mr. Antony Douglas, the apothecary of Bardsley, is here today, and he has confirmed that the snuff was poisoned. You started coughing and vomiting because you had stolen a dead woman's snuff."

All the blood seemed to have left Bernard's face. His swagger was now completely gone.

"Mr. Coram, you may be seated," the judge said. "Mr. Douglas, if you would come to the front?"

A stooped man, in the row in front of hers, stood and walked up. In his hand, he held a green plant with purple flowers, tied with a bit of string. His face was lined, but his green eyes were bright.

"Is that true, Mr. Douglas?" Judge Faulkner asked.

He nodded. "Mr. Lathrop brought it to my shop, and it took me a fair amount of time, but I was finally able to narrow down the ingredients: tobacco leaves and mandrake oil. It appears that someone distilled the roots and the leaves to make an oil. Mandrake root is known to make its victims vomit, which is probably why Miss Doddridge was found in her own sick and why Mr. Coram was also ill."

The judge scooted his chair back from the table and the poisonous jar.

"It won't hurt you, Your Honor, unless you ingest it," Mr. Douglas explained. "And quite a bit of it. It's actually used for many remedies, from stomach complaints to arthritis, but the dosage is low. I brought a bit so you could smell it and compare."

Judge Faulkner looked tentative as he picked up the sprig and sniffed it. He then set it down and picked up the snuffbox.

He nodded his head. "Mr. Lathrop, do you know where Miss Doddridge acquired the poisoned snuff?"

Samir's jaw tightened. "The snuffbox was a gift from her employer."

Tiffany heard several men say, "The duchess?"

"Constable, are you trying to implicate the Duchess of Beaufort in the murder of her lady's maid?" Judge Faulkner said. "For if you are, you should know that even members of the nobility are hung if they are convicted of murder."

Samir shook his head. "I am not, Your Honor. I believe that whoever procured the snuff for the Duchess of Beaufort was trying to poison her. It was only by chance that she was not harmed."

"And why was she not harmed?"

"The duchess stopped taking snuff on her physician's suggestion," Samir explained. "According to her new lady's maid, Miss Emily Jones, she only pretends to take it now." His eyes briefly focused on Tiffany. "That is why the duchess gave the snuffboxes to her employees. She likes to see that it is used."

Tiffany's jaw dropped. She was certain that the duchess was the poisoner. But had both Uriah and Miss Doddridge died by unlucky chance? If neither of them was the intended victim, then who was trying to get rid of the Duchess of Beaufort? And why? It couldn't be for her money. She knew from Uriah that the duchess's son was only six years old and already being sent to school. He would inherit his father's title and estate as well as his mother's money.

"And who gave the Duchess of Beaufort the jar of snuff, Mr. Lathrop?" the judge asked.

Samir shook his head. "The duchess said that it was procured for her in London. I do not know precisely how or by whom. A duchess does not run her own errands, Your Honor."

There were a few sniggers in the crowd. Mr. Ford raised his hand.

"You, sir," the judge squeaked. "What do you wish to say?"

Mr. Ford stood, leaning on his good leg. He cleared his throat. "My name is Mr. Simeon Ford, Your Honor. I am the butler to the Duke and Duchess of Beaufort. I travel with the family to London and to their other seats, including Astwell Palace. Thomas runs errands for the Duchess of Beaufort while she is in London. He would have procured the jar."

All eyes were again on Thomas. Tiffany had to admit that hers were as well.

"Do be seated, Mr. Ford. Thank you for your testimony," the judge said. "Mr. Montague, please stand. Where did you procure the snuff?"

Thomas got shakily to his feet. Typically, the accused were not allowed to speak at their own trial. The revelations of the courtroom seemed to surprise him as much as they did everyone else. "From the tobacconist shop on Bond Street, Your Honor. The same place as always. I did not notice anything different or special about this jar."

"Is the Duchess of Beaufort a fair mistress?" Judge Faulkner asked.

"Yes, Your Honor," Thomas said, looking directly into the judge's eyes.

"Did she purchase you from a slave trader?"

"Yes," he whispered. "I was two or three years old at the time."

Tiffany squeezed her handkerchief in silent indignation. No child that small should be stolen and forced into servitude in a foreign country.

"And she has provided for you since?"

"Her Grace sent me to Astwell Palace to live," Thomas said. "I began working as the first footman about three years ago."

"Was Bernard Coram already a footman at that time?"

"Yes, Your Honor. He was the second footman," Montague said, bowing his head in assent. "But when the first footman died of a fever, I was offered his position."

"Over Mr. Bernard Coram?"

"Yes."

"And why?"

Thomas shrugged his shoulders slightly. "I could not say, Your Honor."

"Mr. Ford, is it?" the judge said, pointing his gavel at the butler. "Do you know why Mr. Montague was promoted over Mr. Coram?"

The butler got to his feet and bowed to the judge before speaking. "No, Your Honor. But it was at the Duchess of Beaufort's insistence. Typically, the butler gets to make decisions about the staff."

"Thank you, Mr. Ford," Judge Faulkner said. "Again, you may be seated."

The butler sat down, and as he did so, he gave Thomas an apologetic glance. His testimony had injured the young man.

The judge pounded the table with the gavel. "If there are no further witnesses, we will wait for the jury to come up with their verdict."

Tiffany watched the twelve jurors put their heads together. She hoped they would give Thomas the benefit of the doubt, for there was no actual proof that he had harmed anyone.

★ ★ ★

A quarter of an hour later, Doctor Hudson stood up, holding a piece of paper. Judge Faulkner pounded his gavel against the table. "May the accused please stand."

Thomas got to his feet and faced the twelve men who held his fate in their hands.

Doctor Hudson cleared his throat. "It is the judgment of this jury that Mr. Thomas Montague, the first footman of the Duke of Beaufort, in the parish of Mapledown, is indeed guilty of the poison and murder of Miss Sarah Doddridge, lady's maid to the Duchess of Beaufort, on the day of September fourteenth, 1784, and that a week later, he attempted to murder Mr. Bernard Coram and the Duchess of Beaufort with the same poison. The prosecution's witnesses were Sir Walter Abney, Baronet; Mr. Bernard Coram; Mr. Simeon Ford; and Mr. Antony Douglas."

Tiffany wanted to cry. Prejudice had overcome justice.

Judge Faulkner banged his favorite gavel against the table. "Mr. Thomas Montague is to be hung from the neck until he is dead. His sentence will be carried out two days from now."

The once-silent crowd again began to murmur. Some stood and threw rotten vegetables and eggs at Thomas and Samir. Others shook their fists.

Tiffany sprinted out of the room, barely reaching the side of the building before losing the contents of her stomach. She wiped her mouth with her handkerchief and walked slowly back to Astwell Palace, tears falling down her face. Despite all of her and Samir's efforts, Thomas was still going to hang.

CHAPTER 31

Her father had often sent Tiffany to her small room for a "period of introspection," usually after she had said or done something he hadn't liked. But sitting in Uriah's room, with the window cracked open to the night, she couldn't help but look in on her own soul. Thomas was going to hang in two days because his skin was a hue of mahogany. Not because he had murdered anybody. Shaking her head, Tiffany knew that she hadn't done enough for him.

She could confess to Judge Faulkner and the jury that Uriah had also been poisoned, but she didn't think that it would do any good. It would only give the jury the name of another person to accuse Thomas of having murdered. She stood and went over to her pitcher and basin and gave herself a sponge bath. But she still felt dirty, the sort of filth that taints both your insides and outside. Rubbing her arms, she felt the beginning of an autumn chill in the air. It was too cold for a dip in the lake.

It was foolish even.

Fie!

Tiffany found herself pulling on Uriah's old boots and leaving her cottage in nothing but his nightshirt. The moon was only a slim silver crescent, but she'd walked the path to the lake so many times that she could have done it with her eyes closed. Shucking off the nightshirt and boots, she stepped into the cold water. Goosebumps formed on her arms and legs, but she didn't let that stop her. She took a few more steps into the freezing lake before diving underneath its dark waters. Slowly, she felt the injustice, the filth of prejudice, the sins of envy and hate, wash from her skin and her soul.

Perhaps it was the cold or the quiet, but Tiffany knew that she could not yet give up on poor Thomas. She had to come up with some sort of plan to find the true murderer, but what? And how, with only two days to do it in?

She kicked her feet and poured water over her face before wandering back to the side of the lake where she'd left her effects. When she reached down for her nightshirt, she saw him—Samir. Surprised, she stood back up, only to duck back down and pick up the nightshirt and attempt to cover herself with it.

"Tiffany?" he said, only five feet away. "I thought you were gone. Your brother said that you had left Mapledown."

A dozen impossible lies floated through her mind, and one impossible truth: if you loved someone, you could trust them with your secrets. A slight breeze caused her whole body to shiver.

"Turn around," she said between chattering teeth.

"What?" Samir stepped forward. "I didn't quite hear."

"Turn around so that I can get decent," Tiffany said more loudly, deliberately enunciating all of her words.

He brought a hand to his cheek and turned his back to her. "Oh. Of course."

She pulled on the large nightshirt. Which should have been easy, but it wasn't. The material kept sticking to her wet skin. At last, she was able to pull the bottom past her knees and slip into the boots.

"You can turn around now," she said, her teeth still chattering from the cold.

Samir gave her a tentative smile that shadowed the strong contours of his face in the moonlight. "I did not know if I would ever see you again."

"I am sorry."

He took another step toward her until he was only an arm's reach away. "Don't be sorry. I have never been so glad about anything in my life."

She shook her head.

Samir's smile fell from his face, and his eyes focused on the lake, instead of her. "Forgive my insolence, Miss Woodall."

Tiffany put her hand on his arm. "I would forgive you anything, but I don't know if you will forgive me when I tell you the truth."

His opposite arm crossed his chest, and he covered her hand with his. "You're freezing."

A giggle escaped her clenched teeth. "It is the end of September."

"Not quite the usual swimming season," he said. "But then you're the only woman I know who swims unclothed in lakes."

"Men do it all the time."

Samir smiled at her, and somehow her heart warmed even while goosebumps covered every inch of her skin.

"In the summer."

"Perhaps we should return to my cottage for the rest of our conversation?" Tiffany said. "I might turn into an ice statue if we stay out here much longer."

"Won't your brother object?" Samir asked. "I don't think he will approve of me talking to you alone, or seeing you swim for that matter."

"He's not there. I mean he is, but he isn't. I will tell you all once we get inside, I promise."

"Are you certain?"

"As death," Tiffany said, stepping closer to put her arm through his. "Would you mind escorting me home, Mr. Lathrop?"

Samir touched his hat. "It would be my honor, Miss Woodall."

They walked quietly to her cottage, and Tiffany led him back to the kitchen. It was nearly black in there. "If you'll take a seat, I will start a fire and make us some tea."

He didn't sit down, but instead bent down to pick up a couple of logs. "Perhaps I should start the fire. I would hate for you to catch your clothes ablaze again."

Tiffany laughed and left him to change.

When she returned to the kitchen, she fetched the teapot. Measuring out the tea leaves, she watched Samir stoke the fire. A warm orange hue seeped through the darkness. He glanced back at her. He looked so handsome that it took her breath away. If only her hair wasn't a stringy, wet mess, and she wasn't wearing an old, plain work dress.

Her own wetness reminded her to add water to the teapot, something that she had managed to forget while in Samir's incandescent presence. Her bucket still had water, but she would need to fetch more in the morning from the well. Bringing the kettle over, she placed it on the hook by the fire.

Samir had moved two of the kitchen chairs from the table, closer to the open range.

"So that you don't freeze to death," he explained, smiling.

As if on cue, Tiffany shivered again. Not from the cold, but from the warmth of his smile. Would he still smile at her after he knew the truth? She trusted now that he would not arrest her or publish to the world her masquerade, but would he still care for her?

She sat down and crossed her ankles. Samir had been right; it was much warmer by the fire. She felt her face grow hot, but perhaps that was caused by her embarrassment. He sat down in the chair beside her and waited for her to speak.

"I thought you were marvelous today during the trial."

He nodded. "I didn't know that you were there . . . I only wish that the jury had come to a different verdict."

"Do you truly believe that the murderer was trying to kill the Duchess of Beaufort?"

"It seems like the most logical explanation to me," Samir said, stroking his chin that had a slight dark shadow of hair on it. "The snuff jar was in her possession."

"Are you sure that she isn't the murderer?" Tiffany pressed. "If she does not take snuff, why does she even have a jar of it? It seems mightily suspicious that she gave it to the two people who died."

"Two? Only Miss Doddridge died. Bernard was only ill from the poison."

It was time to tell the whole truth and nothing but the truth.

Tiffany shook her head. "Miss Doddridge was not the first victim of the poisoned snuff. My half brother, Uriah, was."

Samir blinked and leaned closer to her. "That cannot be. I saw your brother only this morning. He was at the trial."

She took a deep breath in and then released it. "The first night that you caught me swimming in the lake, I was washing because I had just buried my half brother in the back garden."

He leaned back in his chair. Not necessarily away from her, but as if his whole body and brain were taken aback by her words.

Tiffany hurried on. "I found Uriah in his bed that morning, covered in his own sick. It was not uncommon for Uriah to vomit. He has had stomach problems for years, and I more often threw out sick from the chamber pot than I did urine. But that morning, I found him dead in his bed, and I panicked. With Uriah dead, I had no money and nowhere to go. We have no close relatives whom I could call on for aid. This cottage would go to the duke's next librarian, and I would be homeless, with no other choice but to throw myself on the mercy of the parish. But with Mr. Shirley as the rector, there is not much mercy in our parish."

"So, you have been dressing as your brother to keep his position and your home."

"Yes," she said. "I tried to be both Uriah and myself, but it proved impossible."

He nodded again. "Mr. Shirley was trying to court and marry you."

"I had no other choice but to send 'Tiffany' away and to become Uriah all of the time," she said. "I was going to tell you the truth the day that I brought the snuffboxes to your bookshop."

Samir leaned toward her again, his blazing brown eyes boring into hers. "Why didn't you?"

Tiffany bit her lip. "I—I was going to, but then I saw the pamphlet on *The Female Husband*, and I panicked. The illustrations are horrific. I was afraid of being charged of a crime and whipped half naked in the town square."

"You thought that *I* would do that to you?"

"The men in my life have not been kind."

"I assumed that we were friends," he said, sounding hurt by her doubts.

She shook her head and shrugged her shoulders. "I didn't want to believe you possible of it, but I was afraid. So very afraid. And I wouldn't blame you for hating me now. What sort of good person buries her half brother without a proper church service? What sort of good woman wears a man's clothes and masquerades as one?"

Samir was quiet for several moments. The only sounds in the room were the cracks from the fire and the pounding of her heart in her chest.

"The sort of good person who is desperate," he whispered. "The sort of good woman who has no other options."

Tiffany covered her mouth with her hands. Tears fell from her eyes and dropped on her old dress. "Can you forgive me?"

"For not confiding in me?"

She sniffed. "No, for what I did to Uriah."

"That is easy to forgive," Samir said, a ghost of a smile on his lips. "I never liked him anyway."

"Nor did I."

"But his death does change the murder case, from one to two," he said thoughtfully. "It also changes the time line. Mr. Woodall died at the beginning of September. The poison would have been placed at that time or before."

"Unfortunately, my brother's death does not shed any further light on the case besides confirming that the poison was administered through snuff," she said with a sigh. "It doesn't give us any knowledge of who committed the crime. Or why. And the only way we will be able to save Thomas is to find the true killer."

"We need to know more about the Duchess of Beaufort's enemies," Samir said. "We have to know who would want her dead."

"I don't know if she will see us again. She kept you waiting for hours last time."

"You're right," he said. "Perhaps you could ask the other servants?"

"I don't think that will help," Tiffany said. "They do not associate with the duchess's friends. They do not understand the nuances of her position and class."

"What about your friend, the Duchess of Surrey?" he asked. "I am sure that she would not refuse to see you, and who better than her to know if the Duchess of Beaufort has any enemies."

Tess.

"I would have to go as myself," she said. "She snubbed me when I was dressed as Uriah the other day."

"The Duchess of Surrey is not aware that you have gone visiting to Manchester?" he asked with a smirk.

She shook her head slightly. "Only yourself and Mr. Shirley. I delivered him a letter irrevocably ending the engagement that I never entered into in the first place."

"You didn't?"

"No!" she said so forcibly that he laughed. "The rector tried to propose to me over Miss Doddridge's dead body. I was telling him that I was flattered, but we were interrupted before I could refuse him. He assumed that flattery meant assent and read the banns without a word to me."

"What a *gollumpus.*"

Laughter poured out of Tiffany. A large, clumsy fellow was the perfect description of the skeletal rector. Samir laughed with her, and the bond between them seemed to tighten. Their friendship was growing stronger. She hoped that someday it would become more.

The kettle whistled and Tiffany remembered the tea. She grabbed a cloth and took the kettle off the fire. She poured both Samir and herself full steaming cups.

"I will have to go tomorrow," she said, handing him his saucer.

"The sooner, the better," Samir said.

CHAPTER 32

Crawling up into the attic space the next morning, Tiffany fished out her trunk. It would be dangerous to be seen as herself by any villager. They might tell Mr. Shirley that they'd seen her, which would prove disastrous, but she had to risk it. Her silk dress was on top and a little wrinkled from the trunk. She would have to steam it by the fire before she wore it. Tiffany would have to look like a lady, or she feared that her old friend would snub her. Cut her acquaintance by refusing to see her. And while Tiffany was ready to let their old friendship die a natural death, she was not about to let Thomas die an unnatural one.

Tiffany's hands shook as she walked the familiar path to Astwell Palace. She entered the servants' door and walked the few steps down into the sunken dining room.

"Miss Woodall? Is the Duchess of Surrey expecting you?" Mrs. Wheatley asked.

Tiffany bit her lip and shook her head. "She is not, but I was wondering if you might ask her if I could have a word."

"I cannot talk to the duchess."

Tiffany's heart fell to her stomach.

"But I can ask her lady's maid to pass on a message to her mistress," the housekeeper said. "Would that be agreeable?"

"Very."

"If you wouldn't mind taking a seat," Mrs. Wheatley said, "I saw Miss Homer washing her mistress's gloves down the hall only a few minutes ago. I can go and ask her right now."

"Thank you," Tiffany said, and out of habit, took her usual chair on the right-hand side of the men's table. She had nothing to do but tap her fingers against the tablecloth and wait.

A severe-looking woman with black hair and a nose like a knife came into the servants' dining room. She was dressed in a fine but simple blue silk dress.

"Her Grace says that you may come visit her briefly in her boudoir, Miss Woodall," the woman said, her voice as sharp as her nose. "If you would please follow me."

Tiffany stood and trailed the lady's maid out of the servants' quarters, past the library, and up the grand staircase. Tiffany expected the severe woman to lead her down the hall where she had placed all the books in the guestrooms, but instead, the woman led her in the opposite direction, to what appeared to be the wing of family rooms.

Curious.

Tess must be a great friend of the Duchess of Beaufort. The lady's maid opened a door that was ten feet tall and elaborately carved. The room inside it was more beautiful than anything Tiffany had ever imagined. The canopy on top of the bed was over twenty feet high. Silk damask curtains streamed from the four corners. The bed itself was wide enough for six people to sleep across. The coverlet on top of it was finer than any piece of clothing Tiffany had ever worn as herself or as Uriah.

Inside the bed, sipping her morning chocolate, was Tess. It was the first time Tiffany had seen her friend without her wig or her makeup in twenty years. She was still pretty, but she looked all of her forty years. Tiffany could see the lines around her eyes and her mouth. Her chest was also quite diminished in her lacy nightgown. As she'd done with her false hips, Tess must have also padded her breasts to make them look larger. The person she presented in her silks, wigs, and panniers was an exaggerated copy of herself.

Tiffany awkwardly walked forward, passing a marble fireplace and a settee with legs that looked to be made of gold. She curtsied to her old friend, bobbing on her feet. She'd become too used to bowing.

"Thank you for agreeing to see me, Your Grace."

"Oh, fie!" Tess said. "Come sit on my bed with me and share my breakfast."

"I've already eaten."

Tess giggled. "I can guarantee that it wasn't as good as what is on my tray. Come, let us chat as we used to."

Tiffany gulped and stepped forward. She sat on the edge of the bed. The fabrics were even more stunning up close. She doubted that even the king and queen of England had anything as fine as this.

Tess didn't appear to be awed by her surroundings nor worried about getting crumbs on the silk. She took a large bite of an egg, with some sort of yellow sauce, on a slice of bread. "Now, my dear, I am so glad that you have come today."

"You are?" Tiffany said, unable to keep the surprise out of her tone.

"Indeed," Tess said, "for I am leaving this morning, and I do not know if I would have had the time to come and see you at your cottage before my carriage left."

Tiffany tried to picture Tess in the small parlor of her cottage, but she couldn't. She was glad that Tess had never come.

She didn't want to be ashamed of the loveliest home she'd ever had.

"Is the house party breaking up?"

"Oh no," Tess said, pausing for another bite. "My son arrived last night. He was ever so upset that I was here without his knowledge."

"The duke?"

"No," Tess said with another giggle. "My second son, Theophilus, although he has the manner of a duke."

"He disapproves of your visit?"

"Theophilus fears that if I return to my old friends, I'll return to my old sinful ways," she said, unable to smile this time. "He read scriptures to me for hours yesterday evening, and I do feel that it is for the best that we leave together today."

Tiffany would never be a duchess, but she did know what it was like to be told what to do by a man. That Tess would be treated like a child by her own son seemed absurd.

"Don't you have your own money and your own dower house?"

Tess sighed. "I do, but it is not as simple as that. You don't have children of your own, so you don't understand."

Tiffany's sympathy drained from her like tea from a kettle. She hated how mothers treated women without children as lesser and as inexperienced in family affairs. "You're right. I do not. If I had my own income and my own home, I wouldn't allow any man, no matter his age or relation to me, to tell me what to do."

"He is my son, Tiffany," she said. "My older son, Osmond, is entirely my husband's creature, but Theophilus is my little darling. My everything. And he swears that he will have nothing to do with me if I do not repent. And even though I have not sinned during this visit, he believes to put myself so close to temptation, to be in the same house as my lover, is not only foolish but morally wrong."

Tiffany thought of Lord Talgarth. "I saw how you hung on his arm."

Tess snorted. "That's not a sin. Oh, Tiffany, I wish I was still as innocent a creature as you."

Tiffany said nothing. Despite Tess's teasing her, she still felt sorry for her old friend. She understood what it was like to love someone who disapproved of you. But no matter how hard she had tried to change for her father, it had never been enough for him, and it had never been enough for Tiffany. She'd felt like a loaf of dough smashed into a tin and shaped into something—someone—that she was not. Uriah had also tried to mold her and to cut off the bits of her that he didn't like.

No love was worth changing one's true self.

"I have come to talk to you about the Duchess of Beaufort."

"Catharine?" Tess said, smiling again, although her eyes shone with unshed tears. "I daresay no one knows her better than myself, for we have been the dearest friends for over fifteen years."

Tiffany couldn't help but wonder if Catharine had been her replacement, but that was neither here nor there.

"I was wondering what you know about her relationship with Thomas."

"Such a shocking case," Tess said, waving her fork. "I would never have believed it. As a boy, he was so devoted to Catharine, and she positively doted on him."

"Her slave?" Tiffany clarified, moving further on the bed.

"She might have purchased him, but he was never her slave," she said. "You see, poor Catharine longed for a child of her own. When she saw a little slave boy with a British captain, her heart broke for him, and she was determined that he have a good home and a good life. She treated him like a son. Played with him, sang to him. She would always buy presents for her 'Little Thomas' whenever she was in London and was always eager to return to Astwell Palace after the season to see him."

"I thought that she had a son."

"She does," Tess agreed. "Dear little Peregrine was quite unexpected. She'd given up hope of ever bearing a child. I daresay he is six years old now. Such a little rascal. School will be good for him."

"Did the duchess's relationship to Thomas change when her own son was born?"

"I thought it would, frankly," she said, "but it didn't. She even hired Thomas a tutor and raised him as a gentleman. Thomas is also quite devoted to little Peregrine. They tease and wrestle like brothers."

"Then why is he the footman?"

Tess's countenance fell again. "Rumors of Thomas's origins began to circulate among the *ton*, and the duke felt that an honorable position in service was more compatible to his station in life. Catharine was much upset, but she has reconciled herself to having Thomas with her always. He travels with her wherever she goes. Or at least he did."

"She seemed rather cold to him when I last saw her," Tiffany said. Thinking of how she had paraded Thomas like a spectacle to be seen.

"Their relationship is rather strained at the moment," Tess admitted. "Catharine did not want him to become betrothed to her lady's maid. She felt that the girl was not worthy of him.

The maid was rather loose, shall we say. They got into a mighty row over it and have been distressingly civil to each other since."

Tiffany sighed. Instead of finding another person who would want to kill the duchess, Tess had given Thomas an even greater motive for killing her. The only other person who would be motivated to kill the duchess was Miss Doddridge, but she was already dead.

"I am sure since you know about Thomas's case," Tiffany said. "That you have heard that it was the Duchess of Beaufort's poisoned snuff that killed her lady's maid."

Tess clasped her flat chest above her heart. "To think my dear Catharine was so close to death makes me positively ill."

"Did the duchess have any enemies that would wish to see her dead?"

"Catharine is beloved by all," Tess assured her. "I cannot think of one lady or lord who would wish to harm her. Her parties are always the hit of the London season, and everyone who is anyone longs to claim her as an acquaintance . . . Why do you ask?"

"I was hoping to learn something that might help Thomas."

She shook her head. "Such a pity. He was the sweetest little boy, but I suppose he couldn't help growing up."

Tiffany stood up. She and Tess had also grown up. "Thank you for your time, Your Grace."

Tess leaned over her tray and took Tiffany's hand. "It has been good to see you, Tiffany. Take care of yourself. I will probably not be able to come and visit Astwell Palace again. But I am so glad that I got to see you one last time."

Tiffany squeezed her old friend's hand back. She'd always been envious of her. Jealous even of her position and privileges. But now, she had no desire to change places with her for all of her jewels, fancy houses, and servants. Tess was still a prisoner of her sex, but the cage was prettier than most and love of her son kept her inside it.

"I wish you every happiness, Tess."

A solitary tear fell down Tess's cheek. "You finally said my Christian name."

"We were the terrible twosome," Tiffany said, mustering a small smile.

"Off to accomplish some derring-do, see a mermaid, and fight a pirate too," Tess finished their old secret motto. "I will always cherish our childhood memories, back when the world was large and our imaginations were without bounds."

Tess dropped her hand, and Tiffany left the room.

Left her oldest friend.

Leaving behind her past self.

Tiffany was determined to forge a new future. One hopefully without pirates but always with the possibility of mermaids.

CHAPTER 33

Tiffany walked into the servants' quarters and planned to thank Mrs. Wheatley before she left. There was already a man talking to the housekeeper. Tiffany could not see his face, but she could tell from the back that he was not wearing the livery uniform of the male servants. Not wishing to linger longer than was necessary, Tiffany turned to leave, but the sound of her footsteps must have alerted them both.

"All done with Her Grace, Miss Woodall?" Mrs. Wheatley asked.

The man by her side was none other than the rector, Mr. Shirley.

"Miss Woodall, what are you doing here?" he demanded.

"I am—I was here to speak to the Duchess of Surrey," she said quickly. "I only wished to thank you for your assistance, Mrs. Wheatley. I'll bid you both a good day."

Tiffany had barely finished bobbing a curtsy when Mr. Shirley's talon-like fingers sank into her upper arm.

"You're not going yet," he said. "You're not going anywhere. You're betrothed to me, and you will not escape me again."

"Mr. Shirley, please release my arm," Tiffany said. His grip was bruising. "If you have anything to say, you may speak to my brother about it."

"I shall do so at once," he said, dragging Tiffany with him. "Mrs. Wheatley, please take us to the library."

The housekeeper glanced from the rector's grim face to Tiffany's imploring one.

"I am afraid that Mr. Woodall is not allowed to have guests while he is at work," Mrs. Wheatley said.

"I am not a guest. I am the rector. If you will not show me, I will find him myself."

Mrs. Wheatley cast Tiffany a sympathetic glance before bidding Mr. Shirley to follow her. The rector continued to drag her along behind him like a sack of wheat. Tiffany tried to struggle out of his hold, but he merely tightened his grasp. She didn't want to make more of a figure of herself, so she allowed him to pull her to the library, which she knew was empty.

"Where is Mr. Woodall?" Mr. Shirley demanded.

"I don't recall seeing him come to the palace this morning," Mrs. Wheatley said. "But I'd be happy to give him a message from you."

"If the man's not here, he must be at home. I will speak to him today," the rector said, and tried to yank Tiffany back to the servants' quarters.

She went limp and allowed her knees to fall to the floor. "Release me, sir. You cannot treat me like a doll that a child drags behind them."

A bit of color stole into his skeletal cheeks. "If you don't want to be treated like a child or a doll, I suggest that you act like a woman."

"And I suggest that you act like a gentleman and not a brute," Tiffany spat back. "You are supposed to be a man of the church."

The rector finally released his hold on her arm, only to backhand her across the face with the same hand. She fell on her back in surprise, her face smarting from the impact. For all of Uriah's faults, he'd never physically harmed her. She'd never been hit by anyone before. Even her father had believed that violence against women or children was reprehensible.

"Mr. Shirley, that is quite enough," Mrs. Wheatley said. "Such behavior is not allowed in the duke's home. If you do not leave this moment, I will report it to him."

Mr. Shirley glared at the housekeeper and then at Tiffany. "The law upholds that a man can beat his wife with his hands or any object the same size of his thumb or smaller."

"I am not your wife!" Tiffany said, getting to her feet.

"The banns have been read," he said. "You're as good as my wife."

"They were read without my consent. You assumed that I would say yes. Well, let me make it abundantly clear to you now, sir. I would not marry you, if you offered me this palace. I do not like you, nor do I respect a man who would use his authority to prey on those who are weaker than him. Have I made myself clear?"

The rector's narrow nostrils flared, and he lifted his hand as if to strike her again.

"Mr. Shirley," a soft male voice said.

Tiffany turned to see Mr. Ford walking toward them languidly with his decided limp. She dipped into a curtsy. Mrs. Wheatley echoed her movement, and even the horrid Mr. Shirley bowed.

"I do believe that it is time for you to go, sir," Mr. Ford said with the dignity of a duke. "I don't recall you receiving an invitation to the palace, nor do I allow such behavior among the lower or the upper staff."

"She is my affianced wife, Mr. Ford," Mr. Shirley said between tight lips.

"Only a fool would continue to press his suit when a woman has made it clear that it is repugnant to her," the butler said. "I will be having words with the Duke of Beaufort about your behavior. His cousin is your bishop. I suggest you return to the rectory and begin preparing your explanation to him, *Rector*."

Mr. Shirley jerked another bow and stomped off.

Mr. Ford's eyes were focused on Tiffany's throbbing cheek. She longed to cover it with her hand. Shame filled her soul. Tears of embarrassment sprang to her eyes.

"I am aggrieved that you were treated such in this home, Miss Woodall. Please accept my humblest apologies. I will talk to the duke today and inform him of Mr. Shirley's unseemly behavior. I feel confident that it will not be repeated."

Tiffany mumbled her thanks.

The butler turned to the housekeeper. "Mrs. Wheatley, see that her brother walks her home and stays with her for the rest of the day. We do not wish for her to experience any further unpleasantness."

The housekeeper curtsied, and Tiffany held her breath as Mr. Ford walked away slowly, favoring one leg. He was out of sight before Mrs. Wheatley said in a whisper, "Since your brother is not here, shall I send Bernard to accompany you?"

Tiffany shook her head. "Thank you for your consideration and for not telling him that my brother is not here."

"It was the least that I could do," she said, her voice still low. "It was my fault that he was here. He came to bring me Sarah's death certificate."

"I don't want a man to walk me home."

Mrs. Wheatley put a reassuring arm around Tiffany and led her back to the servants' quarters and the entrance. Emily was scrubbing the steps that led down into the servants' dining room.

"Put your bucket away quick-like, girl," the housekeeper said. "You're to escort Miss Woodall home . . . she's feeling unwell."

Emily glanced up at Tiffany's face, her eyes focusing on the bruise forming on her cheek. She nodded, grabbing the scrub brush and dropping it in the bucket. She hurried to put them away. The young maid was only gone for a few moments, and when she met them at the door, she was wearing a shawl and a straw hat.

"You may stay as long as Miss Woodall requires you, Emily," the housekeeper said, and then pulled her arm back that had been resting on Tiffany's shoulders, giving her comfort and reassurance from another woman.

Emily opened the door and Tiffany walked out of it into the cool sunshine of late September. She continued to the lane and heard Emily's steps behind her. Once they reached the lake, Tiffany stopped.

"You don't have to walk behind me," she said. "I would much prefer that you stayed by my side."

"Whatever you wish, Miss Tiffany," Emily said, but hurried her pace so that their strides were the same.

They continued to walk in silence. Tiffany was grateful that the young maid didn't ask her any questions or refer to the swelling on her face. Although why she should feel shame for another person's actions she could not say. But she understood now why other village women made excuses for their bruises or tried to hide them. It was hard to feel weak. It was terrible to look like a victim. And there was a little voice in her head that suggested that it might all be her fault. If, somehow, she had handled the situation with Mr. Shirley better, he would not have harmed her.

When they reached her cottage, Tiffany couldn't help but look around to make sure that no one else was there. Emily waited for her to unlock the door and followed her inside.

"Why don't you sit down, and I'll make you some tea?"

"You are not my servant. You are my guest. I should be waiting on you," Tiffany said.

Emily put a gentle hand on Tiffany's shoulder. "I think you need the tea a bit more than I do right now."

She could only nod in response. The tears that had so nearly fallen at Astwell Palace threatened to fall now. She watched Emily go straight back to the kitchen and pick up the empty bucket. Tiffany was all too aware of the cobwebs in the corners of the room and the unwashed dishes in the basin.

"I can go fetch some water," Tiffany said.

"I saw your well, walking in," Emily said, and left the cottage.

Tiffany sat down on a chair near the table. She breathed in and out with shuddering breaths. Emily returned and started a fire. She put both a pot and the kettle near it, to boil the water. The maid took the pot of hot water and poured it over the dirty pans and china.

"You don't have to wash my dishes."

"It's not your fault," Emily said quietly. "It's not your fault that you were hit."

The blood rushed to Tiffany's face, and the tears began to fall. "I hate feeling so helpless. I should have moved. I should have done something to prevent it."

"My pa has heavy fists," she said. "I used to blame myself when he beat me, but I realized, once I arrived at the palace, that none of the beatings were my fault. They were his."

Emily handed Tiffany a newly washed saucer and cup. Next, she brought the steaming kettle to the table and poured Tiffany a cup of tea.

"Won't you join me?"

"If you'd like me to."

Tiffany smiled through her tears. "Yes, I would like that very much."

Emily fetched herself a teacup and saucer before pouring her tea. Tiffany sipped hers, and the warm liquid seemed to spread throughout her body; calming and warming wherever it went.

"I am sorry that your home life was difficult."

Emily sighed, setting down her teacup. "I've begged my mum to leave him a dozen times, but she won't. She doesn't want her neighbors to think she's a bad woman. But I wish she would, for my little sister's sake. Mary's only fifteen, but there's no position for her right now at the palace, and she often takes the brunt of my father's drinking and anger."

"Do you think she would like to come here?" Tiffany asked. "I don't know how much I can pay her, but I can promise a safe and comfortable home."

"She doesn't need your charity."

Tiffany sniffed. "I think we all need a little charity sometimes, and I should like the company. Besides, someone needs to rid my cottage of spiders. I am doing an abysmal job of it."

Emily smiled first and then laughed. Trust a maid of all work to realize how dirty Tiffany's cottage had become.

"How soon would you want her?"

Tiffany swallowed the tea in her mouth. "Is today too soon?"

"I can fetch her immediately, if you like," Emily said. "Mrs. Wheatley isn't expecting me back at a certain time."

"That would be wonderful," Tiffany said. "But please finish your tea first. It's quite the nicest tasting I've had in years."

So they sipped their tea together, neither woman speaking, but they didn't need to.

CHAPTER 34

Mary Jones looked like a younger, hungrier version of her sister Emily. She had the same bright blue eyes, curly brown hair, and creamy skin. Her woolen dress was coarse and too short, and the apron she wore was dirty. Her arms looked thin and her body undernourished, making her appear much younger than her fifteen years. Such was the fate of many poor families where the food was never quite plentiful enough to go around.

Tiffany had taken the opportunity to change into Uriah's clothes while Emily had gone. She'd powdered the swollen cheek with twice as much white face powder, but it still looked puffy. She needed to go tell Samir what she had learned from Tess (or rather, what she hadn't learned), and she was not about to be accosted by Mr. Shirley again in her skirts.

"Emily, if you would be so kind as to show Mary what needs to be done," Tiffany said. "She's welcome to the room in the back. The sheets are fresh. I need to go into town this afternoon for a little while."

Mary dropped a schoolgirl curtsy.

"What are you going to do in Mapledown?" Emily asked.

Tiffany sighed. "Mr. Lathrop and I are trying our best to find the true murderer, so Thomas can go free. I hoped to learn something useful at Astwell Palace this morning, but I am afraid that I did not."

Emily shook her head. "Then there is no hope?"

"The hanging is not until tomorrow, and I believe Thomas is innocent. I will not stop looking for proof of what really happened. Or who is truly to blame."

"Like I said before, you're a good person, Miss—Mr. Woodall."

Tiffany gave her a lopsided smile. "Thank you, for everything today."

Emily gave her a little nod and Tiffany left her cottage. The walk into town was not a comfortable one. Her nerves were so shot, she half expected Mr. Shirley to spring out from behind a tree and attack her on the path. She'd never been more relieved in her life to step into Samir's bookshop with its familiar smell of leatherbound paper.

Like Mr. Ford's, Samir's eyes went directly to her swollen cheek. He stepped from around the counter and reached out his hand to her face, stopping just before it met the bruised skin.

"What happened? Did you fall?"

Despite Emily's wise words, Tiffany almost allowed Samir to believe that she had fallen. But she didn't want to lie to him again. She shook her head.

"Mr. Shirley was at Astwell Palace," she said. "He saw me dressed as myself and tried to force me to go with him. I refused and he struck me."

His hand that had so nearly touched her face, fell to his side in a clenched fist. "I will no longer stand by while he beats innocent women. I'm going to go over to the rectory and give him a thrashing twenty years in the making."

Tiffany grabbed his arm. "I should like nothing better than for you to knock him down, but we must focus on Thomas. His time is running out."

She felt Samir's arm muscles tense beneath her hand and then relax. She should have released him, but touching him made her feel safe.

"Did you learn anything useful from the Duchess of Surrey?"

Tiffany sighed and shook her head. "She insisted that the Duchess of Beaufort had no enemies and she told me that the duchess had once treated Thomas like a son."

"I had heard rumors of that," Samir said. "English people are much more accepting of dark-skinned children until we grow up."

Tiffany squeezed Samir's arm. "I know it is presumptuous of me to apologize for an entire country, but please know that not everyone condemns you for being different."

Samir looked into her eyes. "Tiffany—"

The door swung open, and the bell on it rang. Tiffany released his arm and wondered what he had been going to say. Hoping that he was about to confess that he cared for her as much as she did for him.

"Constable and Mr. Woodall," Sir Walter Abney said. "Just the two men I am looking for."

Behind the round baronet stood the skeletal Mr. Shirley. Tiffany clutched at the cravat tied around her neck. Her pulse leaped erratically.

Samir stepped in front of her, defensively. "What can I do for you two gentlemen?"

"Mr. Shirley has filed a complaint against Miss Woodall for breach of promise," Sir Walter said, resting his hands on his round middle. "Since Judge Faulkner is still in town until Saturday, he would like him to try the case tomorrow."

"No promise was made," Tiffany gritted out.

"The banns were read on Sunday, Mr. Woodall," the baronet said. "And your sister did not protest them then."

"That was before Mr. Shirley beat Miss Woodall," Samir said, both fists clenched.

Sir Walter turned to Mr. Shirley. "Is that true, sir?"

"She defied me and I struck her," the rector said. "I had to put the woman in her place."

"The only place she should be is as far away from you as possible," Samir said.

Mr. Shirley stepped forward, but Sir Walter held out a plump, restraining arm. "Now, now, Mr. Shirley. Mr. Lathrop and I are servants of the law. We do not handle things with our fists."

"Step forward, Woodall," the rector jeered. "Stop hiding behind the half-breed."

Tiffany was tired of cowering before such a weakling. She stepped forward. "You disgust me, Shirley."

Color stole into the deathly pale face of the rector. He pointed a finger at Tiffany. "Good heavens! It is Miss Woodall dressed in her brother's clothes. See where I hit her face."

Tiffany's hand tried to cover her swollen cheek, but it was too late. Sir Walter stepped closer to her. Her heart fell inside her chest.

"Would you mind taking off the wig?"

With one shaking hand she pulled off Uriah's itchy, horrible wig. Without it holding her hair in place, her braid fell down her back. She glanced at Samir, whose mouth was pinched closed. Nothing he said could help her now. It would only condemn him as well.

"Why are you dressed as a man?" Sir Walter asked.

Tiffany's cheek throbbed with pain, and her whole body hummed in fear. She knew that there was no excuse to satisfy them. She could not produce both her brother and herself in the same room. It was time to tell the truth, and as the Bible said, *"The truth will set you free."* Free from her disguise, but not free from the consequences of it.

"My half brother was the first victim of the poisoned s-snuff," Tiffany said, her voice trembling. "I didn't know then that he had been murdered, only that he had died. I had no money. Nowhere to go. No one to whom I could turn. So I buried him underneath the crack willow tree in the back garden and took his place so that I could keep my home, sir."

A bird could have flown into Sir Walter's mouth, it was so wide. "I-I-I don't know what to say, miss."

"Arrest her!" Mr. Shirley said, his bony finger like the grim reaper's. "Such an indecent display cannot be tolerated in our town. She should be punished. Whipped."

Sir Walter clucked his tongue. "I do believe you're right, Mr. Shirley. Mr. Lathrop, if you would please arrest Miss Woodall and put her in jail. The assizes judge will have to decide her fate."

Samir did not say a word, but took Tiffany by the elbow and led her out of his shop into the main street. Sir Walter and Mr. Shirley followed behind them, as if neither trusted Samir to follow through with their instructions. With every step, Tiffany's heart fell further in her body. By the time they reached the door of the jail, she could feel it beating in her toes. Her life as she knew it was over, and she was worse off than she had been when Uriah first died. The judge had not shown Thomas any mercy in his sentencing; she doubted that he would find some in his frozen heart for her.

CHAPTER 35

Samir unlocked the cell, and Thomas stood up from where he was laying on a cot. The Mapledown Jail was a one-room building with a low roof and only one barred window. At least it was clean.

"I thought it was tomorrow."

"It is. I'm afraid that you have a fellow prisoner," Samir said. "There is only one cell, so you will have to share it."

The relief was visible on Thomas's face. Tiffany watched as all of his features softened. She walked into the cell.

"Mr. Woodall? Miss Woodall?" he said, blinking as if he didn't quite trust who or what he was seeing.

"Miss Woodall," she said, and tried to give him a smile, but her lips would not cooperate.

"I will bring you both your evening meal," Samir said as he locked the door. "I have a body to uncover."

Tiffany turned back to him and grabbed his wrist through the bars. "Emily and Mary Jones are at my cottage. Can you make sure that they are safe?"

"Of course."

"Tell them they can use whatever they need," she said hurriedly. "Also, if the ruling is death, might I make a will? I should like to leave my belongings, the diamond cluster pin, and furniture to them. They should fetch a decent price. I only wish it were more."

Samir's opposite hand covered hers. "I don't think there will be any need for that, but I can assure you that I will personally see to their safety while you are in jail."

"Thank you. Thank you," she whispered, longing to say more. Instead, she released her grip on his wrist. "Uriah is between the two largest roots that reach out toward the cottage."

With a curt nod he left the one-room jail house.

Tiffany turned to Thomas, who was still standing, watching her with open curiosity. She held out her hand.

"I don't think that we have been properly introduced," she said, shaking his hand. "Although, you helped me find the library the first day that I masqueraded as my brother. I am Miss Tiffany Woodall."

"Mr. Thomas Montague."

"I suppose you are wondering why I am dressed like a man and sharing your incarceration?"

He shook his head slightly. "I should have noticed sooner, miss. You changed overnight from a pompous arse to a considerate person."

"I am afraid that my half brother, Uriah, was the first victim of the poisoned snuff," she admitted. "I didn't know that at the time. He has always had stomach complaints. I simply thought that he had died."

Thomas held up his right hand. "I swear to you that I had nothing to do with poisoning the snuff. And I did not murder your brother, nor Sarah. I would have never harmed a hair on her body, no matter what she did."

"I saw in your eyes how much you loved her, and you reminded me of someone I once loved dearly."

Thomas's face softened. "What happened to him?"

"He died," she whispered. "More than twenty years ago now. We were engaged to be married, but he was a sailor in the navy and needed more money before we could marry. He never returned from his voyage."

"Was he African?"

She shook her head slightly. "No. But he was tall and handsome like you. Your smile reminds me of his. The warmth in it. Particularly when you looked at her. It brought it all back to me."

He sniffed. "Does the pain lessen over time?"

"No, but you get used to it so that it is easier to bear," Tiffany said, placing a hand on his arm. "And although the truth of Miss Doddridge's actions will undoubtedly wound you, you should never feel ashamed of your own feelings. They were honest. They were true. And someday I hope you find a woman more worthy of your love."

"That's what Catharine said—I mean, Her Grace."

Tiffany gestured to the cot. "Shall we sit? I do not think there is anything that I can do to save myself, but I think I may be able to save you with a little help."

Thomas sat down on the cot beside her, but his expression was grim. "They're going to hang me tomorrow."

"No, they are going to hang the true murderer," Tiffany said with more confidence than she felt. "But I need to understand more from you about who would try to kill the Duchess of Beaufort, and since you had such an intimate relationship with her . . ."

"I was never her lover," he said sharply. "Those are gross rumors put about by Bernard."

She shook her head. "No, you were and are her son."

Thomas sniffed again. "Not many people know about that. I didn't even leave Astwell Palace until I was seventeen."

"I learned that from Tess."

"Tess?"

"The Dowager Duchess of Surrey."

Thomas's expression grew grim again. *"Her."*

Tiffany sat up in surprise. His tone held contempt, possibly even hate. She had assumed that Tess was the sort of person that everyone loved. She'd been the most popular student at school. The favorite young woman of their town. And now, both the duke and the Duchess of Beaufort treated her like family. Even their servants fawned over her.

"We were schoolmates three and twenty years ago," Tiffany explained. "But I have not had contact with her since. She married a duke and left behind lower connections. I happened to mention to the Duke of Beaufort that I knew her, and he insisted on writing to her. He asked if she wouldn't change her mind about not attending the house party so that she could see me again. The Duke of Beaufort told me that his wife was distraught because Tess was not coming, and it would throw off her numbers for the party."

He huffed and shook his head. "Catharine could only have felt relief if the Duchess of Surrey did *not* come. She has hated her for at least fifteen years. Ever since her husband and the Duchess of Surrey began their long-term affair. The Duchess of Surrey has been a perennial guest since at both their London house and Astwell Palace. I played with her sons, Osmond and Theophilus, growing up."

Tiffany breathed in so quickly that she started coughing. Her hands flew up to her cheeks in surprise. Yet, she shouldn't have been shocked. Tess, herself, had claimed to have affairs outside of her marriage and to have found love with a married man. She'd wrongly assumed that it was Lord Talgarth.

"And the Duchess of Beaufort has known about their affair the entire time?"

Thomas nodded gravely. "At first, Catharine spent more time with me. I was five years old at the time. I think she believed that it would end in a few months, like the Duke of Beaufort's other affairs. But it did not. If anything, the duke became less discreet, and it was widely known among the *ton* that he was devoted to the Duchess of Surrey. He even stopped visiting his own wife's bed."

"That must have been hard for her."

"Catharine grew thin and sad," he said. "A few years ago, she even had an affair with the notorious rake, the Marquess of Harwood, to try to capture her husband's attention; but instead of making him jealous, he was only too delighted to include the marquess in their ménage."

"And what of their son?" Tiffany asked, remembering the Duke of Beaufort's heir was only six years old.

"The Duke of Beaufort acknowledges him as his own," Thomas said. "He is even kind to him, but of course he knows that the Marquess of Harwood is the boy's father."

"Why did the duke claim him?"

He gave a short, mirthless laugh. "The Duke of Beaufort hates his only brother and his son. He was glad to spite them both with an heir. Especially since it was apparent that he was the one in their marriage that was unable to produce children. Not with his wife, his mistresses, or even with the Duchess of Surrey. Although he has been faithful to the Duchess of Surrey all of these years, as he never was to his own wife."

"And then she ended it after her husband's death," Tiffany whispered.

"What?" Thomas said incredulously. "I don't believe it. Now that her elderly husband is dead, the Duchess of Surrey has nothing to inhibit her behavior."

She cleared her throat. "Except her second son, Theophilus. He has become a Methodist and is very religiously inclined. He has threatened to cut her out of his life if she does not change her ways. She told me that she had ended the affair with the love of her life and that she will no longer have extramarital connections."

"Then why did she come to Astwell Palace and stay in the rooms that lead to the duke's?"

Tiffany bit her lip. "I think that the Duke of Beaufort used me. He did write to her and told her that I lived near Astwell Palace. My brother accepted the position as librarian about the same time that her husband died six months ago. She had not returned to Astwell since I had come to live here, and she came to see me . . . I do think that she wanted to repair the rift between us. We had been as close as sisters as children, and young women, before her marriage. Tess also said that she came to test her own resolution to change her ways. I assumed that her lover was one of the other male guests, Lord Talgarth. I had no idea that it was the Duke of Beaufort."

"Francis likes to use people."

She got to her feet and began pacing the small cell. Thomas watched her movements. "What if . . . what if the Duke of Beaufort poisoned his wife's snuff?"

"Francis?"

"Yes," Tiffany said with more assurance. "He has been in love with Tess for fifteen years, and she is finally free. If

Catharine, the Duchess of Beaufort, was out of the way, he could marry her. Especially now, since Tess will no longer continue their affair because of religious reasons. Tess still loves him. I don't think that she would be opposed to marrying a widower. And the Duke of Beaufort would also have had access to the duchess's dressing room and could have added the poison to her snuff."

Thomas slumped back in his seat, his back resting on the stone wall. "I believe that Francis is capable of it. He is the reason that I am a footman in the house, and not a son. He wouldn't allow Catharine to formally adopt me, nor to give me money from her own inheritance."

Tiffany blinked in surprise. The proud and cold Duchess of Beaufort truly did love Thomas as a son. He must have been the reason that she had come to speak with Samir and Tiffany that day in the library. She'd been trying to help her son, not to find the murderer of the devious Miss Doddridge.

"Why did she not come to your trial?"

"I am sure that Francis forbade it," Thomas said. "He appears to be affable and charming in company, but in private, he is manipulative and controlling."

Tiffany held out her fingers and counted off. "The Duke of Beaufort had the means, the motive, and the opportunity to commit all the murders."

"He also didn't know that Catharine gave up snuff earlier this year," he explained. "Her physician said that it was bad for her teeth. But since she is famous in society for her snuffboxes matching her gowns, she continued to purchase it and only pretended to take it . . . As much as your theory makes sense, we have no proof. Only the theory of a woman who is being charged for dressing as a man. The assizes judge will easily throw out your testimony, even if he agreed to give me a second trial. We have no solid proof that ties Francis to the poisoned snuff."

His words were not meant to wound her, but they did. In the society in which she lived; her word meant nothing. As an unmarried woman, she had no standing and no power. Her position was further demeaned by her dressing as her brother. She sat down again next to Thomas and slumped back like him.

"I am out of ideas."

"The situation is hopeless," he said, twisting a ring on his smallest finger.

She grabbed his hand with the ring. "Mr. Hickenlooper!"

"What of him?"

Tiffany realized that she was holding Thomas's hand and released it. "He was being blackmailed by Miss Doddridge."

Thomas groaned and briefly closed his eyes.

"He gave her his ring to keep her silent," Tiffany said. "When I confronted him with it, he said that she caught him doing something that could get him sacked. I assumed at the time, that he preferred male company and I assured him of my discretion. I thought that it had nothing to do with the murder. But what if the company that she found him in was a different kind of compromising? What if Mr. Hickenlooper purchased the poison in London for the duke? All the duke had to do was pour the mandrake oil over the snuff mixture, which he would have full access to, since the duke's and duchess's dressing rooms share a door."

Thomas leaned forward and raked his fingers through his hair. "It is a good theory, but how are we to prove it?"

"We can't prove anything," Tiffany said. "But Samir and Emily can."

"How?" he said.

For the first time, the young man looked and sounded hopeful.

"Samir is the constable," she said. "He can search the valet's room for the bribe—Mr. Hickenlooper could have hardly put coins or jewels in a bank without drawing undue attention. Meanwhile, Emily can scrub the duke's rooms and search for any trace of the poison. If she finds the bottle, we have all the proof that we need."

"But what if she doesn't find it?" Thomas asked. "We cannot prove that the bribe implicates Francis."

"I don't think that Mr. Hickenlooper will hang for the duke," Tiffany said slowly. "Take a bribe and buy poison, yes. But die? No. If he feared for his life, I am sure that he would betray his own mother. He would only be too ready to share with the judge who had paid him to procure the poison."

The young man stood and walked to the wall of bars. He grabbed two and shook them. "If only we could get out of here and search ourselves. Emily would not be allowed into the duke's rooms."

"Then who could we trust to search them?"

Thomas turned back to look at Tiffany. "My mother."

"Do you think she would?" Tiffany whispered.

"Yes," he said, and picked up a piece of paper on the floor. "Mr. Lathrop brought me paper and a quill. I've been writing my goodbyes to her and to my little brother, Perry. Mr. Lathrop assured me that he would deliver them. But I will instead write and beg for her assistance in searching her husband's rooms."

He knelt down on the stone floor and opened the inkpot. He had written nearly a page when Tiffany realized that they needed to ask for one more thing.

"Beg for her to come tomorrow to Mapledown. The assizes judge is going to give me a trial, but she has enough influence as a duchess to demand that you receive a second trial before the hanging."

Thomas brushed the feathers of his pen against his lips. "I don't know if she will directly defy her husband."

"Our plan will only work if she does."

He took a deep breath and nodded. "I can ask her."

CHAPTER 36

The letter had plenty of time to dry before Samir brought them their evening meal. It was already dark both inside and out when he arrived. He held a lantern in one hand and a metal pail in the other. The light from the lantern illuminated his face and his clothes: they were rumpled and dirty. A smudge of mud ran across Samir's usually clean-shaven cheeks.

"Did you find the body?" Tiffany asked, getting to her feet and walking to the wall of bars.

He nodded, his face grim. "If your half brother smelled bad when you buried him, the scent is unendurable now. But Doctor Hudson examined the decaying body and declared that he died of mandrake poisoning from the snuff, like Miss Doddridge."

"Will there be any criminal proceedings against me for not burying him in a churchyard?"

Samir shook his head. "I persuaded Sir Walter to drop that particular charge, but Mr. Shirley still intends to have the judge try you for masquerading as a man."

Tiffany looked down at her rumpled clothes, from her breeches to her cravat. It was hard to deny the truth of those particular charges. She nodded.

"Will you take this to the Duchess of Beaufort *tonight*?" Thomas asked, holding out his letter to Samir through the bars.

Samir put down the lantern and pail. He took the letter from Thomas. "I will, but I cannot guarantee that she will receive it. I'm at the mercy of the staff. Even if they do deliver it, it might not be until tomorrow afternoon."

"We need the duchess to read the letter now," Tiffany insisted.

"Then perhaps Thomas should deliver it himself," Samir said. "That is the only way we can know for sure that the Duchess of Beaufort will receive it tonight."

Thomas grabbed the bars and jerked them. "I would, if I could."

Samir reached into his pocket and pulled out a ring of keys. "You can and you will."

Tiffany watched as Samir unlocked the door and let it swing open. Thomas walked out of it and took the letter back from Samir.

"Aren't you coming out, Tiffany?" Samir asked.

"If I may?"

"You may."

She walked out of the cell, and even though she was still in the same one-room building, she felt free. Breathing in and out deeply, she eyed the pail of food. She hadn't eaten since this morning, and her stomach was making the most embarrassing noises. It chose this particular moment to make a bubbling sort of groan. She took off the lid and picked up a small loaf of bread. Tearing it in half, she handed one piece to Thomas. They ate the bread and the rest of their meal in silence.

"Now you've eaten, we need to get on our way," Samir said.

"How are we going to get through the town without being seen?" Thomas asked.

"It is dim, but not dark enough that someone might not see us," Tiffany agreed, pointing out the barred window.

"I borrowed Mr. Day's wagon to pick up the body from Bristle Cottage," Samir said. "He doesn't expect me to return the vehicle at a particular time. You two can hide in the back with the body until we are clear of town."

Tiffany instinctively shrank back against the wall and took out her handkerchief, covering her mouth. She did not want to see Uriah, or to be near his body ever again. Years of his cruelty to her were still too fresh.

"Clever notion to cover your nose, Tiffany," Samir said, covering his own face with a mask. "The smell of the body is indescribable."

He opened the door to the jail and looked out to see if anyone was there. "Clear."

Thomas and Tiffany crept out behind Samir. He signaled for them to go to the bed of the wagon. He went to the front and hung the lantern on the hook, so that he and the horse could see the road in the dark. Tiffany reached the back of the wagon first but had to step back and cover her mouth with both hands. She couldn't afford to be sick tonight of all nights.

From the lantern, she could see that Uriah's body had been placed in a burlap bag on the left half of the wagon. If she and Thomas lay on their sides, they should both be able to fit. Covering her mouth once again with the handkerchief, she crawled into the carriage and lay on her side, next to the body bag.

"Hurry, Thomas," she whispered.

"Yes, Miss Woodall."

He climbed in beside her, pulling a blanket over them both. They hid underneath it, his face toward hers.

"You might as well call me Tiffany," she whispered. "I would offer you my hand again, but I require it to cover my nose at this moment."

Thomas laughed, a low, pleasant sound.

Samir managed to make a shushing sound turn into a tongue-clicking to urge the old horse forward. Tiffany tried not to breathe until they reached the outside of town. Once the church spire was out of sight, she peeked out of the blanket and propped herself up on her arm.

"Shall we sit up?"

Thomas nodded and they both managed to squirm into sitting positions.

"I thought London smelled bad," Thomas said. "Nothing could possibly describe what we are sniffing now."

Tiffany could only nod, unwilling to take the handkerchief from her mouth and nose again.

"Why don't you two tell me what you have learned?" Samir said from his perch on the wagon seat.

"I," Tiffany started, but saw Thomas nod at her. "*We* believe that the Duke of Beaufort is behind the poisoning of both my brother and Miss Doddridge, but that they were not his intended victims: The Duchess of Beaufort was."

"What? No," Samir said, shaking his head. "I can't believe it. The Duke of Beaufort is the most respected man in our county. He would never harm anyone, especially his own wife. The mother of his child."

Thomas dropped his head into his hands.

"I know that the duke has been good to you, Samir," she said. "When no one else in Mapledown has. I know that he is the reason that you are the constable, but we do not accuse him out of spite, but because of evidence. Evidence that you pointed out in the trial—whoever put the poison in the snuff meant to harm the Duchess of Beaufort."

"Why would he want to hurt his own wife?"

"Because he loves another woman," Thomas said. "And that woman is finally a widow."

"Tess, the Duchess of Surrey, told me herself," Tiffany explained quickly, "that she has had a long-standing affair and that she ended it, when her husband died six months ago, because her second son, Theophilus, has threatened to cut her off if she continues to sin."

"But it wouldn't be a sin if they were married," Thomas added. "The Duke of Beaufort means to murder his wife and marry his long-term mistress."

"What evidence do you have?"

Tiffany and Thomas looked at each other.

"That's what we are going to Astwell Palace to get," Tiffany said. "I—we know that Mr. Hickenlooper procured the poison for his master, and he would have been given money or jewels in exchange for his services. We need to you to search his room."

Samir sighed. "I don't even know where it is."

"I do," Thomas said. "I can go with you."

"But what of the duchess?" Tiffany asked.

Thomas handed her the letter. "There's a secret way into her rooms from the nursery. You push in the pig's snout on the fireplace, and it opens a passage to her rooms. If you hurry, she should still be dressing for the evening meal. Catharine will be able to keep Francis occupied, so that you can search his rooms."

Tiffany nodded, looking down at her brother's inanimate body. Very little stood between her and the same fate: death.

Samir pulled up on the reins, and the wagon shifted to a stop. Tiffany scrambled out of the back as quickly as possible.

Thomas was not far behind her. Samir had halted the carriage in the woods by the lake, just outside the main lawns of Astwell Palace, not far from her cottage. He blew out the lantern so that they were covered in blackness. In the distance, she could see that several of the windows of the enormous building were lit by candles, but the exterior was blessedly dark.

"Tiffany," Thomas said, "I'll lead you to the door nearest the nursery, and then Samir and I will go to the men's sleeping quarters in the basement. We will meet you back here at the wagon."

She held out her hand. Thomas placed his on hers and Samir put his own hand on top of them both.

"To life and liberty," she whispered before dropping her hand.

The three of them stole through the formal gardens and the lawns like ghostly shadows. They followed Thomas to a tucked-away gable that she had never noticed before. With a finger on his lips, he led them behind a bush, to a secret door. He opened it for her, and the creaking sound it made caused her to jump. He pointed for her to go in, and without a word, he and Samir left the same way they had come, through the bush.

Tentatively, Tiffany peered into the dark passage. It looked like the sort of place for specters, evil counts, and dead bones. The perfect den for a blood-sucking villain or even a mysteriously falling helmet meant to bludgeon her to death.

Perhaps she should read fewer Gothic novels in the future.

Steeling herself, she slipped through the door and felt her way up a flight of stairs. She found the end of the staircase when her head hit into wood. Groping around, she found a doorknob and slowly turned the handle, so as to make as little noise as possible.

The room she entered was large and dark, the sliver of moonlight only giving the vaguest of shadows of the furniture in the room. Taking a step, she stumbled over a wooden block and fell with a thud. She crawled for a few yards until she could see the outline of a fireplace across the room. Slowly getting to her feet, Tiffany tiptoed across the room and didn't breathe again until she reached the mantle. She took a few shuddering breaths before feeling around for the face of a pig. The entire mantle was engraved with the faces of different animals carved into the marble. She felt one that she was certain was a cow and another a horse.

At last, her finger ran over an oblong shape with two circles on it. Tiffany touched it, but nothing happened. She pressed harder the second time and felt the stone snout move a little. The third time, she pushed with all of her strength until the snout indented within the carving and she heard a snap. Next to the fireplace, a door had popped open from the wall.

She heard a voice from the other side of it say, "Thomas?"

CHAPTER 37

"No," Tiffany said, stepping through the hidden door and into a bedchamber as sumptuous as Tess's had been. "But I bring a letter from him."

The Duchess of Beaufort was only wearing an exquisite silk robe and no wig on her head. She looked so much smaller without it's added height. Her face had been delicately painted, and it looked like Tiffany had interrupted her toilette. The duchess stepped forward across the well-lit room and took the letter from Tiffany. She raised one perfectly shaped eyebrow at Tiffany's masculine apparel but did not comment on it.

Before she read the letter, she asked, "Is he safe?"

"Not yet," Tiffany admitted. "We are hoping to find the evidence to free him tonight, but to do that, we need your help."

"I'll do everything that I can."

Tiffany could see that the duchess's hands were shaking as she opened the letter and read through its contents.

"Francis," she whispered. "Of course. I should have realized it sooner. I kept hoping that someday he would love me again, but I was foolish. His heart was never really mine to begin with. Ours was an arranged marriage."

The proud, cold woman that Tiffany had seen before was gone. In front of her stood a woman who looked fragile and heartbroken.

Shrunken.

"You cannot save your marriage, but you can save your son's life for the second time," Tiffany said.

The Duchess of Beaufort shook her head.

Tiffany's hopes fell like rain on the floor.

"I did not save Thomas's life when I purchased him from that slave captain," she said. "I saved mine. My sons have been the joy of my life."

"And they can continue to be if we are successful tonight," Tiffany said hurriedly. "I need you to finish dressing and to keep your husband occupied for as long as possible, so I can search his rooms."

"Very well."

"And you must come to my trial in the morning," she said. "Mr. Lathrop is going to ask the assizes judge to retry Mr. Montague's case, based on the new evidence found. And convicting a duke of murder will not be an easy thing to do."

The Duchess of Beaufort took in a deep breath. "I will tell my husband that I am going to the hanging. That I don't want Thomas to be alone in the end."

"Anything to ensure your presence at the trial. Your husband's too, if possible."

"We will be there," she said. "And I am trusting that you will have the proof that we need to see Francis hung."

Tiffany nodded, but inside she was far less certain.

The duchess took Thomas's letter and cast it into the fire. "Stay in here, Miss Woodall. Wait at least a quarter of an hour before you go through that door." Her elegant finger pointed to an entrance that was covered in the same wallpaper as the room. "It's the private entrance to Francis's room."

"I will."

The duchess sniffed and then left Tiffany standing alone in the center of the bedchamber.

"Thank you for waiting, Emily," she heard the duchess say from an adjacent chamber.

"Is everything alright, Your Grace?"

"As right as it ever will be."

Tiffany felt vulnerable out in the open, so she crept around the bed and crouched behind the bed-curtains.

There was not a clock in the room, so it was impossible to say how much time had passed. If she was too quick, she would run into the duke or his valet, Mr. Hickenlooper. If she were too slow, Samir and Thomas would begin to worry and might even risk coming back inside the palace to find her.

She counted to one hundred for the tenth time before stealing quietly across the room to the door that led to the duke's suite. Her heart stopped as she turned the doorknob. Pushing the door open, she saw that no one was in the room and that a fire was lit in the fireplace. There were no other candles lit in the room because the duke was not currently there.

Glancing around the room, she saw that there was another enormous bed with a canopy and curtains. There were three wardrobes. A table with a drawer and assorted chairs. She started first with the wardrobe closest to her, rifling through a stack of starched cravats and silk stockings. There was nowt but clothing there. The next wardrobe was filled with shirts and breeches, but again, there weren't any trinkets or vials that could have held poison. The last wardrobe was full of elegant jackets and both long and short waistcoats. She felt the pockets of each one thoroughly, there was nothing.

Tiffany began to fear that she had given Thomas false hope. For Samir was right. Without concrete evidence, there was no way to prove that the Duke of Beaufort had been trying to murder his wife.

But she couldn't give up yet. She opened the drawer, which was not locked. There were a few papers, quills, and an almost empty inkpot.

All that was left in the room was the enormous bed. She pulled off the coverlet first and shook it out. Nothing. The pillows only had feathers. She tugged at the sheets, and again there was not anything in them. Running her hands along the curtains, she tried to feel for a secret pocket. But there was nowt but silk. She touched the wooden canopy for any secret compartments, like the door from the nursery to the duchess's rooms. Again, she found nothing. Lifting the mattress, she pressed down on every square inch of it, only again to be unsuccessful. She crawled on all fours and touched every baseboard, wainscotting, and stone carving in the fireplace.

Where could the poison be?

If she had something damning to hide, where would she put it?

In plain sight.

She hadn't hidden when she masqueraded as her brother. She had attended church. Gone to Uriah's work. Talked to his friends. She had tried to act as unsuspicious as possible.

And what could be more unsuspicious in a gentleman's room than a pot of ink sitting in a writing desk? Tiffany hurried to the desk and pulled open the drawer. Picking up the almost empty inkpot, she uncorked it and took a sniff. It smelled floral, like the snuff and not at all like ink. She swirled the liquid around and it was not the slack consistency of ink, but thick, like oil.

Clutching her proof, she ran to the door, only to glance back at the mess she had made in the room. The duke would know that someone had been here. That someone suspected him. That wouldn't do at all. Pocketing the poison, Tiffany picked up the sheets and painstakingly made the bed. She smoothed out every single wrinkle in the coverlet before carefully closing the drawer to the writing desk.

Once she was satisfied that she'd left the bedchamber exactly as she had found it, she took her leave through the door that led to the duchess's room.

"What are you doing here?"

Tiffany pivoted to see Emily turning down the duchess's bed.

"I-I can't explain right now," she said. "But if you care for Thomas, please do not mention to anyone that you have seen me."

"I won't," Emily said. "And Mrs. Wheatley said that my sister could stay here tonight with me."

"I'm glad that you are both safe."

She went back to the door that led to the nursery. Happily it was still slightly ajar, for Tiffany did not know how to trigger it from this side. It was with relief that she stepped into the darkness of the nursery, closing the hidden door behind her. She crossed the room without any noise and slid down the steps of the secret passage on her bottom. Opening the door to the outside, Tiffany finally felt as if she could breathe.

CHAPTER 38

A pair of strong arms grabbed her. Tiffany opened her mouth to scream for help, but closed it again when she heard the voice.

"You're safe," Samir said, pulling her into a tight embrace.

Tiffany's body melted against his, and it was more wonderful than she had even imagined. It was as if their frames were made for one another, she fit so perfectly with him. She could feel his warm, sweet breath on her cheek, and she longed for his lips to kiss hers.

"We were so worried," Thomas said from behind them.

With those words, Samir gently released her. "Did you find the poison?"

"Yes," Tiffany said, pulling the inkpot from her pocket and handing it to him. "It was hidden in plain sight . . . Did you two find the bribe?"

"Yes," Samir said.

Tiffany heard a muffled voice and movement in the back of the wagon. Surely, Uriah's corpse was not moving? Such things only happened in novels. She touched Samir's hand, and he intertwined his fingers with hers.

"And Mr. Hickenlooper," Thomas said.

She laughed out of relief. "H-how?"

"He happened on us while we were searching his room," Samir explained. "Thomas had the foresight to subdue him."

"I hit him on the back of the head."

"Once he was knocked cold," Samir continued, "we searched his room twice before we found four rubies sewn into the bottom of the mattress. We then retrieved the ring and carried him here with us."

"After gagging and tying him up," Thomas added.

Tiffany whistled. With such jewels, Mr. Hickenlooper could have sold them for a small fortune and lived comfortably for many years. Perhaps even the rest of his life. It was no surprise that the valet had been tempted by the bribe.

"What do you intend to do with him for the night?" she asked. "Our jail cell is a trifle crowded already."

Samir squeezed her fingers. "You may sleep in your own cottage tonight. Thomas can bunk at my home, and the only person who will spend the night in the jail cell is Mr. Hickenlooper."

She let out a sigh of relief. "I thought Thomas and I were going to spend the whole night fighting over which one of us would sleep on the floor. Both of us insisting that it should be ourselves."

"If you'll allow me to walk you to your home," Samir said, and then added over his shoulder, "Thomas will follow in the wagon, and then, once you are safely inside, we will drive back to Mapledown together and put Mr. Hickenlooper in jail where he belongs."

"Thank you," Tiffany said.

She was pleased that Samir didn't release his hold on her hand but started to sedately walk toward her cottage. It was not much farther down the road from where they had tied the wagon, but she still enjoyed every moment of being by his side and feeling the warmth of his hand in hers.

"You'd best be in town by nine o'clock in the morning at the latest," he said.

"Of course."

She could feel his eyes on her.

"And it would probably be good if you were dressed as a woman when you see the judge," he suggested blandly.

A laugh bubbled out of her. "Probably."

All too soon they reached her door. Tiffany turned once more to look at Samir.

"Thank you for all that you have done for me," Tiffany whispered. "Especially tonight. For trusting me enough to believe me."

"Tiffany, there's something that I need to tell you—"

She cut his sentence off by kissing him on the cheek. She hoped that she knew the words he was going to say, but either way, it was best that she not hear them yet. For tomorrow she might hang, and such words would only make the time harder.

Without another word, she entered her cottage and shut the door.

CHAPTER 39

How does one dress to die?

Tiffany thought that perhaps a dark gray work gown would be the most appropriate. She lifted it up against her body and looked in the mirror. She appeared drab and guilty.

No, if she was going to hang today, she would wear her finest dress and her father's diamond pin on her collar. Stepping into the silk gown, she carefully buttoned it up. Even though the duke had paid for it, it was she who had lovingly stitched and embroidered it. The duke had already taken so much from her; she would not let him ruin the loveliest gown she had too.

She painstakingly craped her hair and left it unpowdered. She was tired of pretending to be someone else. Of looking like someone else. Tying her hair in a simple ribbon in the back, she declared herself ready. She would not put on face powders or paint her lips. If she died today, she would die as herself. The bruise on her cheek was now a rainbow of colors: yellow, green, and purple. But she was not embarrassed by it, nor would she try to hide it. The only person who should feel ashamed of it was Mr. Shirley, who had given it to her.

The color blue caught her eye on the dressing table. She still had the peacock-blue snuffbox with the dried snuff. She might need it as evidence today to prove that she'd had nothing to do with Uriah's death. Unfortunately, ladies' dresses did not have pockets. She could put it in the linen envelope underneath her skirt, but that was hard to access in public. She opted to store it in her bosom. A vulgar place to be sure, but a safe one.

She looked around the room, trying to memorize every detail. She opened the doors to the two other bedrooms on the upper floor: the guest room that had never been used and her old bedchamber—the room that she had meant for Mary Jones. Slowly walking down the stairs, she went first to her kitchen and last to the fine little parlor in front, where she had never once entertained a caller. The furniture had been a part of her mother's dowry. Each chair had so many memories. On her mother's embroidery table sat three beautifully bound leather volumes: *Evelina*, the first book that she had ever owned and had never had the time to start reading.

Lovingly, she ran her hands over the binding of the top book. Despite her possible end, she could not regret her decisions. At least for one month of her adult life, she had lived to the fullest. She would never have traded that for another forty years of genteel poverty and submitting her will to another's.

She locked the door to the cottage and, with her head high, walked one last time to Mapledown. The main street was fuller than she'd ever seen it. In the center of the square, three vagrants were in the stocks. Their hands and necks were held in place by the circular wooden cutouts. She would be lucky if her punishment were only the stocks. More likely, it would be on the scaffold behind it. She saw two circular ropes hanging on the wooden platform, ready to send her and Thomas to their maker.

A loud shriek caught her attention. Several townsfolk were pointing at her and covering their mouths. Others held baskets of rotten fruits and vegetables. No doubt, those projectiles were meant for her. She continued to walk past them and entered the building where the trial would be. Samir, Thomas, and Mr. Hickenlooper already sat on the first bench. The valet was not bound and gagged, but he still looked like a prisoner.

She took a seat next to Samir.

He briefly touched her hand. It gave her the extra support that she needed to keep her fragile composure. Most of the villagers must have followed her inside, for the room was twice as full as it had been for Thomas's first trial. This time, there were as many women as men, and they jeered at her louder than their husbands.

"Strumpet!"

"Yer a disgrace!"

"And she calls herself a lady!"

Tiffany would never have believed that she would be glad for the entrance of the assizes judge, but at least the crowd quieted a little when he entered the room. Sir Walter Abney followed behind him like an obedient dog.

"All rise and be quiet for His Honor, Judge Phineas Faulkner," Sir Walter yelled.

The judge and Sir Walter were followed by the members of the jury. They were the same twelve men who had condemned Thomas only days before. Tiffany and the rest of the room remained on their feet until both the judge and the jury members sat down.

Judge Faulkner picked up his gavel, hammering it three times on the table.

"Hear ye, hear ye," the judge began. "Constable Lathrop, I believe that I have already sentenced that young man there. He should be hanging in the square."

He pointed at Thomas with the gavel.

Samir stood. "There has been new evidence in the case, Your Honor. I respectfully request that you allow the jury to hear all the facts before you and they make a final decision on Mr. Montague's guilt or innocence."

"I am not here for murder, Constable," Judge Faulkner said. "I am here to judge the appalling case of a woman abandoning all decency, not only to deny her sole brother a proper burial but to masquerade as a man."

This time the judge pointed his gavel at her.

"Your Honor," Samir said patiently, "if you would but hear me out. The cases are not separate. Mr. Uriah Woodall was killed by the same snuff that poisoned Miss Sarah Doddridge."

His announcement seemed to stun the crowd, for there were shouts of "Hear him out!" and lots of stomping of feet.

Judge Faulkner pounded his gavel against the table so hard that the legs shook. "Quiet! I repeat, I have already sentenced that case, and I will not reopen it."

"Let him speak," one man called.

There were more yells from the crowd.

Tiffany and Thomas glanced at each other, their mutual dismay apparent on their faces. Again, English law would fail to give them justice for his color and her gender.

Bernard opened the door to the sessions room, and behind him, in all of her majesty, came the Duchess of Beaufort; and on her arm, her husband. She looked commanding, with a large, wide-brimmed blue hat and matching dyed plume. Her dress was also a deep shade of blue and parted in the middle to reveal her white petticoat, which matched the delicate lace around her collar and sleeves, trimmed with deep rose ribbons. Every inch of her looked like a duchess.

Judge Faulkner must have recognized them, for he stopped pounding the table with the gavel.

"Is there a problem, Your Honor?" the duke asked.

"Constable Lathrop wishes to retry Mr. Montague's case and combine it with Miss Woodall's."

"Then I suggest you hear him out," the duchess said. "I, for one, would like to know all of the details."

A hush fell over the entire room, and the occupants of the second bench all stood and moved to other seats. The duchess sat down on the bench, pulling along her husband. The duke looked less polished and assured than before. Bernard sat on the end of their row and cast a dirty glare at them. Tiffany wished that she could give that young man his due.

"Mr. Lathrop," the duchess said, "we are now ready to hear what you have prepared."

Samir bowed to her and then stood so that he could address both the judge and the jury members. "Mr. Uriah Woodall was the first person to be poisoned by snuff."

"Your proof?" Judge Faulkner interrupted.

Tiffany fished the blue snuffbox out of her front and handed it to Samir. He opened it up and set it in front of the judge on the table. "Miss Woodall found her brother dead in his bed, covered in his own waste and sick. At the time, she was unaware that he had been poisoned. Mr. Woodall had been plagued by stomach problems his entire life."

"Why didn't she report his death?" the judge asked.

"Miss Woodall is a spinster," Samir said, and the word hurt her coming from his lips. "She has no other family, nor means of support. Without her half brother and his position as the librarian of Astwell Palace, she would no longer be able to stay at Bristle Cottage. And she had no funds of her own and nowhere to go. In desperation, she buried her brother in the back garden and took his place as librarian."

Tiffany braced herself as a barrage of taunts and jeers fell on her like rain. It would appear that the rest of Mapledown was not quite as understanding as Samir. It was with relief that she heard the gavel hit the table and the judge called, yet again, for quiet.

"I am not here to pass judgment on Miss Woodall, only to state the facts of the case," Samir continued. "For without Miss Woodall, I would never have found the true murderer."

His statement was met with oohs and sighs.

"It was Miss Woodall who first made the correlation between Miss Doddridge's use of snuff and Mr. Coram's sickness. It was on her recommendation that I requested the jar of snuff from Her Grace, the Duchess of Beaufort. As you are aware, Your Honor, the apothecary from Bardsley, Mr. Antony Douglas, confirmed that not only were the snuffs the same from Miss Doddridge's rose snuffbox and the jar, but that they were both poisoned by mandrake oil. If you would care to look in this blue snuffbox, you will see that it contains the same snuff and the same poison."

Tiffany saw some of the jurors stand and others move in their seats, to get a better look at the peacock snuffbox.

"I grow weary of your words, Constable Lathrop," Judge Faulkner said. "I am already aware that the duchess's jar of snuff was poisoned and that Mr. Montague procured it for her."

"When Mr. Montague picked up the snuff from the tobacconist shop in London, it was not poisoned," Samir said loudly, over the whisperings of the crowd. "The poison was administered afterward. As you are no doubt aware, snuff is a wet mixture. The murderer poured the mandrake oil over the jar of snuff and waited for the poison to kill the Duchess of Beaufort."

There was gasps from the crowd.

Even Judge Faulkner's stone face appeared to be surprised.

The jurors stomped their feet.

"But as I have already related," Samir said. "The poisoned snuff did not kill the duchess. It first killed her librarian, whom she gave this blue snuffbox to. The Duchess of Beaufort, who was unaware the snuff was poisoned, gave it next to her lady's maid, Miss Doddridge, in the rose snuffbox. She died. Mr. Bernard Coram took the snuffbox after her death and was made ill from the contents, but luckily did not die. He did, however, accuse his rival Mr. Montague of poisoning not only his fiancé, but Bernard himself, with no proof. Indeed, with nothing but malice for a young man who had a higher position in the household than himself."

"Bleeding—" Bernard began.

"Quiet, sir," the judge said. "Do not speak unless you are given permission to. Constable Lathrop, you have shown the time line of events, but you have not proven who the murderer is."

Samir bowed. "You're right, Your Honor. Once Miss Woodall and myself established that it was the Duchess of Beaufort who was the intended victim, we sought to understand why. Or who would wish to harm Her Grace."

He paused, his face uncertain as he glanced at the duke—the man who had given him a chance when others would not have. His eyes then turned to the jury.

"And did you discover this person?" Judge Faulkner pressed.

"Yes, Your Honor," Samir said. "It was her own husband, the Duke of Beaufort."

Tiffany turned to see the reactions of the crowd. Again, most faces in the crowd were wide-eyed in surprise. Shock.

Some in disbelief. The duke's face was impassive, as if he were bored of the meeting.

"And what proof have you to accuse a duke of His Majesty's realm of such a horrid crime?"

Thomas handed Samir a small wooden box. He opened it and took out the nearly empty inkpot that Tiffany had found in the duke's bedchamber. Placing it before the judge, he uncorked the lid and set the blue snuffbox by it.

"If Your Honor would be so good as to smell both the inkpot and the snuff," Samir said, "You will see that they possess the same odor of mandrake. This inkpot was found in the duke's bedchamber, in his writing desk, where he placed it after pouring the poison on his wife's snuff."

The judge tentatively lifted the inkpot and then the snuffbox to his nose. He then nodded. "They do smell the same. They both have the odor of poison, but you have no proof that another did not place this incriminating evidence in the duke's room. In fact, Mr. Montague himself might have done so; hence, he knew where to find it."

"Alas, Your Honor, you are incorrect in that assumption," Samir said in a louder voice. "Mr. Montague is much attached to Her Grace and knew from her own lips that she had ceased the consumption of snuff earlier that year, at her physician's suggestion. If he had wished to harm her, he would have chosen a different method."

The judge turned to the duchess, and she bowed her head to him in assent.

"I have shown Your Honor and the jury the means by which the Duke of Beaufort poisoned his wife's snuff," Samir said. "He had access to Her Grace's rooms, opportunity, and motive. His Grace, Lord Francis Erskine, the Duke of Beaufort, has held a long-time love affair with the recently widowed Duchess of Surrey. He wished to kill his wife so that he could marry his lover. Wisely, the duke did not wish to implicate himself. He had his valet, Mr. Hickenlooper, purchase the poison for him. But what the Duke of Beaufort did not know was that Miss Doddridge had seen Mr. Hickenlooper acquire it and that she was blackmailing him."

Samir took the ring out of the box and held it up for all to see. "Mr. Hickenlooper gave Miss Doddridge his ring to keep quiet. This ring was found among her possessions after she died. Is that not right, Mr. Ford?"

Tiffany shifted in her seat to see the large butler sitting several rows behind them. "It is, Mr. Lathrop."

"But for the last piece of evidence . . ." Samir said, taking out the four shining rubies, all at least the size of a farthing.

At the sight of the jewels, the crowd went wild with jeers and yells. Judge Faulkner got to his feet and hammered the table with his gavel. Doctor Hudson and Mr. Canning both stood up to get a closer look.

"Quiet! I said, quiet," Judge Faulkner demanded, then pointed the gavel at the valet. "Stand, Mr. Hickenlooper."

The small man shuffled to standing, his head hung low.

"Did the Duke of Beaufort ask you to purchase poison?"

"Yes, Your Honor."

"Did he pay you four rubies to do so?"

Mr. Hickenlooper whimpered and began to cry. "Yes, he did, Your Honor. But I didn't know who it was for—or what it was for, I promise."

"But you knew it was poison, sir?"

The valet tried to speak, but his response was unintelligible through his sobs.

The Duke of Beaufort rose to his feet. "I have endured enough of this farce of a trial," he said, turning to face the jury. "Are you seriously considering charging a peer for murder when before you sit an African and a woman who has masqueraded as a man—and all on the words of an Indian?"

The honorable Judge Faulkner paled and did not speak.

All of the jurors sat back down.

"Sir Walter Abney, will you stand for this?" the duke asked.

The plump baronet fumbled with his quizzing glass.

The small light of hope that had begun to grow within her chest seemed to have been snuffed out like a candle. The judge, Sir Walter, and all twelve men on the jury now knew that Thomas was innocent of murder, but that didn't change their racial and class prejudices.

The judge raised his gavel one last time. "I, Judge Phineas Faulkner, do hereby . . ."

The Duchess of Beaufort got to her feet. "What about on *my* word, Your Honor?"

"Catharine, sit down," the duke said.

"I will not," she said, her voice ringing through the room. "The proof is abundant that my husband has tried to murder me and has instead managed to kill two of our servants. For my own safety and the well-being of my staff, I insist that you, gentlemen of the jury, make Francis pay for his crimes."

Judge Faulkner glanced from the duke to the duchess, to the jury, his expression unsure of what to do.

The crowd of spectators was more certain. She heard their calls:

"Hang him!"

"He's a murderer!"

"Don't let the duke get away with it!"

Judge Faulkner stood and the room quieted. "I await the decision of the jury."

Tiffany watched the twelve men again form a circle and talk in whispers. She prayed that they would come to a different verdict this time.

★   ★   ★

After a few minutes, Doctor Hudson brought a folded piece of paper to the judge, who nodded and opened it.

"Mr. Septimus Hickenlooper, gentleman's valet, you are guilty of the horrid crime of murdering Mr. Uriah Woodall on September third, 1784, and Miss Sarah Doddridge on September fourteenth, 1784, through the use of poison hidden in an inkpot. The prosecution witnesses were Lady Catharine Erskine, the Duchess of Beaufort, Mr. Samir Lathrop, Miss Tiffany Woodall, Mr. Antony Douglas, Mr. Simeon Ford, and Mr. Thomas Montague.

"You are sentenced to death by hanging," the judge concluded.

The valet's sobs turned into loud wails, but they were drowned out by the sounds of cheers and clapping from the crowd.

"What about the duke?" someone called from the back.

The judge hammered his gavel once more and waited for quiet. "I will continue with the jury's verdict.

"Lord Francis Erskine, the fourth Duke of Beaufort, member of the House of Lords, of the Mapledown parish, you are guilty of the horrid crime of murdering . . ."

Tiffany did not hear the rest of the sentencing. The yells, catcalls, and stomping were too loud.

The duke stood up and tried to leave. Bernard let him out of the bench, but men from the town stepped into the aisle and blocked him. Then two men grabbed the duke by his arms and pulled him from the room. A few others grabbed the sobbing Mr. Hickenlooper and awarded him the same treatment. Sir Walter followed the crowd out to the scaffold, but the judge and the jury stayed in their seats. The duchess also sat back down, her eyes on Tiffany.

There was still one more trial that day.

Hers.

The courtroom was as quiet as a church until there was the unmistakable sound of the wooden trapdoors opening. Tiffany was glad that she did not have to witness either the duke's or Mr. Hickenlooper's deaths. Hearing them hang was quite awful enough.

A few minutes later, the villagers filed back into their seats on the benches. Sir Walter, still twirling his quizzing glass nervously around his index finger, came to the front of the room.

"The other case that Judge Faulkner will be reviewing today is that of Miss Tiffany Woodall," Sir Abney began.

"I don't think that will be necessary," the Duchess of Beaufort said in the stateliest manner. "I believe that we should all return to our homes and places of work."

Mr. Shirley ambled to the front, his bony finger pointing at her. "Miss Woodall has committed the grossest of crimes."

"The only crime I see is on her face, Rector," Samir said through gritted teeth. "And you were the one who put it there."

Tiffany stood up so that the jury and the crowd could see the large bruise on her cheek. Any sympathy that the rector was hoping for from the crowd was gone at that statement. A tomato splattered against his cheek. It was followed by rotten eggs. Mr. Shirley tried to cover his face and finally dashed out of the room. His departure was greeted with a cheer from the villagers.

The Duchess of Beaufort sauntered to the front of the room and stood before the judge. "Miss Woodall's masquerade was instrumental in saving my life," she said. "I will vouch for her character. Miss Woodall, do you promise never to dress as a man again?"

"I do," Tiffany squeaked out. Her voice and her heart still clenched with fear.

"There," the duchess said. "I am sure Sir Walter is willing to drop his charges against my *dear* friend. There is no need for a trial or a jury."

The piercing look that she gave the baronet would have melted a much stronger man. He looked as if he'd swallowed his own tongue.

"Of course, Your Grace," he finally said. "But what of the jewels?"

The judge's narrow eyes looked at the four rubies on the table greedily. Every eye in the room stared at the small fortune.

"I believe Mr. Lathrop has more than earned them," she said. "Sir Walter, you may see me to my carriage."

The baronet rushed so quickly that he fell on his face at her feet. Standing back up, he offered the duchess his arm. She lightly placed her fingers on it, and they left the room like royalty.

Tiffany looked at Samir, and he smiled back at her as he shook Thomas's hand. The men in the village surrounded Samir, patting him on the back, waiting for a turn to shake his hand. For once the outsider was not only included in the circle, but he was the center.

CHAPTER 40

Tiffany slept soundly that night in her cottage. Even in Uriah's old room. For the first time it really felt like it was hers. Besides, her old room was currently occupied by Mary Jones, who had also attended the trial and then walked home with Tiffany afterward.

She sat up in her bed and stretched her arms. She had lost much, but she had retained her liberty. At this very moment, she could have been swinging from the scaffold with the duke and his valet. Instead, she was safely in her cottage, and all charges against her had been dropped. Uriah would finally receive a proper church burial.

And Tiffany would lose Bristle Cottage.

It would go to the next librarian, a position that she could not hold because she was a woman.

Now that she was no longer masquerading as Uriah, she could sell his wig, clothing, and some of her mother's furniture. It would hopefully be enough to afford her a rented room in the village until she found a position that was proper for a poor gentlewoman. She could make inquiries about becoming a teacher, a governess, a companion, or possibly even a housekeeper. She could hardly be picky. Her only regret was that poor

Mary Jones would have to be sent back to her abusive home when she did. Until then, the young woman could remain with her.

She thought of Samir and the words that she hadn't allowed him to speak two nights before. She didn't want him to marry her because she needed a roof over her head and money to live. She wanted him to ask her to be his wife because he couldn't live without *her*. Just as she was finding that she could not live without *him*.

Tiffany got out of bed and happily put on a clean chemise and sturdy work gown. She would not leave her cottage in any condition less than pristine. Combing through her hair, she fluffed out the crape curls in the front and braided it in the back. She put on her apron and went down to make the tea. Mary fetched the eggs from the chickens, and Tiffany boiled them. It was nice to sit down to breakfast with another person.

"What should we do first, Miss Woodall?"

"Tiffany."

"Miss Tiffany," Mary said with a shy smile.

She pushed the hair out of her face, and Tiffany saw the remnants of a purple bruise on her upper cheek. The young woman blushed and tried to cover it again with her hair.

"It would appear that we are a pair."

"What do you mean, Miss Tiffany?"

Tiffany touched her tender bruise. "We have matching cheeks."

Mary giggled and no longer tried to hide her face.

"The first thing we need to do is plait your hair," Tiffany said. "Then we will scrub up the dishes and start beating the rugs."

Mary touched her tangled curls. "I'm sorry that it's not tidy. I'm not very good with hair."

"Your hair is beautiful," Tiffany assured the girl. "And I happen to be excellent at plaiting, a skill that I have not been able to use in many years. It would be a treat for me to do yours."

A shy smile formed on the young woman's face.

Tiffany fetched her brush and, with long, slow strokes, meticulously combed through all of the tangles. It had been many years since school, but her fingers still remembered the pattern of braiding. When she was finished, she put a ribbon on the end.

Mary touched it as if it were sacred. "It's so pretty, Miss Tiffany. I've never owned anything half as nice."

"You are pretty too," Tiffany assured her. "Although you are shorter than me, I do believe one of my gowns would work for you until we have time to sew you a new one."

"A new gown for me? Golly," Mary said. "I've never had a dress made special for me—only ones handed down by my mum."

"You can even pick the cloth." As long as the price wasn't too dear.

Once Mary was dressed in a clean dress and apron, Tiffany led them back downstairs. "Now, help me carry the rugs out to the line, and I'll show you how to beat them."

Tiffany rolled up the rug in the front parlor, and Mary took the other side. They carried it to the back garden, where her washing line was strung out. Tiffany lifted the rug out and unrolled it over the line.

"I pretend that the rug is the face of someone I dislike," Tiffany said, and then whacked the rug as hard as she could with the beater.

She handed the instrument to Mary, who was an enthusiastic rug beater. Whoever's face she was picturing was getting quite the beating. Within a minute, dust encircled the air. Tiffany laughed and coughed.

When the dust cleared, she saw that Mary was not the only person creating a dust. A very fine carriage was on the road in front of her cottage, and it had stopped. Tiffany dashed through her house to the front door.

A footman opened the door to the coach. Thomas stepped out first. He was wearing a fine suit, not the livery uniform of a footman. He held his hand out to help the Duchess of Beaufort. She had on a large green calash bonnet, encircling her hair and face, that matched her gown. Thomas offered her his arm, and they came toward the house.

Tiffany curtsied so quickly that she fell back through the open doorway. She popped back up to her feet. "Please, please come in, Your Grace, Thomas."

The duchess paused at the use of his given name.

"Thank you, Tiffany," Thomas said with a smile, before turning to his mother. "You become quite informal when you share a jail cell."

The Duchess of Beaufort nodded and walked past Tiffany with her usual expressionless face, but Thomas gave her a wink of reassurance. He led the duchess to the nicest chair in the room and sat beside her. It had been her mother's favorite. Tiffany shut the door and cursed herself for choosing her best rug to beat first.

"There is usually a rug in this room," she explained. "It is currently being beaten."

"It is a lovely room," Thomas said.

Tiffany gave him a look of gratitude before turning to the duchess. "I know that you will want this cottage for your next librarian, Your Grace. I will leave as soon as I find lodgings.

Indeed, I am cleaning the cottage at this very moment so that it will be ready for its next occupant."

"There is no need to, Miss Woodall," the Duchess of Beaufort said.

Tiffany's heart constricted. Of course, the duchess had plenty of servants that could come and clean the cottage.

She nodded half-heartedly. "Whatever you wish, Your Grace."

The duchess gave Thomas a pointed look, and he pulled a paper out of his jacket pocket and handed it to Tiffany. She unfolded it slowly, her hands were shaking. It was a deed. The deed to Bristle Cottage and the land surrounding it had *her* name on it.

Tiffany Woodall.

"I-I-I don't understand," she muttered.

The Duchess of Beaufort actually smiled. "I should think that it was obvious, Miss Woodall. You saved my life and my son's. The deed to this cottage is a small gift in comparison to your actions."

"Your son's?" Tiffany said, knowing full well that she meant Thomas. But she had never heard the duchess publicly claim him.

"Yes, Thomas has kindly agreed to help me run the estate now that my husband is dead," she said. "My son has no longer any need to work as a servant, and Bernard has been let go."

"Good riddance," Tiffany said.

Thomas was the first to laugh, but both ladies joined him. The duchess stood up, and he again offered his arm.

"Good day to you, Miss Woodall," she said.

"When will you choose a new librarian, Your Grace?" Tiffany asked quickly.

The duchess shrugged her shoulders slightly. "I don't know. I have yet to ask my solicitor in London to advertise for one. Why do you ask?"

"I was wondering if I could put myself forward for the position," Tiffany said. "I know that I am not a man, but no one loves the written word as much as I do."

The duchess glanced at Thomas, who gave her a small nod. "I suppose the position is yours, Miss Woodall . . . on one condition."

"Anything," Tiffany said. She would have fallen on her knees and begged to continue to be the librarian.

"You must promise me that you'll buy more Gothic romances," the duchess said with a small wink. "And no more of that dull stuff."

"I promise," Tiffany said with a nervous laugh.

Thomas touched his hat. "Good day, Tiffany."

She managed to say her disjointed farewells, mixed with awkward thanks. The duchess simply bowed her head briefly and had her son lead her to her carriage. Tiffany watched Thomas help his mother in before entering the carriage. The driver urged the horses forward. She was still standing on her doorstep when Mary came out and stood beside her.

"I am done with the rug."

"Excellent," she said. "We have five more rugs to go."

"Then we have to leave," Mary whispered.

Tiffany held up the deed in her hand to show it to the young woman.

She shook her head. Mary did not know how to read. Tiffany would need to teach her.

"This paper means that this cottage and the three acres around it are now mine, and we don't have to leave."

"Never?"

"Never," Tiffany said, and they walked into *her* cottage, together.

Author's Note

In eighteenth-century England, there were over two hundred hanging offenses, and sentencing was swift. The trials only lasted one day; the first criminal trial to last longer was in 1792. Executions by law were required to take place within two days of sentencing. In London, trials and sentencing happened quickly, but in the country, a prisoner could wait for almost a year for an assizes judge to arrive in the county for the trial. Following the execution, the criminal's body was either given to a surgeon to dissect, or hung in chains in a gibbet, usually at a crossroads. This was the practice until 1832.

There was no formal police force in small towns. In 1750, John and Henry Fielding founded the Bow Street Runners in London, but they were more like private detectives than a formal police force. In the country, the constable was chosen yearly by the local justice of the peace. It was not a paid position. The constable's duties were to keep the peace and apprehend wrongdoers. In 1829, London began having full-time and salaried constables; but not until 1856 for the countryside.

While Samir Lathrop, as a person of color, would have been an unlikely choice for constable, the backing of the Duke of Beaufort would have made it possible. There is historical proof that persons of color *did* hold prominent positions in the community. Dean Mohammed was born in Patna, India, in 1759; joined the British army in 1769; and eventually moved to London, where he opened several coffee houses. Brian Mackey was biracial (half White and half Black). He received an Oxford education and was the parish priest of Coates in Gloucestershire, a position he held thanks to the influence of his White father. Nathaniel Wells (1779–1852) was the son of a White man and a Black slave. He was freed when his father died, and he inherited his father's plantations. He went to Britain for an education. There he bought Piercefield House, near Chepstow, and married a White woman, Harriet Este, the daughter of King George II's former royal chaplain. In 1803, he was appointed justice of the peace, and in 1818, Wells became the deputy lieutenant of Monmouthshire.

Great Britain's first proper census was conducted in 1801; however, it did not include information on race or origin. It is impossible to say how many persons of color lived in England at this time. We do know from historical accounts that persons of color did live, marry, and sometimes thrive in Georgian England. Slavery was legal in Britain until 1772. After that, Black people were freed, and if they continued as servants, they were paid wages. The Slavery Abolition Act was passed in 1833 and abolished slavery in most British colonies, freeing more than 800,000 enslaved Africans. That same year, British abolitionists garnered over 1.3 million signatures on their petitions to end slavery. Abolitionists in England had opposed the transatlantic slave trade since the 1770s. Fanny Price, in Jane Austen's *Mansfield Park* (1814), asks her uncle about slavery in the West Indies: "Did not you hear me ask him about the slave-trade last night?" While many Englishmen and women opposed slavery, that did not mean that they believed in full equality between the races.

William Holland wrote in his diary in 1805 about meeting Brian Mackey, "I am not very partial to West Indians, especially to your negro half-blood people."

Thomas Montague's character was inspired by several historical figures. Julius Soubise (1754–1798), a Black man born a slave in Jamaica was brought to England when he was ten and given to the Duchess of Queensbury as a gift. The duchess saw that Soubise was well educated, played the violin, fenced, and rode. Soubise became a dandy and ran up many debts, all of which were paid by the duchess.

Ignatius Sancho (1729–1780) called himself "the Black Falstaff." He was born on a slave ship and became the butler to the Duke and Duchess of Montague. Sancho was both a writer and a composer. He eventually owned his own property in London, so he had the right to vote. Although he was accepted by some of London society, like actors and writers, including David Garrick and Laurence Sterne, every day he experienced prejudice. One night, he went to Vauxhall Gardens with his Black daughters. Sancho wrote, "We went by water—had a coach home— were gazed at—followed, &c &c—but not much abused."

Dido Elizabeth Belle (1761–1804) was the daughter of a Royal Navy captain, John Lindsay, and an enslaved African woman. She was raised by her great-uncle, the Earl of Mansfield at the family estate, Kenwood. She inherited money from both her father and her great-uncle, eventually marrying John Davinier, a White French servant. Even though Dido had money, her social status was uncertain because she was a "natural" (illegitimate) child of a nobleman. She was above a servant but below a gentlewoman, even though she was educated and accomplished. The Daviniers had children and lived in a middle-class neighborhood in Pimlico.

Dr. Samuel Johnson's manservant and friend, Francis Barber (1742–1801), was born in slavery in Jamaica. Johnson not only educated Francis but also made him his heir. Francis Barber married a White Englishwoman named Elizabeth Ball. Interracial marriages were acceptable in Britain as long as the man and woman were of the same social class.

Silvester Treleaven, a rector, describes the marriage of a Black man in 1808:

> Married with a license Peter the Black servant to General Rochambeau to Susanna Parker. The bells rang merrily all day. From the novelty of his wedding being the first negro ever married in Moreton [Devon] a great number assembled in the church yard, and paraded down the street with them.

The upper social classes saw Black servants as a novelty and a way to appear more "White" in comparison. Author Paula Byrne explains that

> Black children were seen as adorable pets, and dressed in brightly colored silks and satins with turbans. Little surprise that when they grew older and lost their 'cuteness' they were often sold back into slavery, and sent to work on plantations. (Byrne, 2014, p. 104)

Byrne also notes that, although a few exceptions like Soubise and Sancho existed, for the most part, Black people who lived in London were poor and denied basic rights. There were fewer Black women than men, and their choices were servitude or prostitution.

Kathleen Chater extensively studied the Black population in England from 1660–1807. She noted that most Black people lived as domestic servants. Other occupations Black people held: parish constable, parish priest, churchwarden, barrister, victualer, coal trader, cabinet maker, actress, drummer, gardener, groom, market gardener, member of the militia, sailor, seaman, soldier, teacher of sword-fighting, sheriff, and justice of the peace.

Women were able to inherit both money and property if the estate was not entailed on the eldest male heir. In *Pride and Prejudice* (1813), Mr. Collins explains that Miss de Bourgh is "the heiress of Rosings, and of very extensive property." Mrs. Bennet wisely says, "then she is better off than many girls." Unfortunately, Tiffany Woodall is like many women of her time. She did not inherit any money or property from her father. When she is given the deed to Bristle Cottage, it is legally hers unless she marries. *The What-not, or Ladies Handbook* of 1859 explains that all a woman "has or expects to have becomes virtually the property of the man she has accepted as husband."

SELECTED BIBLIOGRAPHY

Adkins, Roy, and Lesley Adkins. 2013. *Jane Austen's England: Daily Life in the Georgian and Regency Periods*. New York: Penguin Books.

Burney, Frances. 1782. *Cecilia: Or, Memoirs of an Heiress*. London: T. Payne & Son; T. Cadell.

Burney, Frances. 1778. *Evelina: Or, The History of a Young Lady's Entrance into the World*. London: Thomas Lowndes.

Byrne, Paula. 2014. *Belle: The Slave Daughter and the Lord Chief Justice*. New York: Harper Perennial.

Fielding, Henry. 1784. *The Female Husband*. [pamphlet] [reprint].

Goldsmith, Oliver. 1766. *The Vicar of Wakefield*. London: R. Collins.

Lyall, Andrew. 2017. *Granville Sharp's Case on Slavery*. Oxford: Hart.

North, Susan. 2018. *Eighteenth Century Fashion*. New York: Thames & Hudson.

Peacock, John. 2010. *The Chronicle of Western Costume*. New York: Thames & Hudson.

Pool, Daniel. 1994. *What Jane Austen Ate and Charles Dickens Knew*. New York: Touchstone.

Reeve, Clara. 1778. *The Old English Baron*. London: Edward & Charles Dilly.

Reeve, Clara. 1783. *The Two Mentors: A Modern Story*. London: Charles Dilly.

Ribeiro, Aileen. 2002. *Dress in Eighteenth Century Europe, 1715–1789*. New Haven, CT: Yale University Press.

Richardson, Samuel. 1748. *Clarissa; or, The History of a Young Lady.* London: S. Richardson.

Walpole, Horace. 1764. *The Castle of Otranto.* London: William Bathoe.

Acknowledgments

Being an author is a lifetime dream of mine, and I still can't quite believe that it has come true. I am so grateful for the support of my family: Jon, Andrew, Alivia, Isaac, and Violet. You guys are my world. I am also blessed to have a great agent who advocates my work; thank you, Jen Nadol. There are not enough letters in the alphabet to express my gratitude to Crooked Lane Books for publishing my story. To my editor, Faith Black Ross, thank you for taking a chance on Tiffany Woodall, spinster extraordinaire. I appreciate the incredible copyeditors, and I want to thank Sara Horgan for her beautiful cover design. And last, but not least, I want to thank my readers. You make this all possible.

DISCUSSION QUESTIONS

1. What's the worst thing that has happened to you on a birthday? Particularly your fortieth.
2. What would you do if you were Miss Tiffany Woodall and found your half brother dead? Was she justified in burying him behind the cottage?
3. Tiffany was surprised that Samir Lathrop was the constable. Were you?
4. Mr. Hickenlooper said that Miss Doddridge deserved what happened to her. Do you agree?
5. Mr. Shirley's marriage proposal over a dead body is certainly surprising. Where did your spouse propose?
6. Tiffany believes that "if you loved someone, you could trust them with your secrets." Do you agree?
7. Should Tiffany forgive Tess for cruelly ending their friendship twenty-three years ago?
8. What is the true relationship between Thomas and the Duchess of Beaufort?
9. What does Tiffany fear will happen to her if her masquerade is discovered?

10. Did Thomas receive a fair trial by White men? Or do you agree with Tiffany that "prejudice had overcome justice?"
11. Do you think love or hate is the most powerful motive for murder?
12. How does one dress to die? What would you wear?